HOW TO RECOGNIZE A GREAT NEW DAD

1) He'll let you and his dog play tag anytime you want.

2) He'll help you with your reading...especially sounding out the big words.

3) He'll make the world's best pancakes (psst...don't tell your mom!).

4) He'll help you build a humungous spaceship.

5) He'll do LOTS of fun stuff with you and your mom.

6) He'll let you watch him shave for when you're all grown up.

7) He'll make your mom get all goofy when he's around!

Please address questions and book requests to: Silhouette Reader Service
U.S.: 3010 Walden Ave., P.O. Box 1325, Buffalo, NY 14269
Canadian: P.O. Box 609, Fort Erie, Ont. L2A 5X3

Born in the USA

MINNESOTA

NIKKI BENJAMIN

Emily's House

Silhouette Books

Published by Silhouette Books
America's Publisher of Contemporary Romance

SILHOUETTE BOOKS
300 East 42nd St.,
New York, N.Y. 10017

ISBN 0-373-47173-4

EMILY'S HOUSE

Dear Reader,

I first fell in love with the state of Minnesota almost twenty-five years ago. As newlyweds, my husband and I traveled to Duluth to visit college friends. That summer we stayed with them in their charming old home, built by a logger baron at the turn of the century, and spent our days exploring the city and surrounding areas. Drawn back many times over the years by the beauty of Minnesota and the hospitality of our friends, we had lots of excellent adventures. Most memorable are the times we canoed and camped in the boundary waters around Gunflint Lake.

When I started work on *Emily's House*, Duluth, Minnesota, seemed like the ideal setting, and our friends' house the perfect place for my heroine to live. And since I had a young son just starting school, it seemed only natural for Emily to have one, too. Thus, I could share the joy of motherhood with Emily Anderson while writing my book. And of course, Duluth, Minnesota, would be only a daydream away!

I hope you have as much fun reading *Emily's House* as I had writing it!

For my husband, Mike,
and my son, Nicholas…
thank you for giving me
the time and space.

Prologue

He was running, running with the speed of a man half his age. He tore through the thick jungle foliage, ignoring the vines and branches that ripped at his face and clothes.

The sun beat down with tropical intensity. The air was thick with humidity and the cloying stench of rotting vegetation. His sweat-stained uniform clung to his body. His heart pounded with dread. Yet he forged ahead, calling on every ounce of willpower he possessed.

Had to find him...had to warn him...warn him of the danger...warn him that death was waiting...waiting....

"No!"

With a muffled groan, Major Joseph Cortez pushed himself up on his elbows. Drawing one ragged breath after another, his eyes probing the cool, quiet darkness, he tried to get his bearings. As he focused on the series of weights and pulleys anchoring his left leg in midair, he cursed long and low. Reality was almost as bad as the dream. Almost...

At least his stay at the army medical centre near San Antonio was temporary. The second operation had repaired the last of the damage done by the explosion in the restaurant in Santa Maria, and his leg was mending. In a few months he'd be ready to return to active duty.

The dream, however, had a frightening permanence about it. It had begun to disturb his sleep almost a year ago, but instead of fading over time, now it awakened him nearly every night. Why? Why, after almost twenty years in the military, was he haunted by the death of one man, a stranger who had died because he'd been in the wrong place at the wrong time?

Easing back on his pillow, Joseph turned slightly, opening the narrow drawer in the nightstand. Groping blindly, he searched for the package of small, thin cigars. When his fingers found nothing but a half-used book of matches, he cursed again, slamming the drawer shut. He'd forgotten that the nurse had caught him smoking last night and confiscated the pack.

He couldn't move and couldn't smoke, and no matter how hard he tried, he couldn't forget Professor Eric Anderson. His hands balled into fists as he tipped back his head and stared at the ceiling. He wanted to vent his frustration at the top of his lungs, but all that would earn him was a visit from the resident psychiatrist. So he closed his eyes and sought yet again the reason why he was obsessed with one man's death.

When he'd been advised following the ambush that a civilian was among the dead, Joseph had assumed he was a reporter and had dubbed him a fool for venturing into a war zone with a pack of rebels. He had glanced at the man's passport, and ordered his lieutenant to send the body to the United States embassy. Then he had turned and walked away from Professor Eric Anderson, lying dead in a jungle clearing in the small Central American country of Norteña.

But there had been something about the big, blond man, something young, almost innocent, something undeserving of death—something that had slipped through the hard shell with which Joseph had sealed his soul. It had lingered at the edge of his mind, along with the memory of sunlight glinting off a wide, gold wedding band.

Eventually, almost against his will, Joseph had called in a few favors and had learned a lot about Eric Anderson. He had been a history professor. He had lived in Duluth, Minnesota. He had had a wife, Emily, and a son, Daniel. And he had been in Central America researching a book when he was killed as an indirect result of Major Joseph Cortez's orders to shoot to kill.

With a sudden movement that jarred his leg painfully, Joseph pushed himself up again and reached for the book on the nightstand. The glossy dark green cover sported in white block letters the simple title, *Vietnam*, and the author's name, Eric Anderson. It was a thoughtful book, full of warmth and insight, and it was so much more than the history of a country or the history of a war. It was a story about people, real people, written by a man who had taken the time to listen, to understand and to care.

Joseph's hand tightened on the book for a moment. How long had it been since *he* had taken the time to do anything except get the job done? How long had it been since he'd cared about people like Eric, Emily and Daniel Anderson, cared about them as individuals rather than as part of a nameless, faceless "common good"? And how long had it been since he'd accepted the responsibility for the way his decisions affected people like them? Because of him, their lives would never be the same.

With a violence born of desperation, Joseph hurled the book across the room. It hit the wall with a dull thud. As it tumbled to the floor, Joseph fell back against his pillow, rubbing a hand across his forehead.

"What do you want from me?" he muttered softly, closing his eyes as pain and a bone-deep weariness rolled over him. "What do you want?"

He had asked himself the question too many times over the past year. As it had before, the sense of honor and integrity drilled into him by his grandfather and father dictated the answer. He couldn't bring back Eric Anderson. But he *could* do something for the widow and her son, for Emily and Daniel. At the very least he could make sure they were all right. And if they weren't? Then he would find a way to take care of them. Now was the time.

He had to recuperate somewhere. Why not Duluth? He could spend some time with Richard Mendoza. He hadn't seen the old professor since his mother's funeral two years ago, and Richard had helped Joseph in the past when his spirit had needed mending.

And while he was there...while he was there...

As the night sky faded into dawn, Joseph Cortez finally drifted off to sleep.

Chapter One

He shifted on the seat of the dark blue, late-model car he had rented at the airport, trying unsuccessfully to ease the throbbing pain in his left leg. Afternoon sunlight, slanting through the branches of an ancient oak tree warmed his face, but the breeze drifting through the open window promised an early autumn. The narrow, tree-lined street was quiet. Drawing deeply on a thin, black cigar, Joseph Cortez leaned his head back against the headrest. It had been a long time since he'd been anywhere as peaceful as Third Street in Duluth, Minnesota.

Eyes narrowed against the smoke curling off the red tip of his cigar, he studied the elegant old homes that stood on neatly manicured lawns along either side of the street. If the service station attendant's directions and description of the house were accurate, 235 East Third Street was the three-story, gray stone house on the corner, diagonally across the street.

Ruffled white curtains fluttered at the open windows, and small pots of bright flowers stood at attention along the stone porch railing. Two tall pine trees swayed in the breeze, shading the front yard. A solarium full of leafy green plants clung to one side of the house. On the opposite side a gray stone garage lay at the end of a long, slightly curving driveway.

Unlike most of the stately homes on Third Street, Number 235 looked warm and inviting. Joseph hoped the house's appearance was a reflection of its owner's personality. Emily Anderson, widow. No matter how often he told himself he'd come to Duluth to visit Richard Mendoza, he knew she was the real reason he'd decided to recuperate in Minnesota.

Of course, Mendoza's invitation had made the final decision that much easier. After six weeks in the military hospital, what Joseph wanted, what he *needed,* was a place to lick his wounds, a place far from the war-torn jungles of Central America, a place where Major Joseph Cortez, military adviser, didn't exist. And as the old professor had said, paints and brushes and blank canvas had helped him deal with the realities of war in the past. Maybe his ability to create, to draw, to paint would work its magic on him again.

Joseph drew on his cigar once more, then leaned forward to stub it out in the car's ashtray. He hadn't said anything to Mendoza about Emily Anderson. He had planned to check on her quietly, from a distance, once he'd settled in with Richard. He had driven by her house only out of curiosity. Then he saw the sign on the front lawn.

As if anticipating her master's next move, the German shepherd lying on the seat beside him stretched and sat up.

"Ah, niña, sí. Vamos." He spoke the words softly, in the Spanish that had been his first language.

The dog whimpered, nudging him with her cold, wet nose as he leaned across the seat and opened the glove compartment. "Yes, in a minute," he muttered, as his fingers wrapped around the butt of his Beretta.

He checked it with easy familiarity, then tucked it into the holster he wore beneath his tweed jacket. Old habits, he thought with a bitter twist of his lips, but he had learned the hard way about safe places.

He closed the glove compartment with a slam and sat up, unwanted memories of a noisier, commercial street overwhelming him. He heard again the explosion of the first grenade that had been lobbed among the tables in the busy restaurant. He saw again the still, silent faces of Lieutenant Charley Markham and Sergeant Steve Travers, felt the sharp, slicing pain in his leg that had rendered him immobile. Then, with a shake of his head, Joseph Cortez picked up his cane and opened the car door. This wasn't Norteña; this was Duluth, Minnesota.

"Greta, venga aquí." With the dog pacing along beside him, Joseph limped toward the old house on the corner, leaning heavily on the ebony cane.

"Damn it, damn it, damn it." Her whispered words were harsh and angry, but they didn't help, not really. Neither did throwing the account book onto the kitchen floor, but violent emotions like anger often led to violent words and deeds. And an afternoon spent trying to balance her budget had left Emily Anderson feeling angrier than ever.

It had been over a year since Eric's death, and she was proud of the way she was coping, proud of the way she'd pulled herself back from the edge of depression and despair. For months she had crawled into a shell, barely eating, rarely sleeping, caring for Danny in a daze while the house fell into disarray, the yard ran wild, and unpaid bills piled up.

It had taken a visit from a collection agency representative to snap her out of self-pity and into action. The fact that some sleazy little man had the right to stand on her front porch, demanding three months' worth of car notes or the keys to the Volvo, had hit her like a bucket of ice water. She had lost her husband. If she didn't pull herself together both mentally and physically, she would lose her car, her home, perhaps even her son.

She had thought of selling the house, but it had been in Eric's family since 1912, and by rights it was Danny's inheritance, not hers. She had applied for a teaching position, but none of the schools in a fifty-mile radius needed a social studies teacher this year. Her parents, as well as her in-laws, would have helped, but Emily was determined to make it on her own.

She had, for instance, discovered she could earn as much money typing at home as she could working full-time in an office.

Now she was getting by, barely, and it was the *barely* that angered her. The income from the third-floor apartment and her typing service was adequate to pay the bills. Unfortunately, taxes and utilities seemed to go up every month. And with winter just around the corner, her heating bills would double, even triple.

Of course, she could finish the book. Eric's editor had phoned again, offering a sizable advance if she was ready to commit herself to a deadline. She had worked with Eric on the other books; the actual writing wouldn't be difficult. But if she agreed to finish the book, she'd have to open the box of research information he'd shipped home from Norteña just before he was killed.

The thought made her palms sweat and her heart pound. She wasn't ready to face the notebooks, the diary, the tapes, the photographs. In addition, she still had too much hatred, too much bitterness brewing inside her toward the United States government and its military machine to produce a fair analysis of Central America, its history, its people and its politics. The book would have to wait a while longer.

In the meantime, to make ends meet, she had decided to try to rent the extra bedroom and the small studio on the second floor. She wasn't thrilled with the idea of sharing her home with a stranger, but at the moment it was the lesser of two evils.

Uttering a sigh, Emily bent to retrieve the account book, placed it on the table and stood up. She crossed the kitchen and filled her red teakettle. Danny wouldn't be home for another hour, so there was time enough to relax with a cup of tea. While the kettle warmed on the gas stove, Emily gazed out the window at her backyard. It was so peaceful. Birds sang in the trees, and somewhere down the street a dog barked, but the old house itself was very quiet.

For so many years Emily had stood by the window, waiting patiently for water to boil, feeling safe. She'd had no premonition that her husband, her lover, her friend would be killed while doing research in a small country in Central America. He had been a history professor, not a warrior. He had been serious about his work and firm in his belief that the United States had no right to meddle in Central American politics.

He had also been sweet and kind and funny. Though the pain of losing him had eased, she still missed him. And she had begun to feel a little sorry for herself. She had loved her husband and the life they had shared, the laughter, the warmth, the companionship. But he had gone away, leaving her to a bleak and rather lonely future. There would never be another Eric for her.

The whistle of the teakettle interrupted Emily's thoughts. She measured tea into a flowered teapot, added hot water and waited for it to steep. When she judged it to be ready, she filled a pottery mug, walked back to the table and sank into a chair. Propping an elbow on the table, she rested her chin in her hand and stared at the account book. Sorry for herself or not, she was going to have to find another source of income, and she was going to have to do it soon, especially if she wasn't able to rent the rooms. Smiling wryly, she tasted her tea. As she moved to take another sip, the chiming of the front doorbell echoed through the quiet house, startling her.

"Now, who could that be?" she muttered, glancing up at the clock that was ticking away on the wall above the refrigerator. She wasn't expecting anyone, and Danny always used the back door. Hesitating for a moment, she tugged at her short, golden-brown curls and considered ignoring the summons. Since the man from the collection agency had darkened her doorway, demanding her money or her car keys, Emily rarely opened her door to strangers.

Of course, it might be someone interested in renting the rooms. Her telephone number was on the sign, but students had a habit of inquiring in person.

The doorbell chimed again. Whoever it was didn't seem inclined to go away, and she didn't want Danny running into a stranger on his own, especially if it wasn't a student. If he saw someone at the front door, her curious son wouldn't think twice about investigating.

"Okay, okay, I'm coming," Emily murmured. Taking a deep breath, she stood up and padded barefoot down the narrow hallway.

Placing a gentle hand on her head, Joseph ordered Greta to sit. She obeyed instantly, crouching beside him, pressing against his good leg as he stroked her. It was cool on the shaded porch, so much so that Joseph found it hard to believe it was still August.

Shifting his weight slightly to ease his left leg, he debated whether or not to ring the doorbell again. Just as he decided to try a third time, he noticed movement behind the etched glass panel in the door. A moment later the door opened a crack, and a teenage boy peered out at him. Joseph frowned. For some reason he hadn't expected the son to be so old.

In fact, over the past few weeks since he'd decided to come to Duluth, he'd conjured up a very clear picture of Emily Anderson and her son Daniel. Her husband had been a big man, blond and handsome. She would be equally tall, but slender and aloof. She would have long, fair hair, calm, serious blue eyes, and a firm, quiet voice. And her son...

As he stared at the boy, Joseph realized he was being considered with equal care through the narrow opening in the doorway. Wide, curious eyes, pale and silvery green beneath a mop of shaggy brown curls, scrutinized his face, traveled down the length of his body, paused to take in the cane and Greta, then rose to meet his gaze.

"Yes? Can I help you?" The voice was soft and low, neither friendly nor unfriendly.

"Is your mother at home, son?" Joseph maintained an equally neutral tone of voice, although he'd already decided the boy could use a haircut and a lesson in good manners, not necessarily in that order.

"So? Who wants to know?" The door opened a little wider. The pale eyes flashed with something halfway between anger and amusement.

Joseph's frown deepened with annoyance at the sarcastic tone of the questioner. He shifted his weight again, leaning more heavily on the cane. He was tired, his leg was killing him, and today of all days, he simply didn't have the patience to deal with a smart mouth.

"Listen, kid, I'm not in the mood to play games. Why don't you just run along and find your mother for me like a good little boy?"

"A good little boy, huh?"

To Joseph's surprise, the heavy door swung wide open, revealing not a teenage boy, but a short, slender girl. As he took in the gentle curves of breasts and hips, neatly tucked into a pink T-shirt and white shorts, his eyes flickered with surprise and admiration. She stood with hands on hips, her bare feet slightly apart, and her chin had a defiant tilt to it. Anger had won out over amusement. The green eyes were flashing fire. And damned if his second impression wasn't as mistaken as his first. She wasn't a girl at all. The late-afternoon sunlight falling on her face revealed fine lines etched around her eyes, and strands of silver highlighted her short, golden-brown curls.

"Hiding behind that door, you *looked* like a boy."

The words were out before he could stop himself, as if some devil buried deep inside his normal reserve, stomped down by years of self-control, had broken free. As a deep rose blush crept up her neck and onto her face, he made a mental note to let the devil loose more often. Her flushed face and flashing eyes were devastating.

"Intimidation through insult, huh? Well, whatever you're selling, I'm not buying. So do me a favor," she said, pausing for an instant to inflict on Joseph the same look of distaste she would no doubt turn on a rat in a trap. "Take your dog and get off my porch."

"Selling...?"

Almost too late Joseph realized she was slamming the door in his face, and he couldn't, wouldn't let her get away. Not stopping to analyze why, he moved quickly, propping his cane against the door so it wouldn't close. By the look on her face she was going to start screaming any second. And if she chose to swing back the door without warning, he'd probably end up flat on his face at her feet.

"Wait...please. I apologize. Please...?" At the sudden softening of his voice, she stopped pushing against the door, and Joseph moved his cane away. Standing very still, she watched him with wary eyes, waiting. "I, um, I...Mrs. Anderson?"

"You're not a salesman?" Now apparent confusion chased the anger out of her pale eyes as she opened the door a little wider.

"No."

"But you know my name?"

"Saw it on the mailbox." He paused for a moment, thankful he had noticed that small detail on his way to the front door. "I also saw your sign. I'm going to be in Duluth for a while. I need a place to live, close to the university...." God, this wasn't going at all as he'd planned, but then, Emily Anderson wasn't at all what he'd imagined, either. What a fool he'd been to come here.

"My sign?"

Of course, you ninny, your sign offering rooms for rent, Emily answered herself silently, as she studied the strange, dark man standing on her front porch. Who was he, and why was the expression in his fierce, brown eyes so full of disbelief?

Funny, she'd always associated brown eyes with Bambi. But this was no Bambi standing in front of her. Though he had several inches on her, he wasn't tall, yet his shoulders were broad and powerful beneath the tweed jacket, and his skin was deeply tanned. He looked lean and hungry, like a panther on the prowl.

His face was lined and scarred. Both adolescence and age had taken their toll. Thick, black hair slanted across his forehead. It was neatly trimmed at the sides, but long enough in back to curl over his collar. His mouth had settled into a grim line beneath his full, black, bandit's mustache. And his eyes, deep-set under thick, straight, black brows, seemed to reach for her soul, their touch both hot and cold, holding her like a bird in a jungle cat's paws.

If she had any sense at all, she thought, she'd slam the door and run. She ought to be terrified of him, but she wasn't. His soft, slightly accented voice belied his fierce, angry scowl. It intrigued her. Who was this man, neatly dressed in dark gray slacks, a white shirt, and gray tweed jacket? Why was he looking at her with such a mixture of anger and confusion? And why did he want to rent rooms in her house?

"Mrs. Anderson, I'm Joseph Cortez." As if reading her mind and coming to a decision, the man extended his right hand in the traditional gesture of greeting. "As I said, I'm going to be in Duluth for a while. I'm going to be working with Professor Mendoza, and I need a place to live."

"Mr. Cortez." Emily offered her hand slowly, allowing it to be held in Joseph's firm, hard grasp far longer than necessary. "It's very nice to meet you," she said, tipping her head to one side and smiling slightly. "But," she continued, unable to control the note of uncertainty that crept into her voice as she slipped her hand from his, "I was hoping to rent the bedroom and studio to a...to a woman."

Joseph hesitated for a moment, trying to decide what to do. If he were wise, he'd thank her for her time, turn around and walk away. He could have dealt with the imaginary Emily Anderson on a daily basis. Ice-maiden intellectuals had never been his type. But the woman standing in front of him was something else altogether. She was hot light and dark night. And when she laid that soft, sweet smile on him, she made him think of sunlight after a storm.

Turn around and walk away. Just turn around and walk away. Easy.

"I'm going to be working with Richard for two, maybe three months." He exaggerated the length of his stay a bit, but he'd work something out. "I'll need a place to paint, too, so a bedroom and studio would be perfect. Would you mind having Greta around?" The dog whined softly as Joseph stroked her head.

"Really, Mr. Cortez, I don't think it would be a good idea," Emily replied, taking a careful step back.

Let it go, pal, let it go. She's right.

The warning rang through his head, but Joseph refused to hear it. Something about Emily Anderson stirred his weary soul. Standing in the doorway of the old house, she seemed so small, so soft and fragile. But her flash of temper assured him that she had her fair share of strength and courage. And her voice and eyes, shadowed with a soul-deep serenity, drew him with the same cool, cleansing promise as a mountain spring.

He wanted to see her smile, wanted to hear her laugh, wanted to bask in her warmth. And more than ever he wanted to be damned sure that she and her son lacked nothing because of him.

"I'll pay you five hundred dollars a month for the rooms and access to your kitchen when you aren't using it."

"Five hundred dollars a month for two rooms?" As Joseph nodded his head, it was Emily's turn to hesitate. Five hundred dollars a month was more than the students in the third-floor apartment paid her.

But he would be living in the house, sleeping across the hall from Danny and herself. Of course, he *was* a friend of Professor Mendoza's, and if he stayed three months, the money he paid would heat the house all winter. It would be nice to have a man around again, too, if only for a short time. He seemed so strong and self-assured, the kind of man a woman could depend on. And life wouldn't be quite so bleak or lonely....

Good God, what was she thinking? For one thing, Joseph Cortez wasn't her type. She didn't like dark, moody men. And even if she had, he didn't look like the type of man who needed anyone, not on a permanent basis. Despite the initial confusion she'd seen in his eyes, he was too calm, too confident, too self-contained. Yet she sensed that he was also very much alone, and his loneliness drew her like a moth to a candle flame.

"No, really, I don't think so." She took another step back, shaking her head, denying the part of herself that wanted to offer shelter. Instinctively she touched the wide, gold wedding band on her ring finger as if it were a talisman.

"If it's the money, I'd be happy to pay whatever you want." Joseph had watched the various expressions chasing across Emily's face, and when she'd looked at him, a hint of sadness in her pale eyes, denying him, he'd had to fight down the desire to shake her. What inner battle had she been waging, and why had he come up the loser?

"No, no, five hundred dollars a month is more than adequate," she assured him. "I just don't think—"

"Greta, then?"

"It's not her. I like dogs—"

"Call Mendoza. He'll vouch for me." He didn't like the idea that she could turn him away so easily. He knew she needed the money he was offering to pay, and the house was certainly big enough for two people, even two people who wanted to avoid each other. Only avoiding her wasn't quite what he had in mind, even if it should be.

"No. Just…no." Taking another step back, almost tripping over her feet, Emily willed Cortez to leave, but he didn't move. And try as she might, she couldn't break away from his dark, steady gaze. It shackled her to him as securely as a set of chains, holding her prisoner in a place as unfamiliar as it was alluring.

It was the crash of Danny's bicycle as he dropped it to the driveway that finally freed her. He called to her from across the lawn.

"Hey, Mom, I'm home."

Her son was bounding up the porch steps before Emily, senses reeling, could say another word. She watched Danny's bright blue eyes, Eric's eyes, as he studied Cortez and the dog. He sidled up alongside his mother, his tumble of honey-blond curls brushing against her arm. Then, with a huge grin that took both adults by surprise, he held out his hand.

"Hi. I'm Danny. Who are you?"

With complete and utter fascination, Emily observed the changes that took place in Joseph Cortez as he greeted her son. He focused his attention on Danny, his features softening. A smile warmed his fierce, dark eyes and turned up the corners of his mouth. Bending slightly to accommodate himself to her son's shorter stature, he extended his hand.

"Hi, Danny. I'm Joseph Cortez."

Instinctively Emily wrapped an arm around her son's shoulders, but instinct also warned it was already too late. Danny's small hand rested in Joseph's larger one, the clasped hands drawing them to each other, leaving Emily feeling very much the outsider.

Danny had never been a shy child, but he was cautious, rarely warming up to strangers on the first meeting. With Cortez he was displaying more interest and enthusiasm in a matter of minutes than he'd yet to show Glen Roberts, the man she occasionally dated. In fact, from the way Danny and Cortez were looking at each other, one would think each had found a long-lost friend.

"I'm six, and I'm going to first grade next week," Danny offered, in answer to some unspoken question, as he withdrew his hand from Joseph's. "Why are you here?"

"He was just leav—" Emily began in a determined tone of voice, but Cortez neatly cut her off.

"I'm going to be working with Professor Mendoza at the university, and I need a place to live. I saw the sign on your front lawn, and thought I might be able to stay here."

"Oh, yeah? Neat. Do you draw pictures like the professor?"

"Yes, and I paint, too."

"Will you draw a picture of me?"

"Danny!" Emily protested, her hand squeezing his shoulder in warning.

Man and boy leveled such fierce frowns at her that Emily caught herself shrugging apologetically. Let them talk all they want, she thought, as she dropped her arm to her side. Cortez was *not* moving into her house, no matter how intriguing he was, no matter how much she needed the money, no matter how nice he was to Danny.

"Of course I'll draw a picture of you," Joseph promised, as he turned his attention back to the boy. Try as he might, he couldn't quite keep the triumph out of his voice. He'd found the key to her, and he'd be damned if he wasn't going to turn it. For her, not against her, he thought, feeling the need to justify his position—for her and Danny, and perhaps most of all for himself.

"Is this your dog? Can I pet him?"

"Yes, she's my dog. Her name is Greta, but before you pet her, let me introduce you, all right?"

"Okay," Danny agreed, nodding solemnly, watching as Cortez took his hand and offered it palm up to the dog.

"Greta, es mi amigo, Danny." The dog whined softly, nudging Danny's hand with her cold, wet nose. "Friends for life now," Joseph added, as Danny stroked the dog's head.

"What did you tell her?"

"I told her that you're my friend."

"Did you tell her my mom's your friend, too?"

"No, but I will."

Before Emily could prevent it, Cortez grasped her wrist. With a sharp tug he pulled her forward, the warning look in his eyes silencing any protest she might make. *"Greta, es mi amiga, Emily."*

He spoke to the dog, but his eyes held Emily's. The warmth of his fingers wrapped around her wrist was so distracting that Emily hardly noticed the dog's cold, wet nose in her palm. Once again he held her, this time with his hand as well as his dark eyes. When she realized it, Emily jerked free. This had gone on far too long. She had to get rid of Cortez before she did something stupid.

"Mr. Cortez," she snapped, pulling herself up to her full five feet, two inches. "I really think you ought to leave—"

"Your phone's ringing."

"What?"

"Mom, he's right. The phone's ringing. You better answer it."

"Oh, damn," Emily muttered as she heard the telephone. She absolutely, positively did not want to go inside before she got rid of Cortez. But Danny, jumping up and down, gesturing wildly, was enough to make her head spin.

"Hurry, Mom, hurry! It's probably Mrs. Stewart. She said

Jimmy could spend the night on Friday, if it's all right with you."

"Okay, okay, I'll get the phone," Emily reassured her son before turning to frown at Cortez. "Mr. Cortez—"

"I'll wait."

Resisting the urge to scream, Emily spun around and stalked into the house. If he interrupted her one more time, she'd slug him, swear to God. The man did not know how to take a hint, she thought, as she reached the end of the cool, dim hallway and grabbed the telephone.

"Hello," she snapped. The only reply was the click of the caller disconnecting.

"Damn." She slammed down the receiver, whirled around, took two steps, then stopped and turned back to the telephone table. She hesitated a moment, took a deep breath, then pulled the local directory out of the drawer. Quickly, before she could analyze what she was doing, she looked up Professor Mendoza's telephone number.

What could it hurt to check the man out? she thought as she dialed the number. Though Richard Mendoza was more of an acquaintance than a close friend, she liked and respected him and would trust his judgment.

On the front porch, Danny turned to Joseph and asked about the time. After checking the slim, stainless steel and gold watch he was wearing, Joseph advised it was almost four-thirty.

"Time for *Mr. Wizard*, my favorite show. Want to come in and watch it with me while my mom's on the phone?"

"I'd like that very much, Danny," Joseph replied. Instructing Greta to stay on the porch, he followed Danny through the open door, closing it behind him. Ignoring the angry glare Emily shot his way, he limped down the hallway and into the living room.

"Actually, Professor, he's here right now," Emily said, turning to face the wall.

"And he wants to rent the bedroom and studio in your house?"

"Yes. He said he was going to be working with you and you would vouch for him."

"I can assure you that Joseph Cortez is an honorable man, Mrs. Anderson. His mother was a good friend of mine, and he was one of my first students at the University of Texas. He's a gifted artist. He's also a very private person. I don't think he would disrupt your home."

"Oh, no, I didn't think he would. It's just that…I…"

"Are you afraid of him, Mrs. Anderson?"

"Just tell me he's not a…not a…criminal, or anything like that."

"No…he's not a criminal.…" The old professor hesitated for a long moment, then continued. "Don't feel you have to rent the rooms to him, Mrs. Anderson. He knows he's welcome to stay with me. However, if you need the money…"

"I do," Emily murmured, more to herself than to Richard Mendoza.

"In that case, I don't think you could have a more trustworthy tenant. Have him call me when he gets settled."

"Yes, I'll do that."

"And I'll look forward to seeing you and your son at the faculty picnic on Monday. Rumor has it Professor Roberts will have the honor of escorting you."

Emily laughed at the suddenly teasing tone in Richard Mendoza's deep voice. "Thank you for the compliment, Professor. I'll look forward to seeing you, too. Goodbye." Cradling the receiver, she stared at the telephone for a moment, smiling slightly. He really was a nice man.

"You called Mendoza?"

The soft, masculine voice calmly questioning her from less than two feet away sent Emily spinning and stumbling around to face Cortez. A few minutes ago he had been in the living room, standing by the sofa. How had he managed to move so quickly, so quietly with a limp and a cane?

"You were listening," she accused.

He nodded and took a step closer, as if eavesdropping on her conversation had been his right. Emily, her back against the telephone table, had two choices. She could stay put and face him down, or she could jump up on the tiny table and start screaming. She was moments away from taking a backward leap when Danny wandered out of the living room and stopped beside Joseph.

"When are you moving in?" the boy asked with an eager smile.

"How about Saturday?"

At least he had the courtesy to ask her instead of her son, Emily thought, as she glared at Cortez. What could she say? She did need the money, and Danny seemed to like him. How could she refuse when the two of them stood there, practically joined at the hip, waiting for her to agree?

"Saturday will be fine," she replied, trying not to sound defeated as she pushed past Danny and Cortez. Stopping at the foot of the stairs, she faced her new tenant and managed a gracious smile. Agreeing to rent the rooms had been relatively painless, after all. "Would you like to see the bedroom and studio?"

"I'll show him, Mom," Danny offered, starting up the stairs to the second floor.

"I seem to remember that before you went to Jimmy's house, we made a deal, young man. If I were you, I'd march upstairs and get busy on your own room."

"Aw, gee, Mom..."

"Danny, did you agree to clean your room when you got back from your friend's house?" Joseph asked, ignoring Emily's startled look.

"Yes, sir," Danny replied in a soft voice. Without another word, he started up the steps. Halfway up, he glanced at Joseph, his smile back in place. "See you on Saturday."

"See you." Joseph smiled, too.

"I could have handled that," Emily murmured. "But not without an argument," she added with a wry smile. "Thanks."

"You're welcome." For a moment he shared his smile with her. Then he turned and started down the hallway toward the front door.

"Hey, don't you want to see the rooms?" Emily asked,

exasperation edging into her voice as she trailed along behind him. One minute he was bullying his way into her house, then he was walking away from her, as if her acceptance meant nothing at all.

"No, not today." He did want to see the rooms, and the rest of the house as well, but he'd been on the leg too long already. Attempting to climb the stairs could prove embarrassing. And there was the small matter of the Beretta pressed against his side. What had seemed necessary out on the street seemed out of place in Emily's house. The Beretta and all the other trappings of his job couldn't be left behind, but when he moved in on Saturday, they could and would be put away. Major Joseph Cortez, United States Army, was on medical leave…indefinitely.

"Well, I guess I'll see you on Saturday then." Emily followed Cortez out onto the front porch. He stood at the top of the steps, his back to her, gazing across the green expanse of lawn. He seemed to be a million miles away.

"You love Danny very much, don't you?"

"Yes," she said, though the question startled her.

"He's a nice boy."

"Yes."

"What did Mendoza say to change your mind?"

"He reminded me that I need the money."

He looked at her, throwing a quick, questioning glance over his shoulder, and felt a nudge of pain that had nothing to do with his leg. Then he turned away again and started down the steps, signaling Greta to follow.

"Until Saturday, Mrs. Anderson," he muttered as he limped down the sidewalk, his back rigid—so strong, so self-assured, so alone, Emily thought, in spite of herself.

"Until Saturday," Emily whispered. Crossing her arms in front of her, she wished she could recall her blunt remark about money, even as she cursed the sudden, unexpected shiver of anticipation racing up her spine.

Chapter Two

Despite the throbbing, aching pain in his left leg, Joseph managed the short walk to the car without faltering, stopping only to remove the Rooms for Rent sign from the front lawn. He opened the car door, stepped back so Greta could jump onto the front seat, then tossed in his cane and the sign after her. Hesitating a moment, he turned to face the house once more.

She was standing on the front porch, arms crossed, watching him. As his gaze settled on her, she smiled and raised one hand. Almost imperceptibly Joseph nodded his head, then turned and climbed into the car. Without another glance, he started the engine and pulled away from the curb.

He knew he should go to see Richard Mendoza, but, fueled by a sense of urgency, Joseph headed for the airport instead. In the hour that had passed since he'd pulled up in front of Emily's house, his plans had changed completely. A two- or three-week visit with the old professor had turned into two or three months in the home of Eric Anderson's widow. He would have to return to the ranch to arrange for a longer stay away. If he went straight to the airport, he could be in San Antonio before midnight, and back on the road to Duluth by the following afternoon.

Talking to Mendoza, either in person or by telephone, would take time, when Joseph had little time to spare. In fact, it was probably wise to wait to talk to Richard until after he'd moved into the house. Richard might be getting old, but he was still sharp as a tack. When Joseph let him know his reasons for moving into Emily's house, he wasn't going to be pleased.

He *would*, however, mind his own business, just as he'd done when Emily had called him. For whatever reason, Richard hadn't said anything to her about the military. If he had, Joseph was sure she would have mentioned it. In fact, from what he'd overheard of the conversation, Joseph felt safe in assuming the two weren't close friends, which worked in his favor. They probably wouldn't see or speak to each other before he returned. And once he returned, Joseph's first order of business would be to persuade Mendoza to keep his past a secret indefinitely.

Over and over again during the long flight to San Antonio he caught himself trying to justify his reasons for living in Emily's house. He tried as well to deny his sudden, inexplicable attraction to her. He knew he was drawn to her warmth, to the peace and quiet of her home. But surely that pull was caused by nothing more than his desire to take responsibility for his actions, coupled with his own need to heal.

Again and again he assured himself that he hadn't forced his way into her house. Again and again he tried to justify the fact that he had. She might be strong enough, courageous enough to hang onto an old house and raise her son alone. But there had been a softness, a vulnerability in her eyes and in her voice that had triggered his urge to protect. Only God knew what she had faced on her own because of him. Now, for a while, he could act as a buffer, making her life a little easier. And at the same time he could determine how best to guarantee her future and that of her son. Then he would leave. She would never have to know who or what he was.

In the past he'd always treasured the quiet hours he spent flying alone, but not tonight. Tonight he wanted down and out of the small plane with the desperation of a claustrophobic in a locked closet. He wanted to finish his business at the ranch and begin the drive to Duluth. For the first time in a long time, someone was waiting for him, someone who needed him. So what if he *was* looking forward to being with Emily and Danny Anderson more than he normally looked forward to fulfilling a responsibility? Before he could ponder the question in any detail, the radio crackled to life, and the San Antonio air traffic controllers advised he was cleared to land.

"And then *he* said...?"

"And then *he* said he'd pay five hundred dollars a month for the bedroom and studio." Emily flashed a grin at her friend Cathy, then turned back to the kitchen counter to finish ladling spaghetti sauce into freezer containers. "Looks like I'll be able to turn on the heat this winter, after all."

"Oh, *really*...?" Cathy drawled, her blue eyes twinkling above the rim of her wineglass, her smooth, dark hair swinging against her shoulders as she tilted her head inquisitively.

"Your mind is in the gutter," Emily declared, as she carried out two full containers to the freezer in the back entryway. "But that's what I like about you."

"Seriously, Em, are you having financial problems?"

"Not anymore," Emily replied, as she refilled their wineglasses. Sinking into a chair on the opposite side of the kitchen table, she propped her chin in one hand. "The typing service was slow during the summer, but it'll pick up once school starts, and the med students moved into the apartment on the third floor today."

"And Mr. Cortez is moving in tomorrow, right? What time do you expect him? And *when* am I going to get a look at him?"

"Not only is your mind in the gutter, but you're subtle, too." Emily grinned at her friend, then took a sip of wine. "I'm expecting him in the morning, but I don't think it would be a good idea if—"

"Half the neighborhood turns out to welcome him?"

"You got it. I don't want to scare him away. I may not be at the gates of debtors' prison, but the extra money is going to make life a lot easier."

"What's he like, Em? Does he look like he scares easy?"

"He's...different." Emily twirled her glass round and round, entranced by the play of sunlight on the pale gold liquid. "Sort of the strong, silent type...dark hair, dark eyes, but he's not what you'd call handsome. I don't think he scares easy, and I know for a fact he doesn't take no for an answer."

"Doesn't sound like your kind of guy, Em. It's just as well, though, since he's going to be sleeping across the hall from you." Cathy's words were solemnly spoken, but her eyes were twinkling as she glanced at her friend.

"Oh, yes, just as well. If he were blond and blue-eyed, with a good sense of humor, he wouldn't be safe in *this* house." Emily's tone was equally solemn. Unfortunately, the effect was ruined as her eyes met Cathy's, and both women burst out laughing.

"Hey, want to see how I spent the past couple of days?" Emily asked, when she finally caught her breath. "We can check on the boys, too. They've been awfully quiet for the past hour."

Wineglasses in hand, Emily and her friend walked down the hallway and up the staircase to the second floor. Danny and Jimmy were building the biggest, best spaceship in the world, or so they said. Since Danny owned three boxes of Construx building pieces, Emily knew the boast wasn't made in vain. Reassured that the boys were all right, the two women moved across the large, circular hallway to the doorway of the guest bedroom.

Two large windows overlooked the front lawn. A brass bed, headboard against one wall, stood on the oak floor, and a braided rug beside it picked up the blues and greens in its patchwork quilt. There was a pale oak wardrobe in one corner and a matching dresser and mirror on the wall across from the windows. A small, round table, covered with white eyelet to match the curtains at the windows, served as a nightstand.

Brass candlestick lamps on the dresser and nightstand completed the warm, country look of the room.

"Is it too feminine?" Emily asked, voicing her major concern. "Maybe I ought to ditch the eyelet and find something more severe."

"Yeah, black serge would be terrific," Cathy teased, then gave Emily a reassuring hug. "It looks fine. How about the studio?"

Across the hall they gazed into the room Eric had used as a potter's workshop. Around noon two students had arrived with a pickup truck to haul away the wheel, kiln, and several bags of clay she'd finally decided to donate to the university. Emily had planned to clean out the room months ago, but until that Friday morning, for one reason or another, the studio door had remained closed. Now, as she stood in the doorway of the clean, empty room, Emily felt as if a burden had been lifted from her shoulders.

Danny, too, seemed happy to have the room opened up again. When he had seen Emily stacking pots in a cardboard box, he'd asked for one to use for the pennies he saved. He had carried his choice to his room, then returned to offer his help with dusting and mopping. As they worked side by side, Emily sensed she wasn't the only one laying a ghost to rest.

Like the bedroom, the studio had two windows framed with white eyelet, looking out over the front yard. The room also had an entire wall of floor-to-ceiling windows that Eric had installed a few years earlier. Thick white draperies could be drawn over them for privacy. A simple rattan mat covered most of the gleaming oak floor, and one wall sported rows of empty shelves, painted white to match the walls.

"Nice. You said he's going to paint?"

"That's what he told me."

"Hmm, interesting." They turned and headed for the staircase. "You're sure it's all right if Jimmy spends the night?"

"Of course. You'll owe me one."

"I owe you more than one. Maybe you'll have an opportunity to collect once Mr. Cortez gets settled, especially since you know he's not a criminal," Cathy suggested with a bright smile.

"I doubt it. He's business, not personal. You'll be by for Jimmy at seven?"

"Sorry to make it so early, but we have to drive down to Minneapolis to visit Hank's mother, then back again in time for the picnic on Monday."

"Don't worry about it," Emily assured her friend, as she took Cathy's wineglass and waved her out the front door. "Have fun tonight!"

"I can guarantee it." Cathy, her eyes twinkling again, waved as she skipped down the porch steps.

Watching her friend walk across the lawn, Emily felt a wave of loneliness wash over her, a wave that was closely followed by a nudge of the self-pity she'd felt on Wednesday. Then, as she'd done so often since Wednesday afternoon, she thought of Cortez. With a sigh, she closed the door and headed back toward the kitchen.

"Hey, Mom, can we have some cookies?"

"It's too close to dinner," Emily called up the staircase. So much for feeling lonely.

As she filled a pot with water and set it on the stove to boil, she reminded herself that she should be enjoying her last night without Cortez in the house. But when she thought about the next day, it wasn't with the dread she'd expected to feel at the idea of having a stranger in her house. Instead, she felt as if something wonderful was about to happen. It had to be the wine, she decided, as she rinsed the glasses and put them into the dishwasher. But as the evening wore on, she never quite convinced herself that the happy haze in which she drifted was caused by alcohol alone.

At six o'clock Saturday morning Greta's cold, wet nose urged Joseph out of a sound sleep. By nine he was turning onto Third Street, slowing to a halt in front of Number 235.

"Witch," he growled, as he sat in the Jeep, staring at the house. Anger at his foolishness rolled through him along with a touch of fear. What if she had changed her mind? What if she glared at him through a crack in the door and sent him away?

For two days the memory of her face and the sound of her voice had invaded his thoughts. He hadn't been able to concentrate on ranch business, causing both his foreman and his housekeeper to stare at him more than once. And he'd driven from Texas to Minnesota, barely conscious of the passing scenery as he tried to balance his fantasies with the reality awaiting him on Third Street.

With a wry shake of his head, Joseph opened the door and stepped out of the Jeep. He slammed the door, then had to open it again to retrieve his cane. His fingers clenched the carved, flat handle. If he weren't so damned dependent on it, he'd vent his anger on it and break it in two. No woman was worth the agony of uncertainty he had experienced the past two days, and he had every intention of proving Emily Anderson equally unworthy.

He stabbed the doorbell with his finger once, twice, a third time. He was breathing hard, as if he had run for miles. He wanted... The door flew open in a heavy whoosh of welcome, and there she was, gazing at him with her wide, pale eyes, her face alight with a radiant smile.

"Mr. Cortez, I've been waiting for you." Her voice was richer, warmer than he remembered. She was dressed in neat, white linen pants and a short-sleeved, red silk blouse. She wore a fine gold chain around her neck and small gold hoops in her ears. Her golden-brown curls framed her face in artful disarray, and touches of color enhanced her cheeks and lips.

He wanted...to do a hell of a lot more than say hello. The realization hit him like a fist. Though the search had been unconscious, every nerve in his body vibrated with the sudden awareness that he'd found what he'd been seeking for so long.

He didn't say a word, and he didn't return her smile. He took a step toward her, ignoring the shred of sanity that warned he was making a mistake. Her face tilted up, her smile wavered, her eyes widened with surprise. She smelled as sweet and pretty as she looked, like a handful of wildflowers. His fingers grazed her cheek.

"Hey, Mom, is he here?" Danny hollered from somewhere right behind Emily. She froze for an instant, as did Joseph, their eyes locked. Then Joseph dropped his hand, and each took a step back as Danny jumped through the doorway.

"Hi! Where's Greta?" he asked, as he scanned the porch and front lawn with bright, eager eyes.

"Danny!" Emily scolded mildly.

"It's all right," Joseph intervened, a smile tugging at his lips as he faced the boy. "She's in the Jeep. Would you like to let her out?"

"You have a Jeep, too?" Danny gawked at the black, hard-topped vehicle parked at the curb, then turned to Joseph, a note of pleading in his voice. "Will you take me for a ride in it?"

"Maybe later, if it's all right with your mother. In the meantime, I think Greta is ready to stretch her legs. There's a leash on the seat. Why don't you take her for a walk?"

"Sure," Danny agreed, as he took off like a shot down the porch steps.

"Well," Emily began, crossing her arms in front of her and lowering her eyes. "I guess you'd like to get settled."

"Yes."

"Come in, then." Turning on her heel, she led him into the house, shivering slightly.

"Cold?" Joseph asked in a low voice, as he followed her along the hallway toward the staircase to the second floor.

"Not exactly," Emily replied without a backward glance. Actually she wasn't cold at all. She was...warm, warm all over, inside and out. Unconsciously she touched her cheek, tracing the path his fingers had taken. What a strange man he was, glaring at her one moment as if he wanted to throttle her, then gazing at her with another emotion she'd rather not define.

At the top of the stairs she stopped and turned around. Cortez was no longer right behind her. "Oh, I didn't think," she murmured, watching his slow progress up the steps. "Your leg—"

"Needs the exercise," he stated, his jaw rigid as he stopped beside her. He could feel the faint film of perspiration on his face, and he had to take a couple of deep breaths to steady himself against the pain. God in heaven, if she offered him sympathy, he wasn't sure he could bear it. He didn't want her pity, even if it was one of the few things he could have from her.

"You'll get plenty of that around here." As if reading his mind, Emily spoke lightly, shrugging her shoulders as she walked across the hallway to the bedroom doorway.

Standing to one side, she watched him roam around the room. He looked good today, very good. He was dressed in faded jeans and a chambray shirt, the sleeves rolled up to his elbows, the buttons undone halfway down the front. His flat-heeled, black leather boots were well-worn. Emily allowed herself the pure pleasure of admiring his broad shoulders, his narrow waist and lean hips. Eric had been a huge, soft teddy bear. Cortez was a black panther, hard and dark. She had been wrong to tell Cathy he wasn't a handsome man.

He opened the closet door, inspected the wardrobe, and stopped to peer out one of the windows. As he crossed the room to stand before her, Emily forced her eyes away from the crisp, black hair shadowing the deep bronze of his chest. She studied her perfectly manicured, pink-polished nails with an exaggerated show of indifference, while her heart tap-danced against her ribs. Suddenly she felt like a shy, silly schoolgirl.

"And the studio?" he asked, his voice cool and polite, as he moved past her into the hallway. He had to put some distance between them, and he had to do it fast. He'd caught a glimpse of her eyes, wide and warm, watching him as he surveyed the room. Was she drawn to him, too, or was it his imagination? In any case, he had to rein in the urge to find out, because he had no right to her, none at all.

"Well?" he asked, raising an eyebrow when she didn't move.

"Over here." Emily walked across the hallway, once again standing to one side so Cortez could enter the room. She wanted to kick him, hard. Then she wanted to kick herself.

He had barely glanced at the bedroom. He hadn't even noticed the fresh flowers on the dresser. One minute he made her feel warm and wonderful, and the next he treated her like a stranger on a street corner. When she'd compared him to a panther, she'd forgotten that panthers never purred. They spat and hissed right before they raked you with their claws.

"This certainly looks like an artist's studio," Joseph remarked, as he prowled around the room, treating it with the same air of indifference as the bedroom, stopping only at the wall of windows to stare at the side street below.

"My husband worked in here. Making pottery was his hobby."

"How long has he been gone?" Joseph asked softly, as he continued to stare out the window. Though he knew the answer, he wanted her to talk about it. Suddenly, standing in the studio Eric Anderson had used, Joseph had to know how the man's death had affected Emily. He had been dead for over a year, yet she still wore his ring. And she was twisting it round and round as she'd done the other day.

"He was murdered last July."

"Murdered?" Joseph wheeled to face her.

"Yes, murdered, by the United States government and its military machine," she retorted bitterly, her eyes cold and distant. "Come on, I'll show you the rest of the house."

Maintaining a brisk, businesslike manner, Emily pointed out her bedroom, Danny's bedroom, and the bathroom Joseph would share with her son, advising him to help himself to sheets and towels from the linen closet as he needed them. Joseph followed her wordlessly, trying to assimilate what she'd said about her husband, the government and the military with what he knew had happened. *Murdered?*

Returning to the first floor, she breezed through the living room, dining room and her office. *What had the State Department told her about Eric's death? And why had she spoken of his death as if he had been gunned down intentionally?* As she led him through the butler's pantry and into the kitchen, a wave of foreboding washed over him.

"And that completes the tour," Emily said, as she stopped

in the center of her cheerful, sunny kitchen. "The basement is down there." She opened a door to one side of the pantry doors and indicated a set of steps. "My washer and dryer are down there. If you use the laundry chute in the bathroom, you won't have to carry your stuff down, but up is another story. As I said, you'll get lots of exercise around here." She closed the basement door, and glanced up to find Joseph leaning against the kitchen counter. "I guess that's all."

"A key?" he asked, searching her face for an indication that she knew about his past.

Crossing to the kitchen table, Emily dug into her purse, extracted three keys and a garage door opener, and lined them up on the table. "Front door, back door, garage door, and for your Jeep. You'll want to keep your Jeep in the garage when it gets cold. There's a special heater in there to keep the temperature above freezing." Turning to face him, she smiled slightly, the cold, distant look gone from her eyes.

Of course she didn't know who or what he was. If she did, she never would have let him in the front door. As relief washed over him, Joseph reached into a back pocket and pulled out a check. "Three months in advance." He held out the check, forcing her to cross the room to take it from him. He wanted her close for just a moment more before he chased her away. He had to think about what she'd said, and then he had to talk to Mendoza.

"Fifteen hundred dollars?" Emily stared at the check. Frowning she glanced up at him. "This is too much."

"I can't guarantee how long I'll be here," he reminded her, as well as himself. "And you did say you needed the money."

"Yes," she murmured, her voice barely above a whisper, as she dropped her eyes. "I do need the money."

If she hadn't moved, he would have touched her again. The urge to protect her, to care for her, almost overwhelmed him. But she whirled around, walked back to the kitchen table and tucked the check inside her purse.

"You ought to put that in the bank while you're out. You *are* going out, aren't you?" he asked, his voice reflecting none of the emotion that was forcing his fingers around his cane in a death grip.

"Um, yes, I was, and you're right about the check." *Liar,* she chided herself, as she clasped her car keys, but she'd die before she let him know she'd dressed for his benefit. "I'll ask Danny to leave Greta on the front porch, if it's all right with you."

"Fine."

"Oh, and this is for you. It was in the mailbox yesterday." Emily indicated an envelope that was propped against the salt and pepper shakers on the kitchen table.

He watched as she slung her purse strap over her shoulder and walked out of the kitchen, head high. He heard her calling Danny, and the sound of a car starting. In the silence that followed, he felt the house shift and sigh around him.

Cursing long and low in Spanish and again in English, he pushed away from the counter. Leaning heavily on his cane, he limped across the kitchen to retrieve the envelope, then moved down the hallway. He had to sit down for a few minutes before he tried to unload the trailer, or he'd end up falling down. And he had to think about what Emily had said about her husband.

Crossing the living room, Joseph sank into the wing chair that stood tucked into the shallow bay of the front window. With a sigh, he stretched out his leg and tipped back his head. Beside the chair a small, round table held an array of framed photographs.

Joseph had noticed them on Wednesday, but he'd been too far away and too engrossed in Emily's conversation to study them. Reaching out with one hand, he picked up the largest of the pictures. As his eyes focused on its subject, he felt a slipping, sliding sensation in his head.

"How many dead, Lieutenant?"

"Ten, sir, ten dead. Three of ours, six of theirs, and one civilian, an American. His name is—"

"I don't give a damn who he is. Probably some hotshot reporter. Damned fool, running with a pack of rebels in the

middle of a war zone. Bag the body and send it to the embassy.''

Staring back at him with bright, blue eyes was a big man, a man with thick, straight blond hair and an easy smile. The man he'd found lying dead in a jungle clearing in Norteña just over a year ago. The man who had haunted him ever since. He was sitting on the lawn in front of the house, holding Emily in his lap while Danny hugged him from behind. With a muttered curse, Joseph slammed the photograph onto the table and stood up, raking his fingers through his hair.

What had she said? That her husband had been murdered by the United States government and the military. But she'd said the words with such anger, such bitterness, such *hatred*. What had the State Department told her? More precisely, what had they failed to tell her? And what would she do if she found out he worked for the government, if she found out he was a part of the military machine she hated, if she found out he'd directed the battle that had resulted in her husband's death? She'd turn her anger, her bitterness, her hatred on him, and would never allow him to help Danny and herself.

Despair clawed at his chest. He had no right to move into her house. Guilt ate at his belly. He should be damned to hell for even thinking of wanting, *needing* her warmth the way he did. A sharp edge of fear sliced through his soul. He risked hurting her badly, when all he wanted was to help her. And he risked hurting himself in a way he'd never been hurt before. The wisest thing he could do was to walk out the door and never come back.

Rubbing a hand over his forehead, Joseph turned his back on the table full of pictures, knowing as he did so that he was turning his back on wisdom, as well.

He needed the time in Duluth—time to heal, and time to sort out his feelings for Emily Anderson, feelings that twined and twisted together with a sudden, painful clarity. His searing sense of responsibility bound him to her, but if he stayed in her house, he must make sure she never found out about his past. Yet without a past there could be no future.

He could stay in her house, but he could not allow their

relationship to exceed the bounds of friendship. The tradition of duty and honor inherited from his grandfather and father wound around him, tying him to Emily Anderson even as it drove a wedge between them. As long as he didn't take her as a lover, as long as they were friends, and friends only, he wouldn't have to tell her who or what he was. And he would have to be damned sure that she didn't find out from someone else.

Mendoza.

Frowning, Joseph studied the envelope in his hand, recognizing the professor's handwriting. Ripping it open, he read the short message. Richard had gone fishing and wouldn't return until sometime Monday morning. He hoped to see Joseph at the faculty picnic Monday afternoon, or in his office Tuesday morning.

With a muttered curse, Joseph limped toward the front door. Since Mendoza wasn't available, he would tackle the trailer first, because he was staying. If he left, Emily would haunt him in a way that would make the jungle nightmare seem like a Disney movie.

Then, Joseph thought grimly, he was going to explore Duluth, Minnesota. Emily Anderson wasn't the only single woman in town, and it had been a while since he'd been with a woman. His attraction to Emily was probably nothing more than rampaging hormones. If he satisfied himself with another woman, he wouldn't be tempted to touch her. And then, God willing, he could take care of her and her son without telling her about his past.

It was one o'clock Sunday morning. She should have been in bed, asleep. Instead she was standing in front of the open refrigerator door, its light forming a halo around her in the dark kitchen as she searched for something to eat. Actually she wasn't hungry, but she *was* tempted to snitch another of his beers. She'd had one earlier, telling herself it was for medicinal purposes, hoping it would help her sleep. A second one would probably do her in, but Emily didn't like the idea of owing Cortez anything, not even a couple of cans of beer.

Thumping the door closed, she glanced at the clock again. It was two minutes past one.

Frowning, Emily wandered out of the kitchen, her long, white cotton nightgown brushing against her body as she moved. She rubbed her hands along her bare arms. She hadn't thought to put on a robe, but then she hadn't planned to visit the inside of her refrigerator when she left her bedroom, just to check the doors one more time. The doors, of course, were as securely locked as they'd been at eleven and at midnight.

"Where is he?" Emily whispered, joining Greta in her vigil at the front door. She peered through the small, clear oval in the etched glass panel for the umpteenth time. The porch light glowed brightly, invitingly, while the street beyond was dark and quiet, as it had been all evening. "Do you think he plans to stay out all night?" Greta nudged her, thumping her tail on the floor. Emily wasn't sure if the answer was yes or no. Smiling slightly at her foolishness, she turned, retracing her path along the hallway and up the staircase. She'd do well to remember Cortez didn't have a curfew.

By the time she'd returned from the bank and a quick trip to the shopping mall, he had moved in and gone out. He'd returned late in the afternoon to shower, change clothes, and leave Greta in Danny's care. Emily had been engrossed in a typing project in her office. She hadn't paid much attention to his coming and going, assuming he'd return again later in the evening. And Danny, in typical little-boy fashion, hadn't asked where Cortez was going when he eagerly agreed to feed Greta and take her for a walk before dark.

Peering into her son's room, Emily assured herself he was tucked under the quilt and sleeping soundly. Then, lured by the glow of the lamp she'd lighted in Cortez's bedroom, she crossed the hallway. He had added very little of himself to the room, she thought as she stepped through the doorway. A long, rectangular pad covered the floor beside the wardrobe, probably for Greta, although Emily imagined Cortez might be spartan enough to use it himself. A small, black travel clock and three books rested on the nightstand, and he'd added a brush and comb and a bottle of men's cologne to the dresser.

Lifting the green glass bottle, Emily removed the cap, closed her eyes, and inhaled the sharp scent of spice. She wanted…to wring his neck for worrying her. Recapping the bottle, she replaced it on the dresser and stalked out of the bedroom.

No, she wasn't worried about him, she told herself, as she retraced her path to the kitchen, opened the refrigerator and retrieved a beer. There was no doubt in her mind that Cortez was capable of taking care of himself, and reporting his whereabouts wasn't something he'd do, even if she demanded it. He was paying a lot of money to live in her house; as long as he didn't disturb her, she had no right to complain. It was her problem, not his, if his presence disturbed her less than his absence.

Popping the top of the beer can, Emily walked up three steps of the staircase, turned and sat down. At the front door, Greta whined and wagged her tail. "To those of us who wait," Emily said, saluted the dog with the can, then enjoyed several hearty swallows of the cold brew. He was probably visiting Professor Mendoza. Or maybe, she theorized as she drained the can, he was out making new friends, or rather, *a* new friend.

Setting the can on the step beside her, Emily drew up her legs, bent forward a bit, and wrapped her arms around her knees. The light from the porch lamp, filtering through the etched glass door panel, combined with the dim glow of the light halfway up the staircase to cast shadows up and down the hallway and into the living room.

It had been quite a while since she'd sat on the steps waiting for a man to come home. But waiting then had been different. She had been waiting for her husband. Tonight she waited for a stranger, a cold, hard man who had offered her nothing but enough money to make it through the winter.

She really needed to have her head examined. But first she needed to sleep. Resting her cheek on her folded arms, she closed her eyes. Just for a minute, one little minute, she swore. Then she'd rouse herself and go up to bed.

* * *

"Madre de Dios," he muttered, his slow progress down the shadowed hallway grinding to a halt. He focused weary eyes on the woman sleeping on the staircase.

He had spent fourteen hours trying to thrust her image out of his mind, driving up one side of Duluth and down the other, then wandering along the shore of Lake Superior, the cool night wind seeping into his bones, only to find her sleeping on the steps like a lost soul. If his urge to laugh hadn't been so strong, he might have been tempted to sit down beside her and cry. No, if he sat down beside her in his present frame of mind, he'd pull her onto his lap, and...

Damn it! Why couldn't she sleep in her bed like a normal person? He wanted to unleash his anger on her. He wanted to grab her and shake her, and send her running up the staircase. But he was honest enough to admit his anger was fueled by guilt and fear, the same guilt and fear that had been eating at him since morning. And he knew why she was sleeping on the steps. Had she been gone, he'd have waited for her, too.

Greta's wet nose nudged his hand. "Yes, you're right, *niña.* We ought to wake her and take her to bed," he said, his voice soft and gentle as the night.

Take her to bed. Now there was an idea, and no more than she deserved, since she had eliminated the possibility of him taking any other woman to bed. He wasn't suffering from rampaging hormones or anything as base as mere sexual desire. In fact, if roaming around Duluth had proven anything, it was that he didn't need just any woman. He wanted, needed, Emily Anderson, and if all he could have with her was friendship, it would be all he had.

Reaching out with one hand, Joseph brushed a soft curl away from her face. Her skin felt warm and silky against his fingertips. "Emily. Emily, wake up." Leaning on his cane, he bent over and ran his hand down her back in a long, slow caress. Her cotton nightgown was almost as warm and soft as her skin, and once again he caught the faint scent of wildflowers. Cupping her shoulder with his hand, he shook her gently. "Wake up, *querida.*"

Emily opened her eyes and sat up stiffly. "You're home."

Her low voice held a hint of relief. "I was wait…um, checking the doors." Groping around with one hand, she found the beer can. "I borrowed a beer…two beers. Must have fallen asleep." Grabbing the stair rail, she hoisted herself to her feet and stood swaying above him. She blinked and wet her lips with the tip of her tongue. "Guess I'll go up to bed."

But Emily didn't move, and neither did Joseph. The pale glow of the hall light, shining behind her, had rendered her thin, cotton gown transparent. Beneath it she wore nothing, nothing at all. She was dressed, yet undressed, and Joseph was sure he'd never seen anything quite so erotic in his life. Slowly, unconsciously, she raised a hand and traced the neckline of her gown, her eyes locked with his. Joseph's fingers opened and closed around the head of his cane, matching the rhythm of his pounding heart.

"Are you coming?" she asked innocently, her voice barely above a whisper.

God in heaven, why are You punishing me? With a mighty effort, Joseph managed to suppress a groan as he felt his body tighten and grow hard with desire. Friendship be damned. By everything that was holy, he was going to forget duty and honor and turn hell into heaven, if she didn't scoot up the staircase, and do it soon.

"Is that an invitation, Mrs. Anderson?" He deepened his voice to a suggestive drawl as he raked her with his eyes.

Mrs. Anderson? She was sure he'd called her Emily a moment ago. And why was he looking at her like that? She felt her whole body flush under the heat of his gaze. "No. No, it wasn't an invitation," she countered with a shake of her head. Crushing the empty can in her hand, she whirled and ran up the stairs.

The back view was almost as alluring as the front, but Joseph forced himself not to follow her. He waited until he heard her bedroom door close with a loud, decisive click. Then he too climbed the staircase, slowly, his legs a bit unsteady.

He was going to have to stay away from her. It wasn't going to be easy to do, not in a nice way, not when she already cared enough to wait up for him. Not when she seemed to be drawn to him in the same way he was drawn to her.

At another time, in another place, he would have been elated by the knowledge that she cared for him, but here and now he was nothing but tired, so very, very tired. He stood in the doorway of his bedroom for a long moment. Then he turned and headed for the bathroom. Despite his overwhelming exhaustion he knew that if he wanted to sleep, he'd have to keep a hot date with a cold shower first.

Chapter Three

By the time Emily crawled out of bed Sunday morning, dressed and trudged downstairs, Cortez was gone. Danny, sprawled on the living-room floor, watching *Sesame Street* and coloring, responded to her question concerning his whereabouts with a shrug of his shoulders. He didn't know where Mr. Cortez was, but before he'd left he'd fixed the best pancakes in the world. Running a hand through her hair, Emily headed for the kitchen, expecting to find a mess. Instead, a fresh pot of coffee beckoned from the clean kitchen counter, and inside the refrigerator Emily discovered a neatly labeled container of leftover pancake batter.

Well into her third cup, she had to admit the man knew how to make a decent pot of coffee; she loved the hint of cinnamon he'd added. His pancake batter was better than hers; she'd eaten a stack of four with butter and syrup. But pancakes, coffee and a clean kitchen didn't make her feel any better about being caught on the staircase. And she certainly wasn't ready to forgive him for insinuating that she'd offered him an invitation to share her bed. That was the last place she wanted to be with him, or any other man.

Emily had planned to take Danny swimming at the Spirit Mountain Recreation Area, but as she loaded her dishes into the dishwasher she noticed dark clouds filling the sky. By the time she'd finished making beds it was raining, and Danny agreed it was a good day to stay home. They spent an hour playing his favorite board games. Then he ran the vacuum cleaner while Emily dusted. Greta, left behind again, followed them from room to room, playing tag with Danny and the vacuum.

The day wore on with no sign of Cortez. Danny added another original building to his growing Lego town, and Emily spent the afternoon completing another typing project. At six o'clock, tired of being cooped up in the house, they donned slickers, grabbed umbrellas and headed for The Chinese Lantern for dinner. They were home by eight, and by nine Danny was ready for bed.

After she kissed her son good-night, Emily prowled from one room to another like a caged animal. *Where was he?* And why had Cortez been so insistent on moving into her house, if he didn't plan to spend any time there? Catching herself in the doorway of his bedroom, she gave herself a firm mental shake. She had too much to do to waste time and energy on aimless wandering, and she wasn't about to have him find her mooning around the house. She strode down the staircase with determination, entered her office and sat down to work. At midnight she checked the doors one last time, walked upstairs, showered and slipped into her nightgown. At two o'clock, when the front door clicked shut, she rolled over, closed her eyes, and finally fell asleep.

It was after ten Monday morning when Emily woke up. She was tired and cranky and in no mood for the University of Minnesota in Duluth faculty's first Labor Day picnic. But Danny had been looking forward to the outing, and Glen Roberts was picking them up at noon. At least the weather had cleared; bright sunshine poured through her bedroom window. With a muffled groan, she climbed out of bed and got dressed.

Danny's room was empty, as was Cortez's, and the house seemed too quiet as Emily walked down the staircase. She was beginning to wonder where they were when she saw the note propped against the fresh pot of coffee on the kitchen counter. He'd taken Danny for the promised Jeep ride, and they'd be back by eleven. Just as she managed to decipher the black slash of the signature, she heard the Jeep idling in the driveway. A few moments later she heard it rolling away, as Danny and Greta crashed through the back door.

Gone again, Emily thought, as she hugged her son and asked about his ride. She should be grateful that Cortez was staying out of her way, but wasn't. In fact, she was going to have to talk to him about keeping more normal hours. For reasons she was too tired to examine, she simply couldn't sleep until he was in the house. And if she didn't start getting some rest, she was going to say or do something rash. Of that she was sure.

He'd made a mistake, another in the long line of errors he'd made since Wednesday afternoon, Joseph thought, as he sat alone on a park bench observing the faculty picnic. Men, dressed in pale slacks, polo shirts and summer blazers shook hands and slapped backs, smiling as they spoke to one another. Women in pastel dresses admired the antics of their sons and daughters, as the children rolled and raced about the lawn, giggling and shrieking with joy. From a distance they appeared to be so at ease with each other.

He had dressed for the part. His khaki slacks, blue shirt and navy blazer were perfectly correct. But he could no more move among them with a polite smile and casual words than walk on the moon. Drowning in the hot, heavy humidity of an Asian jungle, stinking of his own sweat, insides crawling with fear, didn't go a long way toward preparing one for the garden party atmosphere of a faculty picnic. Neither did months of moving in and out of guerilla camps in Central America, nor hours spent on bar stools in village cantinas. He belonged in the jungle, in the camps, on the bar stools. He did not belong here and never would.

But Professor Eric Anderson had belonged, and so did she. She moved among them with poise and confidence, alike yet different in her bright yellow sundress and kelly-green cardigan, sleeves pushed up to her elbows. Like a little parakeet among pigeons. He almost smiled at the thought. Reaching into the inside pocket of his blazer, he pulled out a long, thin cigar and a slim, gold lighter.

"Ah, my friend, I've been looking for you."

Joseph drew deeply on his cigar, slipping his lighter into his pocket. Eyes narrowed, he glanced up, studying Richard Mendoza for a moment through a thin trail of blue smoke. Then, without a word, he turned back to the scene that had held his attention for almost thirty minutes.

With a sigh, Richard sat down on the bench beside Joseph, stretching his legs to match his friend's careless pose. Frowning slightly, he followed the direction of Joseph's gaze.

"It's been a long time, Joseph."

"Too long, Mendoza."

"And yet I don't think you're happy to be here. In fact, I think you're upset about something."

"Why do you say that, Professor?"

"You're smoking. You only smoke those fancy, little cigars when you're upset about something."

Shifting his weight slightly, Joseph sat up and propped his elbows on his knees. Without looking at Mendoza, he drew on the cigar again, releasing the smoke slowly. "You know me too well, old friend."

"I thought you'd stop by the house or call last Wednesday. What happened to you?"

"Had to go back to the ranch. I had to arrange to be away longer than a week or two."

"Your plans changed rather suddenly, didn't they? I was surprised when she called to tell me you wanted to move into her house. And since then I've begun to have the feeling that you didn't invite yourself to Duluth for the sole purpose of spending time with me."

"No." Joseph studied the glowing tip of his cigar, then inhaled once again.

"So why *did* you come here, Joseph? And what do you think you're doing, living in Emily Anderson's house?" Though he hadn't moved or turned to look at Joseph, anger vibrated through Richard Mendoza's words. "You haven't told her about yourself, have you? But by now you must know how her husband died, not to mention how she feels about the military. She's had enough to deal with over the past year. If she finds out about your background, *Major,* she's going to be very upset."

"Yes, very upset," Joseph agreed, his voice rough as he threw down his cigar and crushed it with the toe of his boot. He clasped his hands, staring at the ground. "Especially if she finds out that I was responsible for her husband's death."

"What are you talking about?" Mendoza demanded, rounding on his friend, visibly concerned. "According to what I heard, Eric Anderson was hit by a stray bullet while driving on a back road in Norteña. I don't know any of the details, but I can't believe you were the one who fired the gun."

"So that's what they told her," Joseph muttered, shifting again to lean against the back of the bench.

He was silent for a few seconds, watching the people milling around the park. A cool breeze rustled through the branches of the tree shading the bench, and sunlight slanted over his face for an instant. As the man standing beside Emily put his arm around her shoulders, Joseph frowned and ran a hand across his face.

"When I asked her about his death, she said he was murdered by the United States government and its military machine. She said it as if she believed he'd been killed intentionally. A stray bullet doesn't sound intentional to me."

"Eric had a reputation for pacifism in the university community, both here and abroad. In the late sixties and early seventies he protested the war in Vietnam and, as a conscientious objector, he worked in the veterans' hospital in Minneapolis for three years. More recently, he protested the United States government's policies in Central America, claiming we were headed for another Vietnam.

"Before he left for Norteña to research his book on Central

America, he was warned by the State Department to be careful. When he was killed, and the State Department refused to give her more than a few sketchy details, Emily made it known that she thought he had been assassinated because of his past and present political beliefs.''

"What did you mean when you said you're responsible for his death?'' Mendoza asked quietly, when Joseph failed to respond.

"Eric Anderson was killed in a small, nasty battle along the border of Norteña and Arteaga. He was running with a band of Arteagan soldiers who decided to pay Norteña a friendly little visit. On my orders men under my command ran them off. We were conducting military exercises at the request of the Norteñian government. We weren't there to fight a war, but when somebody shoots at you, you shoot back. I guess that's why the State Department released the stray bullet story.''

Once again Joseph ran a hand over his face, then leveled his gaze at Mendoza. "I was there, Richard. I gave the order to shoot to kill. My lieutenant shipped his body to the embassy. I was responsible for his death. Any way you look at it, I'm responsible.''

"How can you say that, Joseph? You're no more responsible for Eric's death than I am, and you know it. If what you just told me is true, no one's responsible for Eric Anderson's death but Eric Anderson. He was warned about the danger, yet he chose to go. And your men were defending themselves.''

"Is that what you think Emily will believe if I tell her the truth?''

"Is that why you're here? To tell her the truth?''

"God, no. And don't you tell her either, Mendoza. If she finds out, she'll put me out.''

"And well she should, Joseph. What the hell are you playing at? You have no right living in her home under false pretenses. The best thing you could do for her is stay away from her. She's started to rebuild her life. Get out before you say or do something to stir up her anger, her bitterness, her pain.''

"I can't, Richard, at least not yet. Because of me, her husband is dead. Because he's dead, she needs the money I'm paying her to live in her house. It's all I can do for her now, but given time, I intend to find a way to guarantee her future, and Danny's. Once I do that, I'll leave, and she'll never have to know who or what I am."

"I don't like it. I don't like it at all." Mendoza stood up, swept back his jacket and tucked his hands into his pockets. "I don't know her well, but I do know Emily Anderson is a good woman, a woman who has suffered enough. She's also young and attractive and very much alive. I saw the way you've been watching her. How long do you think you can keep your hands off her?"

"You bastard," Joseph snarled, as his fingers wrapped around the head of his cane. He pulled himself up slowly, painfully. Leaning heavily on the cane, he faced Mendoza. "You think I don't know how badly I've hurt her already?" he continued, his voice rough as gravel. "You think I'd do anything to hurt her more? You don't know me at all, do you, old man?"

Joseph limped away through the sunlight and the shadows. "Wait!" his mentor called, but the command failed to halt him. Richard hastened after him, catching Joseph as he opened the door of his Jeep.

"Joseph, I'm sorry. I just don't want to see her hurt, and I don't want to see you hurt, either."

"I can take care of myself." Joseph eyed Richard's hand on his arm with distaste. Turning, he tossed his cane onto the front seat, eased away from Richard's grasp, and climbed in. He fitted his key into the ignition and started the engine.

"I hope so, my friend. I hope so. But I know you too well, remember? And if what I see in your eyes when you look at her is any indication of how you feel about her, you'd better start laying the groundwork for the day you realize you can't walk away from her. That will be the day you'll have to tell her who you are."

Without a word, Joseph reached out to close the door. He glanced at his old friend's face, then away.

"You'll come and sketch with my advanced students tomorrow morning as planned, won't you?"

Joseph knew that whatever Richard Mendoza had said, he'd said because he cared. In fact, he'd offered a first, faint ray of hope along with some very good advice. And Joseph was honest enough to admit he needed the time with Richard as much as he needed the time with Emily and her son. Working with Richard Mendoza gave depth and direction to his artistic skills.

"Yes, I'll be there."

As Richard nodded and stepped back, Joseph shut the door of the Jeep. A moment later he was driving away, leaving Richard far behind.

By the time Emily had convinced herself that she ought to say hello to Cortez, and managed to slip away from Glen and his friends, Cortez was apparently involved in an argument with Richard Mendoza. When Joseph stood up and limped toward his Jeep, Emily wanted nothing more than to grab Danny by the hand and go with her new tenant. But she stayed in the shadows, watching him drive away, turning back to the picnic only when Glen slipped an arm around her shoulders and announced it was time to eat.

Later, much later, Emily concealed an enormous yawn with one hand, and decided she'd had enough picnic for one day. With a touch, a smile and a few soft words, she managed to draw Glen's attention away from the intricate details of a colleague's latest programming coup. Collecting Danny from an impromptu soccer game took only a moment. Fifteen minutes later they were pulling into her driveway behind Joseph's Jeep.

"Looks like you have company, Emily. Were you expecting someone?" Glen seemed only mildly curious as he ran a hand over his thick, straight blond hair and adjusted his horn-rimmed glasses.

"That's Joseph's Jeep," Danny explained. "There he is on the porch. That's his dog, Greta. You haven't met her, so she might bite you." There was relish in the boy's voice as he released his seat belt and fumbled with the door handle.

"Now, wait just a minute, young man. I was speaking to your mother. It was rude of you to interrupt."

"It's all right, Glen." Emily didn't like the way Glen and Danny spoke to each other, but she couldn't trace the origin of their animosity. Most of all she hated being in the middle. Reaching for her door handle, she tried to placate Glen. "The Jeep belongs to my new boarder, Joseph Cortez. He's a friend of Richard Mendoza's." Slipping out of Glen's car without a backward glance, she started across the lawn.

He stood at the top of the porch steps. She could barely see his face in the deepening twilight shadows. Stopping at the foot of the steps, unsure what to expect, she offered a tentative smile. "I wanted to say hello at the picnic, but you left before I had a chance." His dark eyes caught and held hers for an instant, then settled on Glen Roberts as he came to a halt behind her. Danny, with Greta in tow, disappeared inside the house, leaving the three adults alone.

"Glen, this is Joseph Cortez. I was just explaining—"

"Actually, Emily, you didn't tell me anything about another boarder until we pulled into the driveway. I thought you only had room for two, er, students in the apartment."

"I'm staying in the house."

"In the house?" Glen muttered. "Emily, have you lost your mind? You have *that* man living in your house? What was Mendoza thinking to send him here? What about your reputation?" Though Glen spoke softly to her alone, Emily was sure Joseph had overheard.

"Glen, for goodness' sake," Emily protested, her smile fading. "Professor Mendoza didn't send him here. I put a sign on the front lawn advertising rooms for rent. I'm a grown woman with a son and a huge house to support. To be honest, I can't afford to worry about my reputation. Right now I need the money."

"Let me assure you I have no intention of saying or doing anything to harm Mrs. Anderson or her reputation." Eyes narrowing, Joseph leveled his gaze on Glen Roberts.

He was a big blond man, his resemblance to Eric Anderson readily apparent. Joseph knew he should be pleased that her taste in men was so single-minded. He must be part of the new life she was rebuilding. Unfortunately, Joseph couldn't stand the sight of him.

"And I will deal personally, unpleasantly, with anyone who says or does anything to hurt her in any way," Joseph continued, his threat echoing through the growing darkness, all the more lethal because it was issued in such a soft, steady voice.

"Really, Mr. Cortez, I wasn't suggesting—"

"I know exactly what you were suggesting." Settling his eyes on Emily once again, Joseph smiled slightly. "Are you coming, Emily? It's getting cold out here."

"Well, I... Um, nice to meet you, Cortez. I guess I'll be going, Emily. Good night."

Emily, hands clasped in front of her, concentrated on counting her fingers as Glen stalked across the lawn and swung into his car. When the sound of the car's engine had finally drifted away, she allowed herself to look up. The porch was empty, the front door slightly ajar. On the second floor the lights in the studio flickered to life. With a new sense of determination, Emily marched into the house and slammed the door.

"Danny, come on, time to take a bath," she called as she started up the staircase.

She'd get Danny into the tub. Then she was going to talk to Mr. Cortez. She wasn't sure what she was going to say, but he'd pulled his disappearing act once too often. For three days he'd avoided her like the plague. Then he'd stood on her front porch looking and acting like a jealous lover. And she didn't like the way he'd asked her if she was coming, didn't like it one bit. She couldn't remember ever feeling quite so confused and angry in her life.

After the usual grousing around, Danny finally managed to collect a pair of clean pajamas and a couple of toys to play with in the bathtub. Warning him not to splash water all over the floor, and advising him to use soap on his face as well as his body, Emily closed the door and crossed the hallway.

She hesitated for just a moment outside the studio door, listening to the soft strains of symphony music and the rhythmic thunk and clunk of exercise equipment. Along with his art supplies, Cortez had added a small stereo system and a bench with weights and pulleys to the studio. When she'd caught a glimpse of the latter, it had made her think of a torture chamber. She imagined him lying flat on his back on the bench, raising and lowering his leg, his face beaded with sweat, and she almost turned away. But if she waited to talk to him until morning, she risked another sleepless night, and she was so tired.

"Cortez!" she called, rapping her knuckles against the heavy, wooden door, refusing to have any sympathy for the man. "Cortez, I have to talk to you."

The music drifted on, but the thunking stopped. "I'm busy." The thunking started again.

"I don't give a damn. I want to talk to you, and I want to talk to you now." Emily slammed the palm of her hand against the door for emphasis.

"No," he replied without a break in his rhythm.

"Cortez!" Emily reached for the doorknob and tried to turn it. When it refused to budge, she rattled it violently. "You locked the door. This is my house. You have no right to lock a door in my house." Her voice rose a couple of decibels as she slammed her hand against the door again.

"I'm paying you five hundred dollars a month for the right to lock two doors in your house, Mrs. Anderson. The door you're pounding on is one of them. We'll talk in the morning." His voice was calm and courteous, and not once did he break the rhythm of his workout. "Oh, and I'm sorry I chased your boyfriend away."

"You *are* sorry, Cortez. You're a sorry son of—" Emily ground her teeth together, trying to regain her self-control. She was losing her temper, and she *never* lost her temper. It was so undignified. But the man was making her crazy, and he knew it. "If you don't open this door right now, Cortez—"

"Hey, Mom, why are you hollering at Mr. Cortez?"

Emily whipped around to find her son standing behind her, dressed in his pajamas. "I, um, I want to talk to him, Danny," she replied, making an effort to lower her voice. The thunking had stopped again.

"Maybe he wants to be private, Mom. You told me you lock your bedroom door because you need to be private. Maybe he needs to be private, too."

Emily eyed her young son with dismay. They *had* talked about privacy on various occasions, and he was only repeating her own words on the subject. "You're right, Danny," she admitted, embarrassed by her behavior. "Get into bed, and I'll be in to kiss you good-night in just a moment."

"Thanks, Danny." The deep voice rumbled with a hint of laughter.

"You're welcome, Mr. Cortez," Danny replied. Then, catching the look on his mother's face, he scurried across the hall and into his bedroom.

"In the morning, Cortez," Emily muttered, as she turned to follow Danny. "And he's *not* my boyfriend."

"In the morning, Mrs. Anderson," he agreed. The sound of his laughter tickled her spine as she walked away.

"Danny, hurry up in there, will you? It's almost seven-thirty. I don't want you to miss the bus on the first day of school."

"Okay, Mom," Danny called through the closed bathroom door. An instant later Emily heard him giggle.

"Boys!" she muttered to herself, certain she would never understand their universal fascination with bathrooms.

Glancing across the hallway, she noticed Cortez's bedroom door was open, as was the studio door. Both rooms were empty and the bed had been straightened. Greta, lying on the bedroom floor, lifted her head and wagged a greeting. Emily wasn't sure if she was relieved or angry that he'd disappeared again. She was going to have to talk to him, but it might be easier if he had a chance to forget her childish behavior first. And she had to get herself together, too, she thought, as she turned and walked back into her bedroom. He had a way of setting her off that was beginning to threaten her sanity.

As she rummaged around in her drawers and closet, Emily realized that once again she'd let the laundry go one day too many. Danny had his new school clothes, but she was left with a baggy, white sweatshirt, a pair of red silk panties with black lace lips in a rather obnoxious place, and a pair of jeans that had seen better days. She slipped into the panties and sweatshirt, and pulled the jeans off a hook at the back of her closet. She was about to step into them when she glanced at the clock beside her bed. It was seven-forty, Danny was still in the bathroom, and it was awfully quiet in there. Maybe he was suffering from a nervous stomach. The first day of first grade *was* a big event for a little boy.

Clutching her jeans in one hand, Emily strode out of her bedroom. "Danny, honey, are you all right?" Her vivid imagination lent a note of hysteria to her voice as she yanked open the bathroom door, took two steps forward, and stopped dead. "Oh, God, I'm sorry. I didn't realize...I thought you were gone."

Joseph Cortez stood at the basin, razor in hand, clad only in black, hip-hugging briefs and a black T-shirt. As he turned to face her, his arm poised in midair, Emily couldn't help but see that the shirt didn't quite cover his lean, hard belly. With a will all their own, her eyes homed in on his navel, and followed the mat of curly black hair that dipped so enticingly into the low-slung waist band of his briefs. *Don't, whatever else you do, don't look down,* she warned herself, then jumped at the sound of Danny's voice.

"Hi, Mom. Joseph's shaving. Want to watch?"

It took an enormous effort, but Emily managed to peel her eyes away from Cortez's magnificent, masculine body. She had been quite unable to resist temptation. She had looked down. Now she turned to see her son seated on the edge of the old, claw-footed bathtub.

"Danny—" she began, her face burning a bright shade of red, but Cortez's deep, calm voice cut across her words.

"It's all right, Mrs. Anderson. Danny asked if he could watch me shave. I told him it was okay."

As Emily glanced back at Cortez, she saw that he was watching her with a bemused expression in his eyes. His face was lathered with shaving soap. His hair fell in soft, dark waves across his forehead. He looked younger, softer, more vulnerable than she would have thought possible, and she could hardly bear it. Seconds ticked away as she stared at him, caught again in his magic spell.

"You're welcome to watch, too."

Although he didn't smile, Emily was sure she heard a teasing note in his voice. It dawned on her that she was staring at him, and he wasn't dressed. And *she* wasn't dressed. "Do you always wear black underwear?" In her confusion, her thoughts became words. She thought it was impossible that her face could burn more brightly, but it did.

"Not always." Cortez gazed back at her, his dark eyes unreadable as he answered her evenly, all trace of teasing gone from his voice. "How about you? Partial to red, are you? Or are you still celebrating yesterday's government holiday?"

Emily, pressing her lips together in an effort to keep her mouth shut, considered her white sweatshirt, her red panties, and the blue jeans she clutched in her hand. "Just partial to red," she said, trying to keep her voice serious, but her eyes twinkled as she looked at Cortez.

It could have been her imagination, but Emily was sure an approving smile touched his eyes and lifted the corners of the mouth beneath the thick, black mustache before he turned back to face the mirror. As he moved, though, her attention was diverted from his face, and for the first time she noticed his left leg. Running up the side, from midcalf to the top of his thigh, was a thick, angry red weal of scar tissue. She caught her breath, then let it go in a whisper.

"Oh, Cortez, your leg…"

He froze for an instant, the razor still poised in midair. Then, without looking at her, he continued to stroke the steel blade along one side of his face. He couldn't bear to see the pity in her pale eyes, couldn't bear to wonder at the anguish he heard in her voice.

"He's got a zipper in his leg," Danny advised from his seat on the edge of the bathtub. "In case the doctors have to operate again. They operated two times already, and they put the bones back together real good." He waited expectantly for some reply, but when neither Joseph nor his mother responded, he decided, in typically six-year-old fashion, to change the subject. "Those little pants look great, Mom. Are they the ones Mrs. Stewart gave you for a joke?"

Caught off guard, Emily turned to look at her son, almost, but not quite missing the clatter of a razor being dropped into the basin to the tune of a muttered "damn."

"Yes, they are," she agreed absently, watching out of the corner of her eye as Cortez tried unsuccessfully to stanch the flow of blood from his chin with a tissue.

"Well, why don't you wear the little red socks she gave you, too? 'Member the ones with the black, lacy stuff around the edges and the little black bows on the sides. Dad said they were klinky, but I bet Joseph—"

"Daniel Anderson!" Emily rounded on her son, realizing at last where the conversation was heading. She glared at him, trying to ignore the choking sounds coming from Cortez. "I'm going to throttle you if you don't get out of this bathroom immediately. You are to go downstairs—"

"Aw, gee, mom—"

"Immediately!"

As Danny jumped off the side of the bathtub and edged past her, Emily whirled to face Cortez. His dark eyes were sparkling with humor, and his lips twitched as he dabbed at the spot of blood on his chin. She tightened her hold on her jeans and tried to do the same with her temper.

"Klinky?" he asked, his laughter rumbling around the word.

"Mr. Cortez, from now on, when you're using the bathroom, please lock the door," Emily snapped, as she straightened her shoulders and lifted her chin.

"Mrs. Anderson, last night you were upset because I locked a door. Now you're upset because I didn't. You keep changing the rules," he teased.

"Mr. Cortez, this is my house. I can change the rules any time I want. Lock the bathroom door!"

Spinning on her heel, Emily stalked out of the bathroom and into her bedroom. With a mighty shove, she slammed the door, effectively silencing the laughter that was Cortez's response to her order.

The man was impossible, she thought, as she pulled on her jeans and zipped them. He made her feel...what? He made her feel...alive. Yes, for the first time in over a year, she felt *alive*.

For just an instant Emily also felt an edge of guilt as her eyes rested on the photograph of Eric that she kept on her nightstand. She touched the ring on her finger. Then, with a determination that surprised her, she put away thoughts of Eric. She had loved him, she would always love him, but he was never, never coming back. Sliding her bare feet into a comfortable pair of loafers, she wondered if razor cuts to the chin ever proved to be fatal. Well, there was always a first time....

Twenty minutes later Emily switched on the radio on the kitchen counter, swiveling the dial to her favorite light rock station. She poured herself another cup of coffee and sat down at the table. A mellow voice reminded her that the neon lights were bright on Broadway, and the morning paper beckoned. But after her mad dash to the bus stop with Danny, she was content just to sit for a few minutes.

Actually she wasn't just sitting, but sitting and thinking. Thinking about Joseph Cortez in his black underwear. Thinking about every single solitary little detail of his lean, hard body. Thinking about some not so little details, too. Her smile was soft and slow as she sipped her coffee.

"Does the smile mean you aren't mad at me anymore?"

"Oh!" Emily gasped with surprise as her cup banged against the table. She'd been so far away that even with a bum leg, Cortez had managed to take her by surprise.

He was standing over her, one hand resting on the table near her arm. He was so close, closer than he had ever been. His body heat warmed her, and for the first time she caught the scent of spice mingling with a faint tang of cigar smoke. He had used that cologne.

He wore jeans and a black, pullover sweater. He'd pushed

the sleeves up to his elbows, revealing strong forearms covered with crisp, thick black hair that glistened against his dark skin, reminding her of dark hair elsewhere. She wanted to run her fingers along the back of his hand and up his arm. She met his eyes for a moment, and wondered if he could read her mind.

"That depends," she murmured, her voice low and a bit unsteady as she pulled her eyes away from his and stood up. "Why don't we talk about it? Would you like some coffee?"

"Sounds good." His hand rested on the back of her neck for an instant, hard and warm, then grazed her shoulder as he pushed her gently but firmly back into her chair. "I'll get it."

He limped across the kitchen, opened a cabinet and retrieved a pottery mug. He hadn't meant to touch her. He had spent yesterday afternoon and most of the night deciding what he was going to do, and touching her wasn't a part of it, at least not yet. He was going to do what Mendoza had suggested. He was going to try to build a foundation for the future based on friendship, and he was going to try to accept the fact that Eric Anderson shared some of the blame for his own death.

But the warm, wondering look in her eyes had been too much for him. If he didn't put some distance between them, all of his careful planning would be for nothing. He filled his mug with hot, black coffee, and turned to face her, resting one hip against the counter. "I'm sorry for the way I behaved over the weekend, Emily."

"What?" Emily had directed her attention to the newspaper as soon as Cortez had moved away from her, but his words brought her head up with a snap.

"I said I'm sorry for the way I behaved over the weekend. It takes me a while to get used to new places and new people."

"It's all right," Emily replied, studying his face. He seemed sincere, and if he could admit to bad behavior, so could she. Then maybe they could start over, and maybe they could be friends. "I apologize, too. I don't know what's been getting into me. I never lose my temper, and you do have a right to your privacy."

"Friends?" Joseph asked, as he crossed the kitchen and sat down in the chair opposite Emily. He offered her his hand, a smile tugging at his lips.

"Friends," Emily agreed, slipping her hand into his and returning his smile.

"Since we're friends, would you mind if I joined you for dinner in the evenings? You can increase the rent accordingly."

"You're more than welcome to join us at dinner, but I think you're paying enough rent already. You could do the grocery shopping occasionally, load the dishwasher, or fix dinner once a week, though, *friend*." Emily's eyes twinkled as she ticked off her suggestions.

"You've got a deal, *friend*." Joseph's eyes twinkled, too, his hand tightening around hers for an instant before he let it go. It was going to work; it had to work if he hoped to find a way to care for Danny and her after he was gone. But he was going to have to stop finding excuses to touch her.

"How about some breakfast?" Emily asked, feeling a bit flustered as she settled her hand in her lap, curling her fingers around the warmth he'd left there.

"If scrambled eggs and toast are on the menu, the answer is yes."

"You got it." Emily flashed a quick smile his way, pushed back her chair and stood up.

With quick, careful movements she pulled eggs, milk and butter out of the refrigerator and set them on the kitchen counter. She found a bowl, whisk and a small skillet, and popped bread into the toaster. Moments later, as she stirred the eggs in the skillet, the music on the radio faded and the eight-thirty news report began. She turned the sound up a bit and continued to stir the eggs as the announcer read the local news. At the kitchen table, Joseph reached for the newspaper and extracted the sports page.

"And in other news, United States forces resume military exercises in Norteña—"

Without a word, Emily switched the radio off.

From his place at the table, Joseph glanced up and saw the

pain slice across her face. He felt her anger as she pulled a plate from a cabinet, set it on the counter, and filled it with eggs and buttered toast, her movements too quick, too decisive. As she crossed the kitchen, her mouth set in a narrow line, he moved the paper to one side, making room for the plate. She placed it in front of him and turned, but before she could walk away, he wrapped his fingers around her wrist, holding her still.

"Mendoza told me your husband was killed by a stray bullet on a back road in Norteña. What was he doing down there?" His voice was gentle but insistent, and he refused to release her when she tried to pull free.

"He was researching a book." Emily met Cortez's eyes, then glanced away, relaxing the tension in her arm. "He believed Central America was going to end up like Vietnam. He protested against our government's policies, he said the United States had no right interfering down there, that it wasn't our fight, and he was right. No matter what the State Department says, I know that's why he was killed."

"It's not our fight yet, Emily, but unlike Vietnam, Central America is right on our doorstep. And it's my understanding that most of the countries down there don't want Communist dictatorships similar to the one in Arteaga. That's why Norteña and several other countries have requested assistance from the United States in the form of military advisers. One goal is to make their armies capable of fighting their own battles, so we won't have to do it. And the ultimate goal is peace through strength, not war."

"And in the meantime, they murder innocent civilians with the wrong political viewpoint."

"Sometimes innocent civilians, regardless of political viewpoint, end up in the wrong place at the wrong time."

"You seem to know a lot about Central America, Cortez."

"I read *Newsweek*, Mrs. Anderson," Joseph said sarcastically. He freed her wrist and picked up his fork. "And I have a ranch in Texas. I've seen illegal aliens from Arteaga cross the border in droves, seeking asylum in the United States because they're too afraid to stay in their own country. If the

Communists take over in Central America, how long do you think it will be before they decide to take over Mexico, too?''

"Is that how you hurt your leg, Cortez? Were you fighting Commies in the back forty at your ranch?'' Emily asked, her voice equally sarcastic as she crossed to the counter, unwilling to hear what he was saying. When he didn't reply, she swung around to face him, totally unprepared for the cold, dead look in his eyes.

"Not exactly, Mrs. Anderson,'' he said in a level tone of voice.

"I'm sorry. I had no right to say that to you.''

"No, you didn't.'' He met her eyes and held her gaze. "Emily, maybe you're blaming the wrong people for Eric's death. The United States military doesn't murder innocent civilians. Anger at the one who's died is a normal part of grieving. You shouldn't be ashamed to feel angry with your husband.'' For the first time, Joseph voiced the thought that had edged into his mind after his conversation with Richard Mendoza.

"But I wanted Eric to go to Central America. I believed in his ideas. I helped him outline the book. How could I be angry with him? He was working on a project we both believed in when he was killed. If I blame him for ending up dead, I could just as well blame myself for urging him to go.''

"That's something you have to face,'' Joseph said, hardening himself against the anguish he heard in her voice. Suddenly he felt as if he was fighting for his future as well as hers. "If you want to be free of it, you have to face the past in an honest, rational manner. And there's no painless way to do it.''

"You sound like the voice of experience,'' Emily countered, trying to inject a lighter tone into the conversation. They were treading too close to a place she wasn't ready to explore. He was threatening her anger, her bitterness, her last ties to Eric with truths she didn't want to acknowledge. "I'm not the only one with a past to face, am I?''

"No, you're not,'' he admitted, lightening his tone to match hers as he directed his concentration to the food in front of him.

"Maybe sometime we could…we could talk about it," Emily offered, shrugging her shoulders. Then, pushing away from the counter, she walked toward the door leading into the hallway. "But right now I've got to get to work. Are you going to the university?"

"Yes, Richard's expecting me at a morning class and again in the afternoon."

"Well, dinner's at six. If you need anything I'll be in my office. Otherwise, I'll see you this evening." Without a backward glance, Emily walked out of the kitchen.

Alone at the table, Joseph put down his fork and gave up any pretense of eating. He'd almost blown it, spouting off the way he had. Thank God for his conveniently located ranch. At least he hadn't lied to her.

But he'd stirred up her curiosity about his past, and that wasn't good. They needed time, time to get to know each other, as well as time to come to terms with Eric's death. And despite the extended leave he'd been promised, Joseph had a feeling that time for them was in short supply. He hoped he was wrong. He hoped to God he was wrong.

Chapter Four

Safe inside her office, sitting at her desk with the door closed, Emily stared out the front window, concentrating on the sound of Joseph Cortez moving around her house. In her mind she followed his halting steps down the hallway and up the stair-case. She heard the creak of floorboards and the faint tap of his cane overhead as he limped from bedroom to bathroom. Water gurgling through the old pipes muffled his footsteps as he returned to the first floor, but Emily felt the brush of air against the door as he passed her office. When the front door clicked shut, she took a deep breath, then another and another. She switched on the computer, trying to focus on the stack of papers on her desk. But Joseph's words came back to her in the sudden silence, defying any further attempt to block them out.

Was she blaming the wrong people for Eric's death? No, it simply wasn't possible. Was it?

She thought back to the days following the funeral. She had pressed the State Department for more information, for details of any kind. In answer to her letters and telephone calls, she'd gotten nothing but the proverbial pat on the head. They were sorry her husband had been killed, but he *had* been warned about the dangers of traveling the back roads of Central America.

She had given up then, falling into a black pit of despair. After the visit from the bill collector, though, her despair had turned to anger, an anger fueled by her fear, an anger that had become a living, breathing part of her. How close she'd come to losing everything. *They* had murdered her husband. *They* had left her alone to face bill collectors, to hang onto an old house so her son would have some sort of inheritance. *They, they, they...*

Now, sitting in her office, with the cool morning breeze ruffling the curtains at the window, and patches of sun dancing across the gleaming, old oak floor, Emily looked back over the past months. Perhaps she had held onto her anger for too long. Perhaps it was time to let Eric go. Perhaps it was time to review his research notes, study his diary, develop his photographs, finish the book, and truly let him go.

She glanced at the neatly taped and labeled cardboard box sitting in one corner of her office, then turned away from it to shuffle the papers on her desk. No, not yet. She wasn't ready. It was still too soon. She would deal with the past as she'd always done, in her own time, in her own way. And who was Joseph Cortez to say her way was irrational or dishonest? He certainly hadn't been forthcoming about *his* past.

In the meantime, Professor Svenson was expecting that rough draft of his paper on microbiology by Thursday, and Reba Watson would be dropping off her latest manuscript in the afternoon. She had more than enough work to keep her busy, and no time at all to think about anything else. Not if she planned to quit early, so she could fix her famous meat loaf for dinner. Focusing on the papers she'd arranged, Emily loaded a blank disk into the computer and went to work.

Just before six o'clock, Joseph walked into the dining room as Emily set a dish heaped with mashed potatoes on the table.

He had been in and out of the house throughout the day, but he hadn't seen much of her.

When he'd returned to the house for a sandwich between Mendoza's morning and afternoon classes, she had been cooped up in her office, working. Later in the afternoon he'd walked into the kitchen to grab a beer to take upstairs to the studio, and had found her humming along with the radio as she mixed ground meat and seasonings in a huge bowl. She'd flashed a smile his way and mentioned something about meat loaf. He'd smiled, too, relieved that she wasn't upset about their morning conversation, admitted his fondness for meat loaf, and slipped away.

She was smiling now, her pale eyes searching his as she faced him across the dining-room table. With a start, Joseph realized he'd been staring at her, and he wondered if he'd missed something she'd said. He was about to apologize for not paying attention when Danny bounded through the door.

"Hey, Mom, why are we eating in the dining room?" he asked as he came to a halt beside his mother, his bright, blue eyes on Joseph. "Is Joseph eating dinner with us? Neato!"

"I thought it would be nice to eat in the dining room again, and yes, Mr. Cortez will be eating dinner with us."

"Where's he going to sit?"

"Here, across from you." Emily glanced at Joseph. "Okay?"

"Fine," he agreed easily, as he moved past her to hold her chair at the head of the table while she seated herself. Then he took the chair to her right, across the table from her giggling, squirming son.

As they filled their plates, Joseph realized how long it had been since he'd been a part of a family. Since his mother's death two years ago, he'd often shared meals with his sister and her husband and daughters when he was home on leave, but had always felt a little like an outsider. Here with Emily and Danny he felt a sense of belonging, as if he'd come home at last. The thought filled him with unexpected pleasure—and scared him to death. *Friends,* he reminded himself, ignoring the tremor in his hand as he took the basket of rolls from Emily without meeting her eyes.

As the meal progressed, Emily was as grateful as Joseph for Danny's bright, happy chatter. The boy was eager to share all the excitement of his first day at school, and he was just as curious as Emily about Joseph's first day at the university. With a child's unconscious innocence, he eased them through dinner, linking them with mutual respect and admiration. Though Emily and Joseph didn't say much to each other, they exchanged more than one smile and often laughed at Danny's outrageous exuberance.

When they finished eating, Joseph and Danny helped Emily clear the table, then chased her out of the kitchen so they could load the dishwasher and store leftovers. They were arguing the pros and cons of *The A-Team* versus a National Geographic special as she slipped away. Thankful for the free time, she returned to her office to work for an hour before Danny's bedtime.

By eight-thirty Danny was tucked into bed. Emily, stretched out beside him, finished the story she was reading aloud, closed the book and set it on the table beside his bed. She stretched her arms over her head for an instant and shared a sleepy smile with her son. Then she sat up and swung her legs over the side of the bed.

"I really, really like that story, Mom." Danny yawned and slipped down under the patchwork quilt, closing his eyes.

"Me, too. Hug and kiss?" Emily asked, as she brushed a blond curl off his forehead.

"Yeah."

Emily bent to give the boy one of each. Straightening up, she touched his hair again. "Love you."

"Love you, too, Mom," Danny replied, then frowned. His bright eyes searched her face for a moment. "Mom?"

"Something wrong, honey?" Emily asked, a note of concern edging into her voice. Danny rarely frowned, but when he did, it was almost always because he was seriously concerned about something.

"Is Joseph going to eat dinner with us every night?"

"Yes, he is. And I think you ought to call him Mr. Cortez."

"He said I could call him Joseph 'cause we're friends."

"I see." Emily still thought her son should call him Mr. Cortez, but she also thought it would be silly to insist when Cortez didn't mind.

"I'm glad he's eating dinner with us, Mom. It was almost like having Dad there, wasn't it? I like him a lot. Do you like him, Mom?"

In the hallway outside Danny's bedroom door, Joseph Cortez froze. He had come upstairs to say good-night to Emily and Danny, not to eavesdrop on their conversation. He knew he should announce his presence or move away from the door, but he didn't. His hand gripping the head of his cane, he waited for Emily to say something, anything. She would be honest with the boy. Of that he was sure.

Seconds ticked by, one after another, as Emily stroked her son's forehead. Danny was right; it had been almost like having Eric home again. Almost, but not quite. Joseph Cortez was a very real presence in his own right, and he fitted into their life in his own special way.

"I like him," she admitted at last, her words a soft sigh of acceptance.

"A lot?"

"Mmm, yes, a lot."

"He likes you a lot, too."

"Oh, really? And how do you know that, son of mine?"

"I asked him."

"Of course...you asked him. I should have guessed." The smile in Emily's voice was as soft as the one tugging at the corners of Joseph's mouth.

"He's different from my dad." The frown appeared again for just a moment, and was gone.

"Yes, he is. But liking Mr. Cortez doesn't take anything away from how we feel about your dad. We can...like...Mr. Cortez just as much, but in a different way. I think your dad would have liked him, too. Do you understand what I'm trying to say, Danny?"

"Yeah, I think so." Danny hid another yawn behind his

hand, then snuggled into his pillow. "I'm glad he's here," he murmured in a sleepy voice.

"Me, too. Now get some sleep, okay?"

"Okay, mom. 'Night."

"Good night, sweetheart." Standing up, Emily gave the quilt one last tuck, and Danny one more quick kiss. If only all of life's problems were as easily solved, she thought, as she switched off the lamp on the nightstand and stepped out of the room.

She felt his presence before she saw him standing in the dark, silent hallway near Danny's bedroom door. Instinctively she reached for the light switch on the wall beside her, but he caught her hand and held it, keeping the light away.

"I came up to say good night to you and Danny. I have some work to do in the studio." His voice was low as he offered the simple explanation.

"He's asleep now. We were talking." In the darkness his face was a shadow without substance, but the hand holding hers was warm and hard and reassuring. She turned her palm into his. If he tugged just a bit, she'd be in his arms. Without surprise, Emily realized that could be a nice place to be. "We were talking about you."

"Yes, I know." His fingers threaded through hers, and he bent his head, brushing his lips against the back of her hand. For an instant his lips warmed her to her very soul, and his mustache tickled her to her toes. Then, as suddenly as he had taken her hand, he released it. "Good night, Mrs. Anderson."

"Good night, Mr. Cortez," she whispered; he turned and limped away from her. She stood motionless, her heart pounding, watching him until the quiet click of the studio door closing left her alone again.

How long had he been in the hallway? How much of her conversation with Danny had he overhead? Almost all of it, if she was any judge of what he'd said and done, and what he'd left unsaid and undone as he'd held her hand in his.

With quick, light steps she crossed the hallway, stopping in front of the studio door. She rested her hand, still warm from his touch, against the smooth, cool wood. *I do like you. I like you a lot.*

Then, feeling foolish, she pulled her hand away as if the wood had caught fire. Turning on her heel, she headed toward the staircase. She had at least two hours of typing to do, and having a mental conversation with a door didn't go far toward getting it finished.

He remained where he was, his back against the hard wooden door long after she'd gone. Finally the throbbing in his leg forced him to move. Pushing away from the door, he switched on the overhead lights, crossed the studio and stood in front of the easel. He picked up a brush, weighing it in one hand. He had to work tonight, and not only because Mendoza would expect something from him by the end of the week. If he didn't stay busy, he'd go after Emily, and he wouldn't stop with kissing her hand.

The classes had gone well, but much as he enjoyed sketching, it was putting paint on a canvas that really drew Joseph out of himself. After Vietnam he'd slashed at the blank canvases with dark, brooding colors, as he tried to exorcise his demons. But tonight the brush strokes would be smooth and slow, the shades on the canvas pale green, rose blush and golden brown. Her colors. He'd be a fool to hope he could ever have her as more than a friend. But here, in the privacy of the studio, he *would* have her.

Little by little by little Joseph Cortez wove himself into the fabric of Emily's life.

On Wednesday morning she found a fresh pot of coffee and a plate full of warm croissants from the neighborhood bakery awaiting her in the kitchen. In the afternoon she trudged down to the basement laundry, but the sheets and towels she had planned to wash were already clean and dry and neatly folded, ready to be carried upstairs to the linen closet.

At dinner she thanked Cortez for his thoughtfulness. He acknowledged her thanks with a nod and a faint smile. Then he turned his attention back to Danny's description of Skeletor's evil forces, as if their exchange in the hallway had never occurred.

Thursday afternoon Emily decided to move her potted plants into the solarium and mow the yard. She carried in the large plants one by one, then pulled the ancient lawn mower out of the garage. She plowed back and forth across the front yard, hoping it would be the last time until spring. Maybe by then she could afford a new, self-propelled mower.

When she stopped at the edge of the driveway to catch her breath, the two students from the third-floor apartment appeared at her side. She shut off the mower, and they asked if they could finish the yard work for her. Emily stared at them in surprise. Then, shrugging her shoulders, she accepted her good fortune with a smile.

Sweet of them, she thought, as she walked back toward the house, especially since she saw them an average of once a week. Had it been their idea? Glancing up, she saw Cortez watching her from the studio window.

On Friday Joseph and Danny took over the kitchen as soon as Danny got home from school. Emily, barred from her domain for the duration, spent two hours wondering about the unusual, though savory, smells wafting about the house. She wondered about the banging and clanging of what sounded like every pot and pan she owned. And she wondered just how long it was going to take her to clean up the mess she expected to find.

Promptly at six, seated at the dining-room table, Emily was presented with an array of Mexican dishes: enchiladas with chili and cheese, Spanish rice and refried beans. She wasn't quite sure if she was more surprised by the fantastic food, the fact that Danny was actually eating it, or the spotless kitchen she'd glimpsed on her way to the dining room.

On Saturday morning, sitting alone in her kitchen sipping coffee, Emily realized how nice it was to have Joseph Cortez around, and how much she was going to miss him over the weekend.

On Wednesday evening he had mentioned a weekend trip to Minneapolis with Professor Mendoza to visit the Walker

Art Center. Since then Emily had been looking forward to having her house and her son to herself again. But now that Cortez was gone, and Danny was out walking Greta, the house seemed unusually quiet, and she felt unexpectedly lonely.

While Joseph spent most of every day at the university, he did return to the house for lunch; late in the afternoon, he returned to work in the studio until it was time for dinner. Evenings he watched television with Danny for an hour, and twice he'd listened patiently while her son read "Go, go, go. I will go," and countless other simple sentences from his getting-ready-to-read cards. Joseph fixed coffee in the mornings, he wasn't averse to putting a load of sheets and towels into the washer, and he spent a lot of time with Danny. In just a few days Joseph Cortez had become part of the family. And yet...

Sighing, Emily got up and walked across the kitchen. She emptied her cup into the sink and stared out the window at her sunny backyard. Cortez had become a part of the family and yet, once Danny was in bed, he disappeared behind the closed studio door. He hadn't touched her again since Tuesday night. Instead, he kept his distance as surely as if there was a brick wall between them.

If they ended up in the same room, alone together, he found some excuse to leave. He returned her smiles and spoke to her when necessary, but he was so cool, so polite. To Danny he offered his attention and genuine affection. Emily had seen the smiles they shared, heard Danny's laughter at the cartoons Joseph drew for him, and listened to the bits and pieces of their long, earnest conversations, often spiced with the Spanish words Danny was eager to learn. She wanted him to offer her the same attention and affection.

"I'm jealous of my own son," Emily muttered, turning away from the window and folding her arms across her chest. If only he treated her the way he treated Danny...

But of course there could be a good reason why he didn't. What if he'd found a lean, young thing at the university, an art student with dreamy eyes and long, soft hair hanging halfway down her back? Cortez lived in her house and was kind to her and her son, but there was no reason why he should treat her as anything but the landlady she was. No man in his right mind would be attracted to a widow with a young son, not with all those sweet things at the university.

"Well, fine," Emily said, tossing her head as she pushed away from the counter. "Just fine. You want to keep it cool, we'll keep it cool, but—"

"Who are you talking to, Mom?" Danny looked around the kitchen as he walked through the doorway, a curious expression on his face.

"Myself," Emily replied.

"Mrs. Stewart says she only talks to herself when she's feeling crazy. Are you feeling crazy, Mom?"

"Yes, but I have just the cure. Why don't we pack a picnic lunch and take a ride up North Shore Drive to the lighthouse? We haven't done that in a long time."

"All right," Danny agreed, stretching out the words to show his approval. "Greta, too?"

"Greta, too. What kind of sandwich do you think she'd like?"

"Alpo on a hamburger bun, of course. And hold the mustard."

Danny's giggles were catching. By the time they were ready to leave, Emily had almost forgotten about Joseph Cortez. Almost...

He drummed his fingers against the table. The sound was loud and irritating in the quiet, empty kitchen, but for some odd reason, the nervous habit helped him think.

It had been very cool around the house the past couple of days, and it had nothing to do with the temperature on the thermostat in the hallway. The first chill had hit him Sunday night when he returned from Minneapolis, and Emily had been sending icy blasts his way ever since.

He didn't have to exert an ounce of effort to avoid her, because she'd become adept at avoiding him first. When she spoke to him, her voice was cool and polite. Often she simply sent messages via Danny. She didn't smile, and she'd started looking around him instead of at him whenever possible. She didn't seem angry, just…distant. The changes puzzled Joseph, and he didn't like them, not one bit. He missed her warm, happy chatter. He ached for one of her sweet smiles. And if she didn't meet his eyes soon, he was going to grab her and shake her until her teeth rattled.

No, he couldn't do that. Couldn't touch her, not yet, maybe never. But he could shake her up a little, maybe shake her out of her mood or whatever it was. He had to do something to regain control of the situation. But as he reached for his cane and pulled himself to his feet, Joseph had a sudden, unwelcome thought.

What if Emily had been with Glen Roberts while he'd been away? What if Roberts had convinced her she should stay away from him? Danny hadn't mentioned the man, but that didn't mean Emily hadn't seen or talked to him.

For one awful instant, Joseph wondered if his plan to build a foundation of friendship with Emily had backfired into his face. He'd seen desire in her eyes and felt warmth and tenderness in her touch, yet he'd forced himself to stay away from her. What if she'd turned her desire, her warmth and tenderness, toward Glen Roberts?

"We'll see," Joseph muttered, his voice low and angry, as he limped down the hallway toward the closed door of Emily's office. "We'll just see about that."

Emily was sitting at her desk, the warm, sensual rhythm of a David Lanz piano solo weaving its magic as her fingers flew over the computer keyboard. She was so engrossed in the music and the story she was typing that she didn't hear Joseph open her office door. She didn't realize he was in the room at all until she heard his voice, soft and sexy, reading the words printed on the monitor. He was leaning over her shoulder, one hand braced against the edge of her desk, so close that she could feel his heat.

His lips inches from hers, his masculinity poised at her feminine threshold, he growled, "Tell me you want it, baby."

"Oh, Jefferson, darlin', you know—"

With a flip of a switch, Emily darkened the screen, then spun around in her chair to glare at Cortez. Her eyes met his for the first time in days, but she was too angry at his intrusion to be sidetracked by the warmth and humor in their dark depths. "Yes? You wanted something?"

"I've been wondering why you're so anxious to get in here every morning." The fire in Emily's eyes was all the fuel he needed to let the devil loose again. "Does she tell Jefferson, darlin', she wants it...or not?"

"I'm so anxious to get in here every morning because I'm working on Reba Watson's manuscript, *Love's Lingering Lust,* and I promised I'd finish the rough draft by Friday afternoon. As for Jefferson, darlin', don't worry. He gets just what he deserves."

Cortez's eyes were as teasing, as tempting, as the scent of spice and cigar smoke wafting around her. Emily's determination to remain aloof wavered slightly, but only for an instant. By sheer force of will she pulled her eyes away from his, concentrating her gaze on the blank monitor. "Now, what do you want?"

"Grocery list." Without missing a beat, Joseph turned and settled a hip on her desk.

"Oh, yes. Sorry," Emily murmured. She had been so intent on avoiding Cortez before he could avoid her that she'd forgotten about his offer to stop at the grocery store on his way home from school.

She eased her chair away from him, careful not to brush against his leg, and turned to face the opposite side of her desk. He was a kind man, a caring man, a dependable person to have around, and he was making her nervous. He wanted more than a grocery list, or he wouldn't be sitting on the edge of her desk.

Maybe he'd met someone, found another place to live, and

was about to let her down gently, she thought with irrational desperation. Her fingers shook just enough to make the search for the list twice as difficult as it should have been. She didn't want him to move out, and it had nothing to do with her financial problems.

"I need everything this week. Sure you don't mind?" She finally found the sheet of paper with three twenty-dollar bills clipped to the top. Turning, she offered the list to Cortez with a tentative smile. He *was* doing her a favor, she *did* appreciate it, and she couldn't blame him if he chose to move out. But she wished he'd stop looking at her that way, his fierce, dark eyes full of warmth, turning her insides to mush.

"I mind this." Cortez took the list and slipped the money loose, tossing the bills onto her desk. "Otherwise I don't mind at all."

"Now, look, Cortez, I don't expect you—"

"I know you don't expect it, but I'm going to do it, anyway."

"I can pay my bills," Emily protested, tipping up her chin at a proud angle. "For that matter, I can do my own grocery shopping. I'm sure you have better things to do, friends you'd like to see.... I appreciate your thoughtfulness, but I don't expect you to spend all your free time with us." Once again Emily turned to face the blank monitor.

As though a light bulb had suddenly clicked on in Joseph's head, he realized why Emily had been so cool and distant since Sunday. Somehow she'd convinced herself he was avoiding her because he'd met someone else. Either that, or she didn't want him around so she could spend more time with Glen Roberts.

"There isn't anyone else I'd rather spend my time with than Danny and you. But if I'm interfering with your relationship with Glen Roberts—"

"No!" Emily's head shot up and her eyes locked with Cortez's. "I mean, um, I'm not...I don't..." She hesitated, stammering, her face flushed, her eyes bright as relief washed over her.

She clenched her hands in her lap and stared at them. He *wanted* to spend time with them. She didn't know what to say, so she shrugged her shoulders and said the first inane thing that came to mind. "Thanks for doing the grocery shopping."

"You're welcome," he said, brushing a curl off her cheek with one finger. She turned to look at him, a soft, slow smile lifting her lips and brightening her eyes.

He should have gone then; he'd gotten what he wanted. But something had been bothering him since the day he'd first confronted her on the front porch, and her pride in being able to pay her bills had goaded his curiosity. "Emily, are you having financial problems?" he asked, keeping his voice casual. "If you are, I'd be happy to help out with a loan."

"Financial problems?" Emily's smile faded as she gazed at Joseph, a puzzled expression on her face.

"The day you agreed to rent the rooms, you said you needed the money."

"Oh, yes. I mean, no. Actually I would have had to dig into savings to heat the house all winter, but since you're renting the rooms, it won't be necessary."

"Good." Some of the tension eased out of Joseph's face, and for a moment Emily thought he was going to touch her again. But his hand moved to grip nothing but his cane, and he stood up, moving away from her. Limping slowly, he wandered around her office, stopping to study the books on the shelves.

"What's this?" he asked, as he came to the end of the row. He poked at the dusty, cardboard box in the corner with his cane. When she didn't answer, Joseph turned and saw the same stricken look on her face he'd seen in the kitchen a week earlier. He glanced at the box again, focusing on the foreign stamps glued to the upper right corner. Even from a distance, he recognized them and knew that the box had been sent from Norteña. He knew whatever was inside it had to do with her husband.

Damn you, Eric Anderson, he cursed silently, as his fingers tightened around the head of his cane. *And damn you, too, Joseph Cortez,* he cursed himself, unable to escape the stab of guilt he felt each time he reminded himself of the part he'd played in the other man's death.

Emily closed her eyes, pressing the palm of one hand against her forehead. She should have put the box away, she thought, rubbing her forehead, and she would, just as soon as she got rid of Cortez. He'd been in her office much longer than necessary to pick up a grocery list. And no matter how happy she was that he wanted to spend time with Danny and herself, she wasn't going to discuss Eric with him now. But as she opened her eyes and focused again on him, prepared to ask him to leave, her telephone began to ring. Automatically she reached for it and spoke into the receiver.

"Hello...oh, hello, Steve."

Cortez's head went up, his eyes narrowing as he watched her. She swiveled the chair, turning her back on him.

"Yes, I've been thinking about it, but I'm not ready yet." She wrapped the phone cord round and round her fingers, drawing it tighter and tighter until they turned a deep shade of red. "I don't know. Yes, I understand, but I can't...." She closed her eyes, trying to concentrate on the insistent rise and fall of the voice on the other end of the telephone line. "All right... Yes...of course, November 1. Goodbye, Steve."

Slowly she unwound the cord, flexing her fingers to get the blood circulating again. The final notes of the last song drifted away and the tape player clicked off.

As she turned to cradle the receiver, Emily glanced up and saw the unspoken question in Cortez's eyes. She willed him to disappear, but he simply stood there, waiting, and the longer he waited, the more she wanted to confide in him, though she wasn't sure why.

"That was Steve Muehler, Eric's editor. He's been bugging me to finish the book, but I can't do it." Emily risked another glance at Cortez—and didn't like what she saw. She should have remembered his comments, the last time they'd discussed Eric. He hadn't been sympathetic then, and he wasn't sympathetic now.

"Can't...or won't?" His words echoed the challenge in his dark eyes as he held her gaze. "You told me you worked on the project with Eric and you helped him outline the book. You seem intelligent. I find it hard to believe you're incapable of sifting through his research and fleshing out the details you outlined.''

"I'm *not* incapable." Emily shoved back her chair, stood up, braced her palms against her desk and glared at Cortez. "I wrote the final drafts of his papers and the final draft of his book on Vietnam. *He* did the research and the rough drafts. *I* did the polishing. We worked together as a team.''

"Then you *won't* finish his book. Why not?''

The satisfied look in Cortez's eyes assured Emily she'd taken his bait, and she wanted to kick herself. Instead she sat down, switched on her computer and fiddled with the papers on her desk. "The way I feel about the United States government in general, and the military in particular, I can't be objective," she replied without meeting his eyes.

"Can't...or won't?'' Cortez repeated the question in a soft voice, thumping the dusty box atop the papers on Emily's desk. Her head shot up, her pale eyes widening with surprise and dismay.

"Open it, *querida*," he continued in that same, soft voice. "Maybe not today or the next day, but open it soon. Face the past, Emily...honestly, intelligently, before we run out of tomorrows.'' Without waiting for a reply, he limped out of her office, closing the door behind him.

Seconds ticked into minutes as Emily sat and stared at the cardboard box, her fingers clenching and unclenching as Cortez's words echoed in the empty room. Then with a shake of her head she stood, picked up the box and crossed to the room's one, small closet. She opened the door, tossed the box inside, then slammed the door.

Back at her desk, she smoothed the papers into order once again and changed the tape. As the crystal-clear voice of a single flute drifted through the office, she began to type again from Reba Watson's manuscript.

"Oh, Jefferson, darlin', you know I love you.''

Her fingers moved over the keyboard as slowly as a novice's, and one lost, lonely tear trickled down her cheek.

Chapter Five

For the second Saturday in a row, Joseph climbed into his Jeep and headed south. The drive from Duluth to Minneapolis was an easy three hours on interstate highway. The scenery was fabulous. The autumn change of colors had begun, and the roadsides weren't marred by obnoxious signs and billboards. Rest areas and fast-food restaurants were conveniently located for quick, easy access.

Joseph had enjoyed the trip the previous Saturday. He'd had Mendoza to keep him company, and they'd talked about anything and everything, catching up on the years since they'd last seen each other. The only topic they had avoided, as if by silent agreement, was Emily Anderson. In Minneapolis they'd spent the morning wandering through the Walker Art Center and the afternoon wandering through the Institute of Arts. They'd stayed at the Hyatt Regency and eaten dinner at Lord Fletcher's on Lake Minnetonka. Sunday they'd explored St. Paul before driving back to Duluth. It had been a relaxing weekend, unlike the one Joseph had ahead of him.

Alone in the Jeep, he peeled the tab off the plastic lid on

the cup of coffee he'd purchased at a roadside McDonald's. As he guided the vehicle along the wide ribbon of highway stretching before him, a cool, early-morning breeze blew through the open windows, ruffling his thick, dark hair. The blue sky and bright sunshine had a lulling effect on him. He wanted to think of nothing but Emily. Instead he forced himself to concentrate on his afternoon appointment with the specialist at the medical center and his overnight stay in the hospital. He dreaded the poking, the prodding and the testing he'd have to endure almost as much as he dreaded the results.

Joseph was tuned in to his body well enough to realize the leg was healing much faster than expected. The walking and the workouts with weights were adding more strength and flexibility every day. Thanks to Emily's good cooking, he'd also regained some of the weight he'd lost while in the hospital in San Antonio. He didn't need an orthopedic surgeon to tell him he was recuperating well ahead of schedule. There was a good possibility he'd be able to give up the cane in the next week or two, and he had no doubt he'd be ready to go back to work by the end of October, almost a month earlier than he'd anticipated.

They wanted him back, and he wanted to go, he thought as he tasted the coffee and found it drinkable. *The sooner the better, Colonel.* During his weekly telephone call to Washington, a call he had placed from Richard's office, he'd been advised of his promotion to lieutenant colonel. He'd also been advised that military leaders in two Central American countries were requesting his services.

While Arteaga's peace initiative had been greeted with hope, a certain amount of suspicion still existed among her neighbors. They wanted to maintain their military strength, yet didn't want to encourage continued fighting among the countries and the various rebel factions. And they wanted the one man they had worked with in the past, a man they trusted and admired, to advise them on how to achieve a satisfactory balance.

Washington had agreed to their requests for Lieutenant Colonel Joseph Cortez's services.

Joseph was prepared to do the job. In fact, he looked forward to using his knowledge and skills to promote a peaceful settlement. It would be an extremely satisfying way to end his military career. But accepting the assignment meant he'd have to settle things with Emily sooner rather than later.

He had to force himself to ration the time he spent with her, had to remind himself that her feelings for him probably weren't going in the same direction as his own. He was drawn to her more than ever, while his original urge to protect had grown steadily over the past few weeks. And the sense of responsibility, of honor, of duty drilled into him by his father and grandfather never allowed him to forget that he owed Emily and Danny much more than a few hundred dollars.

Though he no longer felt as if he were solely to blame for Eric Anderson's death, Joseph's sense of obligation to Emily and Danny had increased rather than decreased. He had spent long hours trying to devise a way to secure their future, but had yet to find a workable solution. And the more he thought of caring for them in the years to come, the more he found himself toying with the idea of marriage.

He had no illusions about replacing the husband and father they had lost. But he could afford to maintain the house on Third Street while offering them the security of a home on the ranch. And he could help Emily raise her son. From the time he had spent with Danny, it was obvious the boy wanted and needed an adult male in his life. Joseph would be more than happy to be that man.

Funny, he hadn't thought of marriage and a family for years, not since Charlotte. And he was beginning to realize that his feelings for Charlotte had been nothing compared to his growing desire for Emily Anderson. Not for the first time Joseph thanked God that the silly sorority girl he'd dated in college had been too spoiled, too selfish to wait for him when he'd been sent to Vietnam.

He'd been hurt and disillusioned when he'd come home to find she was engaged to another man, so much so that he'd volunteered for another tour of duty in Nam. For years he hadn't wanted a wife or any woman in his life on a permanent basis. He'd been so sure all females were as cruel and careless as Charlotte. By the time he'd outgrown that fallacy, he was married to his career, a career that often kept him in foreign countries for months at a time and exposed him to physical danger on a regular basis.

Not anymore, though. He had begun to think about retiring over a year ago, long before he was injured, and now he was definitely ready. He was ready to have a life of his own, a wife and family of his own. Emily and Danny. The realization hit him like a ton of bricks, forcing him to grip the steering wheel to keep from running off the road.

But he had no right to take a single step in that direction, at least not until he told her about his past and his involvement in Eric's death. The same damn sense of honor and duty that bound him to her forbade him to consider the possibility of a future with her until they'd dealt with the past, with her anger and bitterness, and with the guilt that clutched at his heart and soul each time he entered the house.

She hadn't mentioned the cardboard box or its contents since he'd invaded her office on Wednesday, but Joseph was certain she hadn't opened it. When he'd glanced into her office Thursday afternoon, he hadn't seen it on her desk or on the floor. He could only hope that she hadn't destroyed it. There would be no future for them until she accepted the fact that her husband was dead, and opened the box.

If only she would talk about it. He had given her enough openings the past couple of days, but she had ignored each and every one. In fact she had been too bright, too chatty since Wednesday, her teasing voice and her laughter not quite ringing true. She slipped away from him more than he liked, and she refused to meet his eyes, as if denying the importance of their confrontation in her office. Still he had caught her looking at him more than once, her eyes warm, yet cautious, questioning, as if she wasn't quite sure of him.

It had taken a great deal of willpower to retreat behind the closed door of the studio the past three nights, when all he had wanted to do was hold and comfort her. And the disappointment on her face when he'd told her he was again going to Minneapolis for the weekend was almost more than he could bear. But even though time was running out, he had to take things slowly and easily with her. He had to build a foundation of trust and friendship between them, and he had to help her accept Eric's death, or she would never give him a chance to explain his past.

He crushed the empty styrofoam cup, tossing it onto the floor as the exit sign for the medical center loomed ahead of him. Digging into his shirt pocket he pulled out a small, thin cigar, stuck it between his teeth, and punched the lighter on the dashboard. He needed one last smoke before he entered the chamber of horrors.

He had faced pain and near death in the past, but that didn't make the coming afternoon any easier to anticipate. The thought of having his leg manipulated in six different directions made him shudder, and he hated having to spend the night in the hospital. In all honesty, though, he dreaded none of it quite as much as the look on Emily's face when he told her who he was. For the first time in a long while, Joseph Cortez was truly afraid.

"Do you believe in love at first sight?"

"That bad, huh?" Cathy asked, as she stepped back from her open front door. "Well, come in and tell me *all* about it," she suggested with a smile. "Danny's watching television with Jimmy."

Emily followed her friend into the house. "He's driving me crazy, you know," she said at last, shrugging out of her goose-down vest and hanging it next to Danny's jacket on the brass coat tree in the hallway. "It's come here, come here...stay away, stay away. I thought men were supposed to be decisive."

"Maybe you ought to jump on his bones. If that doesn't help him make a decision, nothing will. Now that you know he isn't interested in some sweet, young thing at the university, I think you ought to go for it. What could it hurt?" Cathy had met Joseph Cortez shortly after he'd moved into Emily's house, and had been enjoying daily bulletins about the man ever since.

"Don't think I haven't considered the possibility," Emily admitted, as she raked her fingers through her mop of curls. "It's just that I'm not sure how to go about it. I've never pursued a man in my life."

"I suggest you stand at the top of the stairs, wait for him to walk down the hallway, and take a flying leap." Cathy's grin widened even more, her eyes sparkling as she ducked the fist Emily aimed at her.

"You're such a help, Cathy. What would I do without you?"

"You'd sit around and mope, and that's a heck of a way to spend a Saturday. Come on," Cathy urged, as she started down the hallway toward the kitchen, "I've got a pan of blueberry muffins ready to come out of the oven any minute. I'll put on a fresh pot of coffee. We can gorge ourselves and talk about Mr. Cortez."

"I thought you said you were dieting when I talked to you yesterday." Emily slid onto a high-backed stool at the island counter. Even though it had been two years since the remodeling, Cathy's kitchen still surprised Emily every time she entered it. No quaint, calico curtains or country cupboards here, although the house was as old as Emily's. Everything was white and wood block with futuristic-looking stainless steel appliances looming up in the strangest places.

"And I thought you wanted to live to see your next birthday." Cathy favored Emily with a nasty look as she plugged in her European coffee maker, but her sparkling eyes belied her threatening tone of voice.

"Hey, let's not talk about birthdays. I don't think I'm ready to cope with the downside of thirty-five yet."

"Okay, no birthday talk and no diet talk." Cathy eased a pan of muffins out of the oven and placed it on a cooling rack. "That leaves us with Mr. Cortez." She slid onto the stool next to Emily. "So, how's it going?"

"I don't know. I *really* don't know. With Eric everything was so simple. We met at a party my freshman year at UMD, we dated, we...liked...each other, we fell in love, we got married, and we lived happily ever after. We had our problems, especially when we lived in the third-floor apartment. The years before his father retired and his parents moved to Florida were rough. And we always fought about the silliest things. But I loved Eric, and I liked being married to him."

"And...?" Cathy prodded in a gentle tone of voice.

"When he was killed, I was certain I'd never feel the same way about another man. I couldn't imagine sharing my life with anyone else. And if by some chance I fell in love again, I thought it would be with someone just like Eric. Then Cortez appeared on my front porch." Emily crooked an elbow on the counter and propped her chin in her hand, staring into space. "I liked Eric first as a friend. Love and...desire...happened later."

"And with Cortez...?" Cathy slipped off her stool to pour coffee into white, china mugs.

"Cortez isn't anything at all like Eric, physically or emotionally. Sometimes I'm not sure I *like* him, much less love him. The first moment I saw him standing on my front porch, accusing me of looking like a boy, he set me off, and he's been setting me off on a regular basis ever since. He stares at me with his dark eyes and my heart pounds, my palms sweat, my knees turn to jelly. Then he'll say something smart or shrug his shoulders and walk away, and I want to slug him. I don't know him, not really. Not the way I knew Eric. I can't be falling in love with him, can I? Maybe I'm just starved for sex." With a sigh, Emily reached out and wrapped her hands around her coffee mug, unconsciously seeking its reassuring warmth.

"If you were starved for sex, you'd have done something about it the first time Glen Roberts asked you to go to bed with him, or the second time or the third time. In fact, if you really wanted or needed an Eric clone, Glen would fit the bill, at least physically," Cathy retorted, as she set out plates and napkins and transferred the muffins to a wicker basket. "Tell me something. How do you feel about Cortez up here?" She tapped a finger against her forehead. "When all is said and done, do you *like* Joseph Cortez most of the time?"

"Yes, I like him," Emily admitted, reaching for a muffin. "He's a kind, thoughtful man, a quiet man. He's strong and dependable, and he has a sense of humor. He keeps the bedroom and the studio clean, he helps with the laundry, he cooks, he buys groceries, and he spends lots of time with Danny." Emily pulled her muffin apart and took a bite.

"Believe it or not, from where I'm sitting he sounds a lot like Eric. If I didn't have Hank, I'd fight you for him. So what's the problem."

"That's just it. I don't know." Emily reached for her coffee and took a sip. "He's kind, he's considerate, he's good with Danny. We've had a couple of serious conversations. I really want to get to know him better." Emily shrugged her shoulders and took another sip of coffee. "But most of the time I get the feeling he's avoiding me. He doesn't necessarily run for the nearest exit when I'm around, but he's always on his way up or down or out. And he's spending the weekend in Minneapolis again. Is there something wrong with me?"

"There is nothing wrong with you, Em." Cathy leaned over and put an arm around Emily's shoulders, giving her a quick, warm hug. "If Cortez cares for you at all, it can't be easy for him, living in the house you shared with Eric. You know as well as I do that you haven't gotten over Eric's death yet, and I'm sure Cortez realizes it, too."

Emily opened her mouth to protest, but closed it without saying a word. She couldn't deny the truth of her friend's statement, not after her confrontation with Cortez in her office on Wednesday. She had tried to block out both his challenging words and the cardboard box tucked in the closet, but hadn't been very successful.

"I know it hasn't been easy for you, Em, but maybe you ought to reconsider finishing the book," Cathy continued, when her friend remained silent. "Eric died working for something you both believed in, and all the anger, bitterness and blame in the world aren't going to bring him back. But something positive like the book would be a lasting tribute to him.

And once it's complete, you'd be free, *really free* to start a new life.''

"You sound like him,'' Emily muttered, tracing a finger over the wedding ring on her finger. First Steve Muehler, then Cortez, then her best friend Cathy, all urging her to finish the book. If she didn't know better, she might be tempted to think they were conspiring against her.

"Oh, yeah? How so?"

"He was in my office Wednesday morning when Steve Muehler called. Cortez thinks I should finish the book, too. In fact, he had the nerve to insinuate I wasn't doing it because I'm incapable."

"What did you say?"

"I told him Eric was a terrific researcher, but we worked as a team on the actual writing."

"No, no. What excuse did you give him for not writing the book?"

"I told him I wasn't working on it because I can't," Emily retorted, refusing to meet her friend's steady gaze. "I'm not ready."

"I don't believe you. It's been over a year, Emily. I think it's time to give it a try. You owe it to Eric, and you owe it to yourself. That book is unfinished business, a part of the past hanging over your future. And you're too smart to spend the rest of your life buried under busywork."

Once again Emily opened her mouth to protest, and closed it without saying a word. Much as she hated to admit it, Cathy was right. But acknowledging the truth and doing something about it were two different things.

"If you're falling in love with him, you'll put the past behind you. You *are* falling in love with him, aren't you, Emily?"

"Cathy, I swear I don't know how it happened. A few weeks ago I didn't know he existed, and even now I can't say I know much about him. But I can't believe he won't always be a part of our lives. I wish I could explain it. He makes me feel safe and secure, and sometimes...sometimes I think I see love in his eyes. Then sometimes he makes me so mad I could spit.''

"Well, don't take it out on my muffins," Cathy teased, trying to lighten the mood.

"Oh! I'm sorry." Emily shook her head ruefully as she glanced down at the blueberry muffin she'd turned into crumbs. "See what I mean? The man is making me crazy."

"And I have just the cure for the crazies. Let's go shopping. We can prowl around the mall and decide what to do about Cortez.''

"Oh, yeah, I can just see us dragging the boys away from Saturday morning cartoons for a trip to the shopping mall. And I don't dare talk about Cortez in front of Danny. He tells the man everything, and I do mean *Everything*."

"Hank offered to baby-sit."

"He *what*?"

"He offered to baby-sit, and yes, I did check—he doesn't have a fever. He's holed up in his study, hoping I'll forget.''

"In that case, what are we waiting for?" Emily slid off her stool, dusting muffin crumbs off her fingertips. Shopping, even when she couldn't afford to spend much money, always brightened her spirits. And she did need some new lingerie.

"Let's see if we can find you something soft, silky and very sexy," Cathy suggested with a sly grin as they walked down the hallway.

"When did you start reading minds?" Emily muttered, slipping into her down vest.

"About the time you started walking around with a starry look in your eyes." Ignoring Emily's wry glance, Cathy pulled a jacket out of the closet and dug into the pocket for her car keys. She hollered up the staircase to let Hank know they were leaving, then turned her attention back to Emily.

"We ought to make some definite plans for our last canoe trip of the season, too. Next Saturday, I think, before the weather turns really cold. Maybe you could invite Mr. Cortez," Cathy suggested as they walked down the sidewalk to the car.

"And maybe you could mind your own business," Emily

retorted. Not trusting the twinkle in her friend's eyes, she stopped, leveling a finger at Cathy over the roof of her car. "You're in big trouble if you ask him, Catherine, big trouble."

"Now, now. Don't get excited. It was just a suggestion. We have all day to discuss it."

"Don't push it. I'm warning you...."

"And I'm shaking in my shoes, really shaking."

"I'm sorry, Danny, honestly I am," Emily said.

It was Friday afternoon, and her son slouched on the living-room sofa, bottom lip extended in an angry pout. It had not been a good week. Cortez had been more distant than usual, despite all the talk about their plans for a canoe trip on Saturday. Emily had hoped he'd invite himself along, but he hadn't seemed very interested. More likely than not, he'd made his own plans for the weekend. And if she didn't think of something fast, Emily realized she'd end up all alone with a very crabby six-year-old for the next two days.

"Jimmy's grandmother is sick. They have to drive down to see her tomorrow. I know how much you've been counting on the canoe trip...." Her words trailed off into silence. She raked her fingers through her curls, then shoved her hands into the side pockets of her jeans, waiting. When Danny finally turned to look at her, his eyes bright with unshed tears, desperation grabbed her.

"Okay, okay. Let me try to get the canoe on top of the car." It wasn't all that heavy, was it? If Cathy and she could manage it between them, then maybe, just maybe she could handle it by herself. "If I can do it myself, then we'll go, just the two of us. All right?"

Danny jumped up, all trace of tears gone. He raced around the sofa and threw himself into Emily's arms. "Thanks, Mom, thanks a lot. I love you."

"I love you, too." Emily gave her son a quick, hard hug. She'd get their canoe on top of her car if it meant traction for a month when they returned. "Now, come on. Let's get started."

Forty-five minutes later Emily had succeeded in attaching

the canoe racks to the top of the car. Twice she had come very close to maneuvering the canoe onto the racks, but its size and shifting weight had been too much for her. The darn thing had come crashing down, and each time it had just missed leaving a dent in the side of her car. The afternoon air was cool, but her hair was damp with perspiration, and her pink cotton shirt clung to her back. She was exhausted, but one look at Danny, sitting on the front porch steps, chin in hand, convinced her she should try again.

"Once more, okay?"

Danny nodded glumly, not saying a word.

Emily turned back to the canoe, positioning it next to the car. Stepping between the canoe and the car, she dropped to her knees, placed one hand on each side of the canoe, and turned it over her head, turtle fashion. Slowly, carefully, she stood up and moved closer to the car. Taking a long, deep breath, she counted to three, then straightened her arms, heaving the canoe up and over toward the racks atop her car.

She heard brakes squealing, a car door slam, a shout. Her concentration wavered, her arms trembled, and she lost her balance. The canoe tumbled to the ground, narrowly missing her head, this time leaving a real gouge in the side of her car. She tightened her fingers into fists and squeezed her eyes shut. "Damn it, damn it, damn it," she muttered, just barely controlling the urge to jump up and down in time with her words.

"What the hell are you doing?"

Rough hands caught her shoulders and spun her around so fast that it made her dizzy. *Cortez.* He towered over her, his mouth a narrow, white line beneath the thick, black mustache, his eyes blazing with anger—and something else. Fear or pity? Emily didn't stop to analyze it. With the last of her strength, she wrenched away from him, turning so he couldn't see the hot tears that suddenly burned her eyes.

"I'm trying to beat my car to death with a canoe. What does it look like I'm doing?"

"It looks like you're doing a good job of it."

At the gentle, teasing tone of his voice, Emily's tears spilled onto her cheeks. She sagged against the car, blinking furiously, swiping at her face with shaking fingers. How humiliating, crying in front of him, but she couldn't stop. The thread of tension that had been tightening inside her over the past three weeks had finally snapped.

"We were supposed to go canoeing with Jimmy. But his grandma's sick. My mom said if she got the canoe up, we could go anyway." Danny hopped off the porch steps and crossed the lawn to stand next to Joseph. Staring up at him with wide, blue eyes, he offered his dilemma to his friend as only a small boy offers his problems to a trusted, adult male.

"I see." Joseph's hand rested on Danny's blond head for an instant. He knew all about the canoe trip. Danny had provided the details Sunday night, and Joseph had spent the entire week hoping Emily would invite him to join them. Perversely, he had also avoided her more than ever. "Well, maybe I can help."

"Help?" Emily asked, sniffling once more before turning to face Cortez.

"What are friends for?" he asked, brushing the last of her tears away with a gentle fingertip.

Emily stared at him in surprise. After days of treating her as if she had the plague, he had touched her twice in less than ten minutes, and she was having a hard time coping with her body's response. He hadn't been so close to her since the day he'd come to her office, and it had been a very long time since his lips had brushed the back of her hand in the hallway outside Danny's room. Now the warm honey feeling he triggered deep inside her threatened to render her helpless. How easy it would be to lay her head on his shoulder and let him hold her. How easy it would be to depend on him to solve her problems. But when he grew cold and distant again, what would she do?

"You don't understand." She took a step away from him, shaking her head, denying her thoughts and desires. "I have to be able to get the canoe up alone, in case no one's around to help at the lake."

"Are you telling me you were planning to go off alone with Danny on a canoe trip? Just the two of you?"

"Yes." Emily didn't like his tone of voice, nor the fact that he was gripping her upper arms again. She was a responsible adult, quite capable of taking her son canoeing. It was getting the damn canoe on top of her car that was the problem. And if he hadn't come roaring up on her the way he had—

"Lady, I can guarantee that's one thing you're *not* going to do."

"And *who's* going to stop?—"

"Mom, Mom," Danny interrupted, catching her arm and tugging it insistently. Emily's eyes flashed dangerously as she pulled away from Cortez and focused her attention on her son. "Maybe Joseph could go with us. I wanted you to invite him." As Emily's mouth dropped open, Danny turned to Joseph. "Will you go with us? Will you, please?"

"Danny, I know we talked about it," Emily admitted, her eyes skittering away from Cortez's sudden, intent stare. "But I'm sure Mr. Cortez has made plans for the weekend."

"No, I haven't." His fingers grasped her chin and forced her face up. His eyes caught and held hers as he gazed at her over Danny's head. "I haven't made any plans at all for the weekend," he said as he released her.

He could have taken the out she'd offered him. It would have been the wisest thing to do. But suddenly the prospect of a long, lonely weekend without her was more than he could face. For the first time in weeks he was willing to admit how much he wanted to be with her, how much he *needed* to be with her, the past be damned.

She needed him, too. He had seen her strong and sure of herself. He had seen her angry and obstinate. He had seen her laughing with childish delight. But he had never seen her shoulders sagging in defeat, her cheeks wet with tears. Yes, she needed him, but he had forced his way into her house. He wanted her to invite him into her life.

He wants me to ask him, Emily thought, as she matched him stare for stare. And she *wanted* to ask him. She couldn't handle the canoe alone, and she couldn't disappoint Danny, but there was more to it than that. In his own way he was offering to spend a day with them. The least she could do was meet him halfway.

In a very short time he'd become an important part of her life. If she didn't let him know it, would she spend the rest of her life dreaming about what might have been? What had Cathy said about his feelings, living in the house she had shared with Eric? Maybe if they spent one special day together away from the house, he'd be able to tear down the barriers he'd put up between them. Maybe he wanted to do just that, but didn't know how. With a soft smile of anticipation in her eyes and on her lips, Emily offered to lead the way.

"So, Cortez, do you want to go canoeing with us tomorrow?"

He felt as if he'd been punched in the gut. She had laid her sweet smile on him so many times the past few weeks, but the smile she offered him now was altogether different. It took his breath away. And her invitation loosened something tight and heavy in his chest. There was the strangest sensation of a wall starting to crumble. His eyes held hers as his hand moved to brush a cluster of damp curls away from her face. He wanted nothing more than to be with them, with her, out from under Eric's shadow.

"My pleasure."

"Oh, boy! Yippee!" Danny shouted, jumping up and down.

Reluctantly Joseph turned away from Emily and began to unfasten the canoe racks.

"Hey, we need those for the canoe!" Emily protested, groaning inwardly, wondering if canoeing was new to him. *Silly girl,* she thought a moment later, as he sent a wry glance her way.

"Your car's taken enough punishment for one weekend. I thought we'd use the Jeep."

"Oookaaay," Danny agreed immediately.

"Fine with me," Emily admitted. "But why do I get the feeling I'm going to be outnumbered every time there's a vote around here?" The look exchanged between Cortez and her son wasn't at all reassuring.

Cortez changed the canoe racks and put her car into the garage. Then Emily helped him position the canoe atop his Jeep. She left him to secure it front and back with special ropes while Danny helped her find life jackets and waterproof packs in the garage. Finding three of each, she sent Danny back to the Jeep with the life jackets, and carried the packs into the house.

Dropping two of the packs onto the kitchen table, she propped the third one on the counter and began filling it with fruit bars, chips, cookies and paper cartons of apple juice. She'd make sandwiches after dinner and add them to the bag in the morning. As she worked, Emily hummed snatches of songs and talked nonsense to Greta who was sitting beside her, waiting for a treat.

Catching sight of her reflection in the kitchen window, Emily hardly recognized herself. Her eyes sparkled and her lips curved up in a happy smile. One day to gether...anything could happen. For the first time in ages Emily had a glimmer of hope for the future.

Joseph walked through the back door, his arm around the boy at his side, and felt that gut-punched feeling all over again. Twilight had brought a definite chill to the air outside, but the kitchen was brighter, warmer, more welcoming than ever. He heard Emily humming softly as she worked at the counter, and admired her spare and easy movements. Greta, sitting beside her, watched, too, waiting patiently for the cookie Emily finally offered.

He tightened his arm around Danny for an instant, reminding himself to slow down. Much as he wanted to cross the kitchen and pull her into his arms, feel her body close to his, he couldn't do it. Not yet. But he would do it soon, very soon, because in that small moment in time he had made his decision. The woman and the boy would be his to care for and protect for the rest of his life.

"Hey, lady, you're spoiling my dog," he growled, as he released Danny and moved to stand beside her.

"I'm just a sucker for big, brown eyes," Emily retorted. She threw him a smile over her shoulder, a smile that faded when she felt the heat of his own dark eyes on her.

"I'm partial to pale green myself," he said softly.

"Is dinner ready yet? I'm starving." Danny's plaintive wail brought both adults down to earth with a thud.

"Almost." The oven stew she'd put together early in the afternoon could be served any time now. "Why don't you guys set the table?"

While Danny pulled silverware and fresh napkins from a drawer, Emily opened a cabinet, reaching for plates and glasses. Turning, she handed them to Cortez. As he took them from her, his fingers brushed hers for just a second, and he smiled before moving away. *Yes,* Emily thought, as she watched him leave the kitchen. *Yes, yes, yes.*

Dinner was a rowdy affair. They argued over what time to leave and where to stop for breakfast. Emily was sure they'd have more than enough time for canoeing if they left at eight. Cortez and Danny threatened to leave her at home if she wasn't in the Jeep by six-thirty. She begged and pleaded for a civilized breakfast at Denny's. They insisted on the drive-thru at McDonald's.

Just like a real family, Emily thought, right down to the bumping and thumping against each other as Danny and Cortez stored leftovers and loaded the dishwasher while she put together ham and cheese sandwiches. And if Cortez's hip brushed hers more than necessary, and if his arms reached around her for no apparent reason, well, what could she say? The kitchen *was* small.

By the time Danny tumbled into bed, much later than usual, Emily was tired, too. She had packed a change of clothes and jackets for Danny and herself, along with a first aid kit, in one of the remaining waterproof bags. The other bag was for Cortez. Making one last check, Emily retrieved it from the kitchen table, then climbed the stairs to the second floor.

Crossing the hallway, she stopped in front of the closed studio door and hesitated. Despite their closeness earlier, Cortez had disappeared inside right on schedule, about the time she had settled down on Danny's bed to read his bedtime story. Since the night of the picnic, when she'd pounded on the door and hollered at him, she hadn't disturbed him when he was in the studio.

In fact, she hadn't been in the studio for weeks. He kept the door closed, and she could think of no good reason to open it. But tonight she had an excuse for disturbing him. She had to give him the bag. Taking a deep breath, and hanging on to the glimmer of hope that had stayed with her all evening, Emily tapped on the door. It opened, and the smell of paint and turpentine assaulted her nose.

"I, um, forgot to give you this earlier." Alone with him in the dimly lighted hallway, Emily suddenly felt nervous. He stared at her with dark, unreadable eyes and didn't speak. "You might want to pack a change of clothes, an extra pair of shoes and a jacket, in case the weather turns bad. It's waterproof, so even if we tip over in the canoe, everything inside will stay dry." She was rattling, and she knew it. Thank God she'd run out of breath.

"Thanks." He took the bag from her, taking care not to touch her hand. "And thanks for asking me to go with you."

"I wanted, um, Danny...we both wanted you to go." Emily glanced down at the floor, then up into his eyes. "I thought you'd be too busy."

Once again he didn't say anything.

"Well, see you at six-thirty," Emily offered. Without another word, she spun around and crossed the hallway. She stepped into her bedroom and closed her door with an unintentional slam. Her heart was pounding as she leaned back against it. If he changed his mind about the canoe trip, she would never, never forgive him.

Standing in the studio doorway, Joseph fingered the dark blue bag in his hand. *See you at six-thirty,* he thought, then frowned. *No, querida, I'm afraid I'll be seeing you much sooner.* Tonight, of all nights, Joseph had no doubt he'd be seeing Emily in his dreams. He, too, allowed his door to shut with a slam. If she changed her mind about the canoe trip, he would never, never forgive her.

Chapter Six

Emily crawled into bed fully prepared for a sleepless night, but the strain of the past weeks caught up with her at last. She slept like a log and woke up just after five, full of anticipation for the coming day.

The glimmer of hope she had begun to feel had lingered through the night. As she snuggled under the quilt on her bed, it blossomed deep inside her, fueled by the sound of Cortez's footsteps in the hallway. Surely he wouldn't be up and around if he had changed his mind, she thought, warmth and happiness washing over her in a long, slow wave.

"Mommy?" Trying not to smile, Emily closed her eyes, feigning sleep as Danny crept into her bedroom. "Mommy, are you awake?" he whispered, his face close to hers.

"Yes!" Emily growled, popping her eyes open and grabbing his arms. He screeched and giggled as she hauled him into bed with her, tickling his tummy and plopping wet kisses all over his face.

"Stop, Mom, stop!"

"Only if you promise to stay and cuddle."

"I promise."

"You're getting so big, Danny," Emily said, as their laughter subsided. "Too bad six-year-old boys don't like to cuddle with their mothers." Her voice was wistful as she brushed his blond curls off his forehead and gazed at him in the dawn light. Her baby was growing up, and she wondered if she'd ever have another. In the space of a single sigh, she imagined a tiny bundle with soft, dark hair and big, brown eyes, and almost laughed aloud at her foolishness.

"I *do* like to cuddle," Danny insisted, snuggling against her for all of ten seconds before hopping off the bed. "Now get up, Mom."

"No rest for the weary in this house," Emily grumbled, though she was grateful for the interruption of her wayward thoughts. She threw back the quilt and swung her feet over the edge of the bed.

When she didn't leap to her feet immediately, Danny tugged at her hand. "All the way up, Mom."

"Okay, okay." Emily stood up and started across the bedroom toward her bathroom. "What's your buddy doing?"

"Joseph? Taking Greta for a walk. He's trying out his leg without his cane. He'll be back way before six-thirty."

"Good. Why don't you use the bathroom while he's gone, and get yourself dressed? Then we can get this show on the road."

Thirty minutes later Emily and Danny skipped down the stairs side by side, as Joseph and Greta walked through the front door. Emily wore jeans with her kelly-green cardigan over a matching green and white plaid, flannel shirt, while Danny wore a red pullover with his jeans and blue, chambray shirt.

"You look like Christmas," Joseph said, as they met at the foot of the staircase.

Also in jeans, and a thick, navy-blue sweater, he looked as dark and dangerous as ever, but the brooding intensity of the past weeks had disappeared. In the dim light of the hallway, Emily saw her rush of relief mirrored in his eyes, and realized that he had been as unsure of her as she of him. Beneath his cool, calm exterior he was just as excited about the canoe trip as she was, and just as eager to make the day a special one.

"I'll take that as a compliment."

"It is, *querida*, it is," Joseph murmured, draping an arm around Danny's shoulders. "Come on, son. You can help with the packs."

"What does that mean?" Danny asked as they started up the staircase.

"*Querida*? It means sweetheart."

"You think my mom's sweet?"

Emily watched them climb the staircase, a soft smile lighting her face as she listened to their conversation. At the small landing halfway up Joseph stopped, turning to meet her eyes.

"Sometimes...."

"Me, too. But sometimes she's really crabby."

"Yes, sometimes she's really crabby," he agreed, turning to follow Danny up the steps, his laughter echoing through the house.

"Really crabby," Emily muttered, but she was smiling as she headed toward the kitchen to tuck the sandwiches into the food bag. They were going to have a wonderful time, just like a real family. She could feel it deep inside.

They pulled out of the driveway shortly before six-thirty, and as planned, they drove through McDonald's to pick up breakfast. As they headed north, following Highway 61 along Lake Superior, they munched biscuit sandwiches and sipped milk from small cartons. In the front seat, Emily and Joseph also shared a thermos of coffee, while behind them, Danny made sure Greta received her fair share of tidbits from everyone. Outside the air was crisp and cool, the autumn colors brilliant against the bright, blue sky.

When they had finished eating, and she had stowed their trash in an empty bag, Emily opened the road map of Minnesota to check their progress. The route to Gunflint Lake was fairly simple; Highway 61 to Grand Marais, where they picked up the Gunflint Trail to the lake. They had agreed to put in at

Trapper's Lodge, since it was on the near side of the lake and Emily had set out from there many times in the past.

Refolding the map, she apprised Cortez of the major turn-offs and when to expect them, then settled back in her seat to enjoy the scenery. He didn't seem inclined to talk, so she contented herself with pointing out an occasional landmark or an unusually startling change of color among the aspens and paper birches bordering the road.

For a while Danny's chatter filled the void, but then he, too, was quiet. Glancing back at him, Emily saw that he had dozed off. Cortez, his hands wrapped around the steering wheel, seemed to be deep in thought, probably a million miles away. Unwilling to disturb him, or the peaceful silence surrounding them, Emily tipped her head back against the headrest and closed her eyes. She was almost asleep when Cortez spoke.

"Did you go on canoe trips with your husband?" His voice was low and rough.

"Canoe trips? With Eric?" Emily sat up, blinking against the sudden, bright sunshine.

She slanted a look at Cortez, but he was concentrating on the road, his grip on the steering wheel anything but casual. He was frowning, much like Danny did when he was upset about something.

What a strange question for him to ask, she thought, as the silence lengthened between them. She wasn't sure she wanted to answer it. Both times they had discussed Eric, it had ended unpleasantly. Then she recalled Cathy's comment about how Joseph might feel living in the house she had shared with her husband.

If in the past someone had told her that one day she would be glad Eric had hated canoeing, she would have told them they were crazy. Now, traveling down the highway with Cortez, Emily thanked God that Eric had been the original couch potato. Suddenly her day with Joseph Cortez promised to be very special indeed. In an odd way it was a small gift she could give to the man who had begun to mean so much to her.

"About ten years ago, after an entire week of begging and

pleading, I managed to get Eric to agree to try canoeing.''
Emily shrugged her shoulders and smiled slightly, remembering. ''He griped about loading and unloading the canoe. He griped about being too cold, then too hot, then too cold again. He griped about the bugs. To answer your question, Eric and I went canoeing once, and we didn't go to Gunflint Lake. He griped about it being too far away. He didn't really enjoy the great outdoors, and he wasn't the least bit adventurous.''

''I see.'' Joseph glanced at Emily for a long moment, surprise and uncertainty alternating in his gaze.

Eric Anderson might not have been adventurous enough to go canoeing with his wife, but he'd certainly managed to get into the swing of things with a pack of Arteagans in Norteña. Unconsciously Joseph tightened his grip on the steering wheel.

In his heart and soul he was furious with the man for choosing the Arteagans over Emily and getting himself killed. Yet he was also glad that Eric Anderson had never gone, nor would ever go to Gunflint Lake with Emily. The two conflicting emotions roiled around inside him, leaving him confused and angry.

''After that you went alone?'' he asked harshly.

''After that I went with friends.'' Emily sensed Cortez's anger. Though she wondered at its source, she didn't want to probe. She wanted only to dispel it before it spoiled their day. ''Now that he's old enough to paddle, Danny and I have been going with Cathy, her husband, Hank, and her son, Jimmy. And today we're going with you,'' she added hesitantly.

''And today you're going with me,'' Joseph agreed.

He reached out and took Emily's hand in his, anger and confusion fading away. Emily was here with him now, and that was all that mattered. Eric Anderson was dead. There was nothing he could do or say to bring her husband back. But he could give her so much, and today would be the beginning.

Inch by inch, the tension eased out of Cortez as they rode again in silence. Threading her fingers through his, Emily wished the quiet, peaceful journey could last forever. If she was any judge at all, their sudden closeness was as good for him as for her, and she didn't want it to end.

By the time they turned onto the dirt road leading to the lodge, Cortez was as close to being relaxed as Emily had ever seen him. As they pulled into the parking lot, he squeezed her hand once, then released her so he could maneuver the Jeep close to the water's edge. It had taken so little, she thought, cradling her hand in her lap, savoring his lingering warmth.

As the Jeep rolled to a stop, Danny and Greta awoke from their naps. Each making excited noises, they tumbled out and headed for the lake. Emily sat still for a moment, admiring the lovely sight of sunlight glistening on the crystal-clear water, and the rich, deep green of the pine forest.

"It's beautiful up here, isn't it?" she asked, turning to face Cortez. He was staring at her, his eyes deep and dark and warm.

"Beautiful," he agreed, his fingers brushing lightly along the curve of her jaw.

Emily's eyes widened with surprise. She felt the heat of a blush climb her neck and settle into her cheeks. But before she could reply, Cortez opened his door and climbed out.

"Come on. Time's a-wasting," he chided gently. Slamming his door, he moved toward the front of the Jeep and began unfastening the line securing the canoe.

It was Emily's turn to frown, but only for an instant. Their time together was too short to squander. Analyzing Cortez's actions since the previous afternoon could wait until later, when she was alone. At the moment, all she wanted was to glide across Gunflint Lake with Cortez and Danny, into a time and place disturbed by nothing more exotic than the call of a loon. Scrambling out of the Jeep, she moved to the back and set to work helping Cortez.

They checked in with Mr. Carson, the owner of Trapper's Lodge, giving him an idea of where they were going and how long they planned to be out. After that, they had their life jackets on and the canoe in the water in record time.

Emily sat in front, Danny and Greta were stowed in the middle along with the packs, and Cortez sat in back. It took only a few minutes to synchronize their paddling so that the canoe moved smoothly through the shimmering, crystal-clear water. Once, about halfway across the main expanse of the lake, it felt as if the canoe wasn't moving, but Danny's giggling gave the game away.

"All right, Cortez, pull your weight, or plan to get wet," Emily threatened, snapping her paddle into the water in such a way as to guarantee him a lapful of icy-cold water. She felt the canoe shimmy and wondered if he'd give in to the urge to stand up. Slanting a glance at him over her shoulder, she saw something very near to admiration in his dark eyes.

"Yes, ma'am," he said, soft and low, with no hint of meekness at all.

Once across the lake, they followed a narrow stream that Emily remembered from past trips. There was one short portage to avoid a set of gurgling rapids, then another narrow, twisting stream that eventually widened into a second, smaller lake. It took them about two hours of steady paddling to reach it. By then it was nearly noon, so they decided to stop for lunch. They beached the canoe and climbed a short, steep path leading up to a flat, grassy area that jutted out over the lake.

Emily pulled a small tarp from the food pack she carried, and with Cortez's help, spread it out in a patch of sun. They polished off sandwiches, chips, fruit bars, cookies and juice in companionable silence, too hungry to talk. Then Danny ventured off with Greta to toss pebbles into the lake. Sighing with contentment, Emily flopped onto her back and closed her eyes, enjoying the contrast of warm sun and cool breeze on her face.

"I'm stuffed. I never should have eaten that last cookie."

"Oh, I don't know. Five cookies, six cookies…not a lot of difference, really." Cortez was sitting beside her, Indian-style, cramming paper wrappers and empty cartons into the pack.

"Smart mouth."

"Sweet mouth." He reached over and casually brushed cookie crumbs off her chin with his fingertips.

"It's too late for flattery, Cortez." Shading her eyes with one hand, Emily squinted up at him but he was clearly trying to figure out how to close the pack to keep it waterproof. "You're pretty good with a canoe, but I'm wise to all the tricks," she continued, her voice smug and self-assured. "Pants still wet?"

"Want to check for yourself?" Tossing the pack to one side, Joseph stretched out beside her, resting his weight on one elbow. His eyes gleamed a challenge as he gazed down at her.

Emily blushed bright red to the roots of her hair for the second time that day. He was so warm, so close, and he was twisting one of her curls round and round his finger. Suddenly she was just a little bit afraid of the fire she was playing with. Instinctively she knew that when he loved her, it would be with a fierce, all-consuming intensity. When...and then...forever? If he loved her, then left her, what would she do?

Pulling her eyes away from his, Emily decided it was time to change the subject. "Did you do much canoeing when you were growing up?"

"My folks used to take my sister and me canoeing on the Guadeloupe River. It's a different kind of canoeing, though. The river's fast, with lots of rapids, especially in the spring. We used heavier canoes and shot the rapids. It's a one-way trip, with pickup points at various locations down the river. I think you'd like it."

"Sounds like fun," Emily agreed, glancing up at him in time to see a grimace of pain cross his face.

Without a word he released her curl and shifted positions on the tarp. Sitting up, he bent, then straightened his left leg again and again, kneading his thigh muscles with his hands while Emily watched.

"How's it doing?" she asked hesitantly, sitting up to face him. She wanted to touch him, but the look on his face kept her still. Much as she wanted to comfort him, she was afraid Cortez would interpret any action on her part as pity.

"Damn thing's stiffening up on me," he growled, as he continued to knead his thigh.

"How did you hurt your leg?" Emily asked, edging a little closer to him, barely restraining the urge to touch him. "You don't have to tell me, especially after that wisecrack I made a few weeks ago...."

Joseph's hands grew still. He couldn't, wouldn't lie to her, because lying now would only make the truth that much harder to tell. But he wasn't going to tell her all the details of his past either, not here, not now. He wanted this day. He *needed* this day more than he'd ever needed anything in his life.

"Maybe another time, *querida*." His gaze held hers for a long moment, then he turned his attention back to his leg. "I don't want anything to spoil our day."

She saw the pain edged with anger in his eyes, heard it in his low, rough voice, and felt it deep inside her soul. She closed her eyes, knotting her fingers in her lap as a shiver raced through her body, sensing that somehow, some way, violence had shattered his life as thoroughly as it had hers, and that he was no more ready to deal with it than was she.

"Maybe a walk would help," she suggested softly, focusing on the thick stand of pines at the opposite end of the meadow.

"A walk would help," he agreed, brushing a hand over her curls in gentle reassurance, letting her know as best he could that he understood and appreciated her retreat. "Feel like going for a walk?"

"What I really feel like is a nap," Emily admitted, turning to face Cortez with a rueful smile tilting her lips. "Five o'clock in the morning is too early for me. I'm sure Danny will go with you, though."

"Trying to get rid of us?" Joseph asked, as he pulled himself to his feet and tested his left leg. A short hike would definitely work the kinks out of it.

Emily allowed her eyes to travel up the length of him and knew an instant of deep desire. He was so dark against the bright, blue sky, but his eyes were soft and warm, and the cool breeze ruffled his hair, making him look young and almost carefree. *I'm falling in love with you. No matter who you are, or what you've done in the past, I'm falling in love with you.* She smiled slowly and shook her head. "What do you think?"

"Ah, *querida*, you don't want to know what I'm thinking," he muttered. He had read the silent message in her eyes and felt his body respond. Turning quickly, he called to Danny.

Boy and dog joined them immediately, and Danny eagerly

agreed to go for a walk in the woods. Checking his watch against Emily's, Joseph promised to return in one hour, allowing them more than enough time to paddle back to the lodge and get onto the road to Duluth before dark. Over Danny's protests, he ordered Greta to stay in the meadow. He didn't plan to go far, but he refused to leave Emily alone. He had a knife strapped to his good leg in case Danny and he ran into trouble, and Greta would die before she allowed anyone or anything near Emily. He knew he was being abnormally cautious about a harmless outing, but he had learned that nowhere in the world was perfectly safe.

Emily sat up long enough to watch Cortez and Danny cross the meadow and disappear into the woods. Once they were out of sight, she stretched out on the tarp, tucking one arm under her head, the sunshine warming her like a thick, wool blanket. Greta curled up beside her, and soon Emily was sound asleep.

Muttering to herself, she rolled onto her back, one hand reaching for a blanket that didn't exist. Cold...she was cold. What had happened to her blanket? And somewhere nearby someone or something was crying; she was sure of it. Slowly she came awake, blinking once, then again, as she tried to focus on her surroundings.

Thick, gray clouds scudded across the sky, blotting out the last patches of clear blue. Emily sat up on the tarp, rubbing her hands over her face in a futile attempt to chase away the muzziness that fogged her brain. She had been sleeping so deeply that for a few minutes she was incapable of doing anything except staring out across the lake in a stupor. A sudden gust of cold air finally cleared her head.

The bright, blue sky, the shining sun and the warmth it offered had all disappeared behind a low bank of heavy, leaden clouds that promised rain, and a lot of it. The refreshingly cool breeze of earlier in the day had turned into a cold, damp wind that whistled through the treetops and across the flat meadow to ripple over the lake. Emily pulled her cardigan around her, shivering as she fastened the buttons with stiff fingers. The damp was already seeping into her bones.

"Getting a little chilly out here, isn't it, girl?"

Greta acknowledged Emily's comment with a gentle nudge, then faced the woods again, ears at attention, dark eyes searching. She whined softly.

"That was you, huh?" Emily stroked the dog's head, the mystery of who had been crying easily solved. She, too, faced the woods, eyes searching. "They should be back any minute now," she said, as much to reassure herself as to comfort the dog. She pushed up her sleeve to glance at her watch.

"Oh, my God," she whispered. Another shiver, this time born of fear, raced down her spine as she stared at her watch, confusion lining her brow. It couldn't be....

Think, Emily, think, she instructed herself, draping an arm around Greta. It had been one o'clock when they'd synchronized their watches, and Cortez had promised to return in an hour. Now, according to her watch, it was almost three o'clock. A thirty-minute walk in any direction wouldn't have taken them too far away. Thirty minutes out, thirty minutes back, one hour. Even with the addition of some unexpected exploration, they shouldn't be an hour late getting back. Cortez just wasn't the type to say one hour unless he meant it. And even if he hadn't meant exactly one hour, the deteriorating weather conditions would have sent the most determined hiker heading for home.

"Where are they, girl?" Emily whispered, as fear shot through her again.

Greta whined and nuzzled Emily's shoulder once more, as if to offer reassurance, but Emily's mind was already turning over all the possible dangers lurking in the woods. Bears loomed high on her list.

In all the years she'd been canoeing and camping in the boundary waters, Emily had never encountered a bear. She knew they lived in the wilderness areas, and knew they were as eager to avoid humans as humans were to avoid them. Yet every bear story she'd ever heard crowded into her mind as she stared at the woods, her heart racing. Even Cathy and

Hank had run into a bear on a recent camping trip. The fool thing had wandered into their campsite one night and sat on their tent. The whistle Cathy kept in her backpack had frightened it away.

The story had been funny, and Hank loved to crack jokes about his experience with "bear buns," but sitting alone in the deserted meadow, the sky darkening around her, Emily didn't feel like laughing. Her vivid imagination conjured up horrible visions of Cortez and Danny, lying on the cold, hard ground, their bodies viciously mauled—

"Stop it. Just stop it," she told herself, grinding out the words through clenched teeth, blinking back a sudden, hot rush of tears. Sitting and shivering, scaring herself silly and crying weren't going to help matters one little bit. Regardless of what had happened to make them late, Cortez and Danny were going to need her.

Another gust of wind caught at her hair, ruffling Greta's fur as well. Emily shook as icy fingers trailed across the back of her neck. God, it was getting cold. If only she had a jacket. But she did, she thought, remembering the packs still secured in the canoe.

She glanced again at her watch. It was ten past three. She would give them another twenty minutes before she took Greta into the woods to search for them. The wisest course of action was to stay put as long as possible, rather than risk getting lost or hurt herself. In fact, if they didn't return by three-thirty, she should get into the canoe and head back to the lodge for help. But she wasn't leaving without them. If she lost Danny and Joseph, life wouldn't be worth living.

"Okay, Greta, you stay here. Stay." Her decision made, Emily reached for the food pack and stood up. Bending, she eased the tarp from under the dog's bottom, folded it, and tucked it under her arm. The dog looked up at her with huge, sad eyes. "I'll be right back. I promise." Greta whined again, then resumed her vigil.

The pack over one shoulder, the tarp clutched in her arms, Emily crossed the meadow and hurried down the steep, narrow path to the canoe. A subtle change in the air warned her that the rain would start soon, and the heavy cloud cover promised darkness at least an hour earlier than usual. It had taken them two hours to get in. With the wind and rain it would take longer getting out. They'd have to be on Gunflint Lake, where the lodge's light could be their beacon, by six.

Don't think about it, she warned herself. *Just take things one step at a time.*

Don't think about it, he warned himself. *Just take things one step at a time.*

Levering himself up against a tree, he put his weight on his left leg, groaning inwardly. Despite the cold wind whistling through the trees, perspiration trickled down his face. If only he'd brought the cane, or had the time to find a sturdy stick to lean on while he carried the boy. But he was over an hour late getting back to Emily already.

"Are you okay, Joseph?" Danny asked in a small, scared voice. He sat on a rock, his face pale, the ankle he'd sprained wrapped in a makeshift bandage.

"Leg hurts," he admitted, resting a hand on the boy's head. "But we're almost back to the meadow. How are you doing?"

"My ankle hurts a little bit. Maybe I could walk...."

"No. Just give me a minute more, and you can ride piggyback again."

"I'm sorry I fell down. You were right about the rocks being slippery."

"Don't worry about it, son. If I could have, I would have been climbing around up there with you. It's fun to explore, isn't it?"

"Yeah," Danny agreed, grinning sheepishly. "Wish we could have gone inside the cave."

"Yeah," Joseph smiled too, as he pushed away from the tree. "Come on. We'd better get going. Give me your hand and use my leg as a step up." Once again he groaned inwardly as Danny climbed onto his back. He swayed slightly as the boy wrapped arms and legs around him. Then he started slowly down the trail.

"Do you think my mom will be mad?"

"I don't know, Danny. I hope not," he said softly, trying to reassure himself as much as the boy.

In reality he was sure Emily would be furious. She had trusted him with her son, and what had happened? He'd allowed the boy to climb up a tumble of rocks to peer inside a small cave, and on the way down, Danny had slipped and twisted his ankle. It had happened thirty minutes into their walk. By the time Joseph had checked Danny for other injuries and bound his ankle with a clean, white handkerchief, it was after two o'clock. The hike back had been slow and painful, and despite the bad weather brewing, he'd been forced to stop more than once to rest his leg.

Now she was going to hate him, and she had every right to do so. It was his fault that Danny had been hurt...his fault. Another kind of pain twisted inside him, as he saw the meadow ahead through a break in the trees. She was better off without him. He was no good to her or any member of her family. First her husband, then her son. He squeezed his eyes shut for a moment, his arms tightening around the boy's legs.

"I hear Greta barking," Danny said as he rested his chin on Joseph's shoulder. "She knows we're coming."

Without a word, Joseph limped toward the clearing, his eyes searching for Emily.

At the canoe, Emily dug out her bright yellow jacket and pulled it on, her fingers trembling violently as she tried to zip the zipper. Having mastered it at last, she tugged Danny's jacket out of her pack, then opened Joseph's pack and found his. She stowed the food pack with the others, arranged the life jackets on top, and covered everything with the tarp, in case it rained before they returned. The trip back to the lodge would be miserable enough, without having to start with wet life jackets.

She refused to allow herself to consider the possibility that they wouldn't be on their way in less than an hour. Clutching the jackets in one hand, she spun around and started up the path, quickening her pace when she heard Greta's excited barking. Breathing hard, her heart pounding, she reached the top of the path—and saw Joseph step out of the shadow of the woods and start across the meadow, with Danny riding piggyback.

He walked slowly, his limp more pronounced than it had been in days. Halfway across the meadow, he stopped and eased Danny off his back and onto the ground, where her son stood, favoring his right leg. Greta, barking wildly, her whole body wagging, circled them again and again, but Emily couldn't move. Her mind whirled. Danny hurt. Joseph hurting, too. *But, God, oh thank you, God, both of them are all right.*

Suddenly, as if freed from a hideous nightmare, she started toward them, first walking, then running, unable to close the distance between them fast enough. With a small cry, she dropped the jackets onto the ground and hurled herself into Joseph's arms.

"Are you all right?" she cried as his arms closed around her. His sweater was incredibly soft and warm and reassuring against her cold, wet cheek. As she squeezed her eyes shut, trying hard to stop the tears trickling down her face, she felt a shudder roll through his body. He swayed against her, then steadied himself. "I was so scared...so scared."

"We're okay, Mom. You don't have to cry," Danny declared in his best, big-boy tone of voice.

"Oh, Danny," Emily murmured, breaking away from Joseph to kneel in front of her son. "Are you really all right?" Hands on his shoulders, she studied every inch of him, then pulled him into her arms for a quick, fierce hug.

"I'm okay, Mom. Now will you *please* stop crying?"

"Yes." Emily sat back on her heels, hands clasped in her lap. She took a deep breath to steady herself, then brushed away the last of her tears with trembling fingers. With every ounce of willpower she possessed, she forced herself to smile. "Better?"

"Yeah. Can I have my jacket? It's getting kind of cold."

Without a word, Emily retrieved the two jackets from the spot where she'd dropped them. She helped Danny into his, zipping it up to his neck. Then she stood up to face Joseph.

She saw the beads of perspiration dotting his forehead, saw the lines of pain and fatigue etching his features. His hands stuffed into the side pockets of his jeans, he swayed slightly, trying not to put too much weight on his left leg.

"What happened to you guys?" Emily asked softly, holding Joseph's dark blue jacket so he could slip his arms into the sleeves.

"I saw a little cave. Joseph said I could climb up and look inside. It was spooky." Danny rolled his eyes and shuddered. "Then I slipped and fell down."

"He twisted his ankle," Joseph added, avoiding Emily's eyes as he zipped his jacket.

"Joseph fixed it. See?" Danny pulled up the leg of his jeans to display an ankle neatly wrapped in one of Joseph's handkerchiefs. "Then he carried me all the way back. It took a long time, 'cause we had to rest a lot."

"Does it hurt?" Emily knelt down beside her son and gently touched his ankle. "It doesn't look too bad. It's just a little puffy."

"It hurts a little bit."

"Emily, I'm sorry—" Joseph began.

"And you're going to be a lot sorrier if you don't get off that leg," she interrupted, as she stood up, dismissing the apology she deemed unnecessary. "I have a feeling you're hurting more than a little bit, so sit," she commanded briskly.

"It's going to rain, Emily. We've got to get going," he protested.

"I know. But I have no desire to pick you up at the bottom of the path to the canoe. I can only help one of you down at a time. So sit, damn it!"

Without further argument, Joseph did as she ordered, indicating to Emily just how badly he was hurting. But there wasn't time to think about it. The first drops of rain were beginning to fall, and in less than three hours, it would be dark.

Thank God, the portage trail was short and straight enough for her to drag the canoe along it. Coming in, Joseph had carried it turtle-style, but Emily wasn't strong enough for that, and Joseph's leg couldn't take much more stress. Getting across Gunflint Lake was going to be hell if the wind picked up any more. She had come across the lake in bad weather a few times, though. She could do it again.

"Come on, kiddo, up." Emily scooped Danny into her arms. "Put your legs around me like a little monkey. Good. But you weigh a ton." Glancing at Joseph over her shoulder, she caught her breath. He looked bad, his face pale and drawn, his eyes dull with pain. "I'll be right back," she promised, then started toward the path.

She was really something else, he thought, as he watched her disappear down the steep, narrow path. There was one tough lady lurking under that fragile exterior. Not tough in the sense that she was hard or cruel, but she had a core of strength and serenity that made her unlike any woman Joseph had ever known. He knew she was frightened, yet she hadn't given in to hysterics. Instead, in her own quick and easy way, she had assessed the situation, decided on a course of action, and knowing he was in pain, had taken over.

Respect, admiration and another, deeper emotion he was afraid to name wound themselves around his heart and settled into his soul. He had never wanted, never *needed* a woman as he did Emily. Yet all he seemed capable of was betraying her trust. Fueled by a full measure of self-disgust, Joseph levered himself up and started limping slowly, painfully toward the path.

At the canoe, Emily tucked in Danny and Greta among the packs, leaving the boy to put on his life jacket under the protection of the tarp. By the time she reached the top of the path again, Joseph was waiting for her, head down, hands deep in the pockets of his jacket.

"I thought I told you to sit." Emily allowed a touch of exasperation into her voice as she came up to his left side and eased an arm around his waist. His left arm settled across her back, his left hand wrapped around her shoulder. "I wanted you to save your strength for paddling."

"Nothing wrong with my arms," he muttered, as they

started down the narrow path. "Listen, I'm sorry about Danny."

She looked up at him in surprise, and saw that his eyes were bleak and weary. She hesitated, uncertain of how to reassure him. Silence stretched between them until Joseph spoke his thoughts aloud.

"You trusted me with him. I should have been more careful. He's just a little boy. I should have had more sense. I'm...Emily, I'm so sorry."

He knew she wouldn't pull away, because he needed her help on the path. However, he hadn't expected the sudden tightening of her arm around his waist, nor the reassuring pressure of her hand on his chest.

"He's a boy, Joseph, and boys have accidents all the time. I expect he'll get into a lot worse scrapes along the way. If he doesn't, *then* I'll worry. I'm just sorry you had to carry him. Was it far?"

"Far enough," he admitted, tightening his hold on her shoulder for an instant.

But he would have carried the boy a hundred miles to hear her call him Joseph again. And she didn't blame him...didn't blame him...didn't blame him. He clung to that knowledge as he clung to her. A tiny seed of hope took root and began to grow deep inside his soul. Would she also understand about Eric's death?

He savored the warmth and weight of her against his chest, savored the feel of her arms around him, holding him as if she'd never let him go. And he wondered if it was possible that her worry and fear had been as much for him as for her son.

"If anything had happened to you..." Emily whispered, unconsciously answering his unspoken question. Her fingers, buried in the thick warmth of his jacket, tightened their hold.

"Everything's going to be all right, Emily. We're going to be all right." He was closer than ever to believing it, as he rested his cheek against her hair. Her head dropped to nestle on his shoulder, and despite the pain shooting up his leg, Joseph Cortez willed the steep, narrow path to go on forever.

Chapter Seven

The first drops of rain settled into a fine, steady drizzle as Emily and Joseph reached the canoe and put on their life jackets. No rain at all would have been best, but the drizzle was better than a torrential downpour, and the wind had cooperated by dying down a bit. They eased the canoe into the water and headed across the small lake, aiming for the channel that would eventually lead them to the portage trail and into Gunflint Lake.

Joseph proved there was nothing wrong with his arms; his paddling was as smooth and rhythmic as Emily's. Within minutes they had crossed the lake and were gliding into the narrow, twisting stream. Tall trees on both banks provided some shelter from the rain, and they were making good time. The lodge lights would be well in sight long before dark, and aside from being cold and damp, they were all right.

Her tension should be easing, Emily thought. But an hour later, as they angled into shore near the tree marked with the trail blaze, she realized she was holding her paddle in a death grip. She was tired, scared, and worried about Joseph. He had swallowed some aspirin before they started, but each time she glanced back at him, she could see the lines of pain on his face, and feel it radiating from his anguished eyes.

What would she do if the strain proved to be too much for him and he passed out? She couldn't, *wouldn't* leave him, even to get help. Waiting for him to return with Danny, she had finally begun to understand how much he meant to her. She had held herself together for him, as if with bits of tape, dabs of glue and scraps of string. Suddenly she was aware of just how close she was to unraveling completely.

As the canoe bumped against the lake bottom, Emily stood up and stepped into ankle-deep, icy-cold water. With quick, deft movements she maneuvered the boat so that Joseph could step onto the gently sloping bank. One shiver chased another down her back.

"I could have done that," Joseph muttered, tugging the canoe onto shore. "The last thing you need is wet feet." Without looking at Emily, he lifted Danny out and began to unfasten the tarp covering the packs.

"And you enjoy having wet feet, right? The perfect antidote for your leg?" Emily couldn't contain the faint tinge of sarcasm in her voice. She was so tired, and her head had begun to ache. "Listen, leave the packs and everything in the canoe. I'm going to drag it."

"Are you crazy?" Joseph exclaimed, glaring at her. "You can't drag that thing half a mile by yourself. If you take the packs, I'll carry it."

It was past time for him to take control of the situation. Thanks to the aspirin he had dug out of Emily's first-aid kit, he was feeling better, and he knew by the tone of her voice that she was nearing the end of her rope. His only thought was to spare her as much as possible, because he was going to need her help to get across Gunflint Lake. Unfortunately, Emily was in no mood to be spared.

"I can, and I *will* drag the canoe. You help Danny."

"*You* help Danny. I'll handle the canoe." His voice cracked like a whip through the dull, gray, rainy day, issuing an order he expected her to obey.

For Emily, wound up tight with worry and fear, it was the last straw. He had chosen the wrong time and the wrong place to resort to Latin machismo. She rounded on him, her eyes flashing, her hands clenched in tight fists, and strode toward him. When she was inches away from him, she propped her fists on her hips and lashed back at him. "Issuing orders to the *little woman* may work where you come from, Cortez, but don't tell *me* what to do. Don't…ever…tell me what to do." Her voice was high and harsh and almost over the edge.

"If you weren't so damned pigheaded, I wouldn't have to tell you what to do. You'd have the sense to do it," he shot back, barely restraining the urge to shake some sense into her.

"Pigheaded?" Emily blinked furiously against the unexpected threat of tears his harsh words had triggered. Her chest rose and fell with every panting breath she took. *Why are we fighting? Why are we standing in the middle of nowhere yelling at each other?* "Pigheaded?"

"Are you going to cry again, Mommy?" Danny, arms around Greta, stared at the two arguing adults with wide, frightened eyes.

"Oh, Danny…" Emily whispered, as she saw the look on her son's face. "I'm sorry." Her eyes traveled from Danny to Joseph. "I'm sorry," she said again.

Without another word, Joseph took a step forward, his arms closing around her. She clung to him, resting her forehead on his chest, as his hands stroked her back and his cheek rested against her curls.

"I don't know what got into me. I just…just…didn't want you to hurt…I need you. Oh, Joseph, I need you so much."

"It's all right, *querida*. I know. But you're getting tired, and I need you, too," he admitted, his arms tightening their hold on her. "We've made it this far. We can make it all the way…together. Okay?"

"Yes. You?"

"Yes. Let's move the damned thing, all right?"

Reluctantly they stepped apart, eyes searching each other's faces. Joseph's fingers brushed a curl off Emily's cheek. She smiled wanly and nodded her head. Together they dragged the canoe down the portage trail, Danny and the dog walking along behind them.

They were halfway across Gunflint Lake when the rain turned hard and driving and the wind picked up again, but the lights of the lodge guided them through the ever-darkening night. Danny and Greta, huddled together under the tarp in the center of the canoe, stayed fairly dry. Occasionally Danny's arm would snake out to bail water from the front or back of the canoe with the small, plastic pail meant for just such emergencies.

Emily was more wet than dry, despite her hooded rain jacket, and her feet and fingers were numb with cold. Exhaustion was setting in. Joseph had to be as wet and as tired as she was, and he had the added burden of his painful leg, yet he continued to paddle with a strong, steady rhythm. Though her arms felt like lead weights, Emily was determined to match him pull for pull. Glancing back, she saw that his face was pale and drawn beneath the hood of his jacket, but a ghost of a smile flickered on his lips and in his eyes.

"Almost there," he called softly.

Almost there, Emily chanted to herself as she turned away and dipped her paddle into the icy, black water yet again. *Almost there.* And then, as if the words were a magic incantation, the bottom of the canoe was scraping against the gravel bottom of the lake.

Dropping her paddle into the canoe and balancing carefully, she stepped out into knee-deep water, and began pulling the canoe the last few feet to the beach. As she helped first Danny and then Joseph out of the canoe, she couldn't contain her feeling of triumph. They had made it…together. Arms around each other, they abandoned the canoe at the water's edge and moved slowly toward the lights and warmth of Trapper's Lodge.

"Glad to see you folks made it back. I was just about ready to send out a search party." Bruce Carson greeted the wet and weary trio with a hearty grin as they tramped into the lodge's main lobby, a wet dog trailing behind them. "I've got a cabin for you if you want to spend the night, and I can have a hot meal ready for you in thirty minutes. Rain's supposed to get a lot worse before it gets better.''

Pushing back her hood, Emily exchanged a long look with Joseph, who had done the same. His damp hair fell across his forehead, and drops of rain glistened in his mustache. Pain and fatigue had scored deep lines on either side of his mouth and shadowed his dark eyes. He was in no condition to drive the Jeep home. She couldn't, *wouldn't* let…

…her drive the Jeep all the way back to Duluth, no matter how capable she was. And he had already admitted to himself that he couldn't do it. Unconsciously he touched her pale cheek, collecting a thumbful of sparkling raindrops. Danny and she were as cold, as wet and tired as he was. A warm, dry cabin, a hot meal and a good night's sleep would go a long way toward keeping pneumonia at bay. His eyes searched hers a moment longer, asking. At her slight nod, he turned to face Mr. Carson.

''Thanks. We'll take the cabin and the hot meal,'' Joseph replied, offering his hand in greeting. ''I'm Joseph Cortez. This is Emily and Danny.''

''Good. Nice to meet you. Now, why don't you go get settled. I turned up the heater in the cabin about an hour ago in case you decided to stay, and there's plenty of hot water. I'll bring a tray down as soon as the food's ready.'' Mr. Carson plucked a key off the pegboard behind his desk and handed it to Joseph. ''We'll take care of the paperwork in the morning, Mr. Cortez. Just go out the door here and follow the path off to your left. It's the third cabin down.''

''Thanks again.'' Joseph took the key and turned to Emily. ''Ready?'' He slipped an arm around her shoulders, and they turned to leave the lodge.

''Yes.'' She felt Joseph sway against her, and her smile expressed her concern. He had taken over so efficiently inside the lodge that she'd forgotten how badly he was hurting. When they were outside, standing on the porch, she turned to face him, braced for an argument. ''Why don't you take Danny to the cabin and get him started on a hot bath? I'll pull up the canoe away from the lake and get the packs.'' But none followed.

"Don't be too long." Joseph gave her shoulder a squeeze, then released her to step out into the rain, his arm now around Danny.

Fifteen minutes later Emily let herself into the cabin. Danny was out of the bathroom and sitting on a bed. He was wrapped in a towel, his sprained ankle encased in an Ace elastic bandage.

"Where did that come from?" Emily asked, as she struggled out of her wet jacket.

"There's a first aid kit in the bathroom better than ours." Danny wriggled his foot, showing off the bandage. "Joseph fixed it for me."

"That was nice of him." Emily opened her pack and pulled out dry clothes for Danny and herself. "Here, put these on." She handed her son clean underwear, a pair of navy-blue sweatpants, a matching sweatshirt and a pair of socks.

As Danny started to dress, she opened Joseph's pack and dug out similar clothes for him. He hadn't lied; he didn't always wear black underwear. The briefs and T-shirt he'd packed were white; the sweats and thick, wool socks were pale gray.

I should be too tired to care, Emily thought, as she opened the bathroom door just wide enough to set the clothes on the counter by the sink, ready for Joseph when he finished his shower. *But I'm not,* she admitted, grinning a Cheshire cat's grin.

A knock on the cabin door interrupted her mental picture of Joseph in white, and announced dinner. Mr. Carson hurried in with a huge, covered tray. Placing it on the table by the window, he whipped off the protective sheet of plastic to reveal bowls of beef stew, hot rolls, slabs of apple pie, a large thermos of coffee and a smaller one of hot chocolate.

"This is wonderful, Mr. Carson. Thank you so much." Emily gave the man a big smile.

"No trouble, ma'am. Put the tray outside when you're finished. I'll pick it up on my ten o'clock round. And we start serving breakfast up at the lodge about six-thirty, if you care to join us.''

"We will," Emily assured the man before he slipped out of the cabin, closing the door behind him. Turning back to Danny, she saw that he was dressed. "Come and eat while the stew's hot.''

"Okay, Mom, but what about Greta? He didn't bring a bowl for her.'' Danny slid onto a chair by the table, his face full of concern for the dog, who was curled up on the floor as close as possible to the heater.

"We'll each save a bite for her, all right? Now get started.''

While Danny ate, Emily kicked off her wet tennis shoes, then peeled off her equally wet jeans and socks. Using Danny's damp towel, she dried off her legs and feet as best she could, then slipped into her own warm, dry, pale blue, fleece-lined pants and wool socks. Joining Danny at the table, she snatched bites of food and sipped hot, black coffee while surveying the cabin.

It was one large room with a bathroom. The round table with four chairs where she sat with Danny was tucked into the slight bay of a big window. Across from the table were two beds, a twin to the right, and a large double bed to the left, both covered with deep green, puffy down comforters. Emily frowned. She'd have to suggest that Joseph use the twin bed. But when he finally limped out of the bathroom, all she could think of was how good the shower was going to feel on her still shivering body.

"Save me any hot water?" she asked, quirking an eyebrow at Joseph on her way into the bathroom. He had probably spent a long time under the shower, yet still looked haggard. He was wearing the gray jogging pants and the white T-shirt, but his feet were bare.

"Some," he reassured her, rubbing a hand across the back of his neck as he eased himself into a chair at the table. "Would you hand me my pack before you go into the bathroom?"

Emily did as he asked. He took it from her, opened it and retrieved a small prescription bottle of pills. He shook out two, swallowed them quickly, then tilted back his head against the wall, closing his eyes.

"Why didn't you take those sooner?" Emily couldn't prevent a tiny edge of anger from entering her voice. He had been in so much pain, yet he hadn't taken anything but aspirin.

"They're pretty strong. They knock me out, make me dopey."

"You *are* dopey," she murmured, brushing a thick fall of soft, dark, damp hair off his forehead. Her fingers sifted through the silken strands. "I could have—"

"No, you couldn't," he interrupted, squinting up at her through narrowed eyes. "And neither could I. We did it together."

"You're right," Emily admitted, still stroking his hair, her eyes soft and warm. "You'd better eat."

"I never realized what a bossy little thing you are until today," Joseph muttered, wrapping his fingers around her wrist, holding her still when she would have moved away. Feeling her hand in his hair was doing funny things to his insides, things he liked altogether too much.

"First pigheaded, now bossy. You really know how to hand out the compliments, don't you?" She bent and brushed her lips against his hair. His fingers tightened around her wrist for an instant. Then he let her go, his eyes drifting closed again. The pills were beginning to work.

"Are you going to take a shower, Mom?"

"Are you trying to get rid of me?" Emily eyed her son; her hand still rested on Joseph's shoulder.

"Yeah, so Joseph can eat. Then we can feed Greta. She's hungry."

"Okay. You two look after each other. I'll take my shower."

Once she was cocooned in the steamy warmth of the bathroom, Emily stayed much longer than she'd planned. She stood under the throbbing pulse of the shower until the water temperature faded from hot to barely lukewarm. When she finally turned off the faucets, she had managed to chase most of the chill out of her bones. Curling up in bed under the thick, down comforter would take care of the rest.

Wrapping her wet hair in one towel, she used another to briskly rub the water from her skin. She slipped into fresh panties. Deciding a bra would be too uncomfortable to sleep in, she pulled on her socks, sweatpants and a matching sweatshirt. Settling down on the small stool she found tucked under the sink, she unwrapped her hair and began toweling it dry.

Fifteen minutes later she had finished with her hair and had sorted the wet clothes from the dry. Sweaters and shirts she hung on hooks on the bathroom door. Underwear she folded and stacked on the stool to repack in the morning. Wet jeans and socks she spread out over the shower rod and towel racks. The damp towels she would spread out over the chairs. She wasn't sure what to do with the large, sheathed hunting knife, so she left it on the countertop next to Joseph's watch, making a mental note to ask him about it. He ought to put on his sweatshirt and dry socks, too, she thought, scooping them up as she opened the bathroom door.

A small lamp on the nightstand between the beds had been lighted, but otherwise the main room of the cabin was dark. The tray had been cleared from the table. In the twin bed, Danny was sprawled on his stomach, blankets pulled up to his shoulders. Greta was curled up at his feet. Joseph lay on one side of the double bed. Stretched out on his back, he had one arm behind his head, the other resting across his chest. He had turned down the comforter, but hadn't pulled it over himself before he'd fallen asleep. In the pale glow of the lamplight he looked incredibly young and vulnerable, unlike the man Emily had come to know.

"Great, just great," she muttered, dropping his sweatshirt and socks onto the table and draping the wet towels over the chairs.

It would be foolish to try to sleep with Danny in the twin bed. It would be equally foolish to wake both Danny and Joseph just to have them change beds. She could move Danny in with Joseph, but her son was such a restless sleeper that, pills or no pills, he'd keep Joseph up half the night with his tossing and turning. That left her with the choice of spending the night on one of the wooden chairs, on the floor, or in the bed with Joseph.

Actually, she thought, crossing the room to stand beside him, that left her with no choice at all. Her heartbeat shifted into overdrive. With a soft smile, she pulled up the comforter around him and gently smoothed his hair off his forehead. When all was said and done, she wanted to crawl into bed with Joseph Cortez so badly that it hurt. Still she hesitated. She had shared a bed with her husband. Granted, this wasn't the same kind of sharing, yet in her heart of hearts, Emily couldn't say that she didn't want it to be the same kind.

She walked around the bed and stood for another moment, staring at the empty place that had her name written all over it. She hesitated a split second longer. Then, with a flick of her wrist, she switched off the lamp and slid under the comforter. She stretched out along the very edge of the bed, her back to Joseph. She stayed there for about a minute, two minutes maximum, the space between them yawning like the Grand Canyon. Then slowly, carefully, so as not to disturb him, Emily closed the gap, easing her body against his. Curling slightly on her side, she fitted her bottom along his hip, closed her eyes and...slept.

Initially it was the dull, throbbing pain in his left leg that led Joseph out of the deeper reaches of sleep. But it was the feel of the soft, warm, feminine body so close to his own that brought him back to full awareness. The dream he had dreamed so many nights, the dream of her curled up beside him in bed, had become reality. She was lying on her side, her bottom tucked firmly against his hip. The slow, steady rhythm of her breathing assured him she was sound asleep.

He wanted to roll onto his side and wrap himself around her, cradling her in his arms, but his leg was making demands he couldn't ignore. Easing away from her, he turned back the comforter, swung his legs over the side of the bed and stood up. After the warmth of the bed, the cabin felt cool, and the patch of floor he crossed on his way to the bathroom was downright cold beneath his bare feet.

A few moments later, cup of water in hand, he limped to the table and rummaged around in the packs. According to the watch he'd left in the bathroom, it was nearly five o'clock. Another pain pill would knock him out for at least four hours, and the leg wasn't half as bad as it had been. Two aspirin from Emily's first-aid kit would be sufficient.

Be honest, Joseph, he admonished himself, chasing the pills with a swallow of water. *Now that you've finally got her in your bed, you don't want to waste time sleeping, do you? And you didn't choose to sleep in the double bed because you expected to share it with Danny, either, did you?* Not really, he admitted, moving back to the edge of the bed. Crawling beneath the comforter again, he stretched out on his side and gazed at Emily in the shadowy darkness.

He wanted to touch her. Ever so gently his fingers brushed over her tumbled mass of short, silky curls, then traced the line of her jaw. He wanted to inhale her warm, womanly scent. Ever so slowly he nuzzled the wisps of hair at the nape of her neck, savoring the sweetness of her skin. He wanted to kiss her. Ever so lightly his lips grazed her cheek and outlined the small, pale shell of her ear.

She shivered and sighed, and suddenly he wanted to feel the weight of her body against him. He wanted to wrap his arms around her and hold her close. He wanted to be over her, inside her. His hand trembled as he traced the line of her shoulder, the curve of her waist, the swell of her breast. She sighed again deeply and stirred, turning toward him. In one fluid movement he rolled onto his back and gathered her into his arms.

She came to him willingly. Eyes closed, she rubbed her cheek against his chest, then nestled her head in the hollow beneath his shoulder. She wrapped an arm around his waist, and drew up one leg to cover his. She sighed yet again, and murmured something unintelligible. Her eyes fluttered open, and she tilted up her head. For an instant her gaze met his. His heart missed a beat as he waited for her to pull away.

"Joseph?" she whispered.

"Yes, *querida*?"

Once again she rubbed her cheek against his chest. Her hand, small and soft and warm, moved from his waist to rest on his chest. "Are you all right?"

"Yes, *querida*."

Her eyes closed, her breathing deepened, her body settled into his.

"Yes," he growled again, deep and low. He tipped his head slightly, laying his cheek against her curls. His arms tightened around her. His eyes drifted shut. "Yes."

Emily awoke slowly. In the dim, gray dawn light that was filtering through the cabin window, she could see very little. But the gentle beat of falling rain and the gentle beat of Joseph's heart brought back memories of the previous day and night. She closed her eyes again, savoring the fine texture of his cotton T-shirt and the rock-hard strength of his chest beneath her cheek. She would indulge just a little longer in the incredible warmth, the safety, the unbelievable security she felt lying in his arms. There she could pretend that she was loved.

She wasn't exactly sure how she'd ended up in Joseph's arms, but as long as he was asleep, Emily had every intention of making the most of the occasion. Tentatively she traced the planes and contours of his body, her hand roaming lightly from chest to belly and back again.

She felt his heartbeat quicken, heard the growl of pleasure low in his throat. So, he wasn't asleep either, she thought, smiling slightly. Urged on by his response and some naughty demon all her own, she grazed first one nipple, then the other with a fingertip, testing, teasing, tempting.

The growl became a groan. Joseph's hand moved with lightning speed, gripping her jaw, turning up her face. Her eyes opened into his and her smile widened.

"Emily, I don't think—" He was trying to maintain his self-control, trying to ignore the devil in her eyes, not to mention the one between his thighs, the strain evident in his low, harsh tone.

"That's good," Emily interrupted, her voice equally low, but inviting. "Better not to think. Just…just…" *Kiss me,* she thought, unable to say the words aloud. *Just kiss me. Once.* Her hand smoothed the dark fall of hair off his forehead again, then settled against his cheek, her thumb along the high ridge of his cheekbone.

Just once. He was going to kiss her once. He would allow himself the pleasure of tasting her, touching her, slowly, gently. Once. He bent his head. She closed her eyes. He brushed his lips against hers.

Good, Emily thought, as he raised his head. *But not nearly good enough.* Her eyes holding his, she moved her hand from his cheek to the back of his head, threading her fingers through his hair, drawing him closer. Her tongue darted out to trace his upper lip. Then she tugged at his mustache with her teeth, a smile in her eyes.

Joseph's tentative hold on his self-control snapped. One kiss, he told himself as he knotted his fist in her hair and opened his mouth over hers, one *real* kiss, one long, slow, deep kiss to last a lifetime.

Cradling the back of his neck with her hand, Emily opened her mouth for him, savoring his taste, the warm, wet velvet touch of his tongue, the rough tickle of his mustache, with every fiber of her being. She moaned softly, wanting, wanting, wanting, cursing the thick layers of clothing they wore. His arms tightened around her. She had never known a kiss could be so wild, so fierce, so…frightening. For an instant she arched against him, her body tight and heavy with desire. Then she drew away, trembling, her eyes wide with sudden uncertainty.

"No, don't pull away from me, *querida,*" Joseph whispered, his words both plea and command. All thought of just one gentle kiss had disappeared along with his self-control. With every ounce of willpower he possessed, he blocked out the past. He would not, could not let her go. He wanted her, needed her, and had waited so long for her. The hunger pulsing through him would not be satisfied by one kiss, wouldn't be satisfied by a lifetime together.

She tried to move away from him, tried to ignore the desire building deep inside her, tried to deny the power of her feelings for him. It was too much, too soon. He was a stranger, and in a few weeks, a few months, he would be gone. She couldn't, shouldn't want to love him so fiercely.

But he refused to let her go. He held her still, one hand in her hair, the other sliding under her sweatshirt to cup her breast, gently yet possessively. His thumb grazed the tight, hard peak of her nipple once, then again and again. He felt her body tremble at his touch. His eyes searched hers and he smiled.

In answer to his unspoken question, she buried her fingers in his hair, pulling his head down, her lips seeking his. His mouth opened over hers once more, the slow, sure rhythm of his tongue pleading, promising, possessing—

"Oh, boy, wrestling!" The bed vibrated violently as a six-year-old boy, followed closely by a ninety-pound German shepherd, landed at its foot.

Beneath the thick, down comforter, Joseph rolled away from Emily and sat up. He was shaking, and panting hard. Emily, slower to react, but also having trouble with her breathing, propped herself up on her elbows. They stared at Danny, then at each other in stunned silence, the same thought in mind. How could they possibly have forgotten about the boy sleeping in the next bed?

"Come on, Greta, let's get them." Seeming pleased with his surprise attack, and totally unaware of what had been going on between the two adults, Danny moved up the bed toward Joseph in his best, slow-motion, tough-guy imitation.

Emily began to laugh. The roller coaster ride of emotions she'd been on the past few weeks had reached another peak. As Joseph eased away from her, frowning, she tried to speak but couldn't. Shaking her head from side to side, her laughter completely out of control, she pointed at Danny, trying without much success to warn Joseph of what she knew was coming.

"Wrestling?" Joseph stared at Emily in confusion, raking his fingers through his thick, dark hair. He wasn't used to having certain activities interrupted by a small boy. In fact, he felt as if he'd been hit with a baseball bat. And what the hell had gotten into Emily? She was laughing like a madwoman and gesturing wildly. *"Wrestling?"*

Emily nodded, still laughing, still pointing at Danny. Poor Joseph...if she didn't warn him soon... With a valiant effort, she pulled herself together. "Watch out!" she gasped, as Danny launched himself into the air. Her advice was approximately thirty seconds too late.

Joseph's "Oomph!" and wildly rolling eyes attested to the fact that Danny had landed with knees and elbows strategically placed to do the most damage.

"Gotcha," Danny crowed. Joseph fell backward, the boy in his arms.

"I'm sorry," Emily exclaimed, catching her breath. At the look Joseph gave her, she started laughing all over again. Then Greta landed on her and started licking her face. "Oh, no! Stop, Greta, stop!" Emily screeched, trying to push the dog away.

"Let's get her while she's down," Joseph instructed Danny, a wicked gleam in his eyes as he shifted the youngster off his lap and onto the bed between Emily and himself. Within seconds, the proposed wrestling match had turned into tickling, and Emily was the main target of their attack.

"Okay, okay. Enough! I thought you guys had bum legs," Emily shouted, after what seemed like an eternity of giggling and rolling around on the bed. Joseph's large, strong hands had moved up her ribs more than once, setting her off in more ways than one. Two male faces hovered over hers as she lay on her back, gasping for breath after the heat of battle had passed.

"What'll you give us if we quit?" Danny demanded.

"How about a kiss?" Emily offered. As she pushed herself into a sitting position, her gaze met Joseph's over Danny's head.

"Aw, yuck," Danny said with a shudder.

"Greta, too?" Emily asked.

"Well, okay. But kiss me first," Danny replied.

Emily planted a firm kiss on her son's cheek, then brushed a light one on Greta's furry head. "Now, go use the bathroom, gather up your clothes and find your shoes."

As Danny and the dog jumped off the bed, Emily, eyes sparkling, turned to Joseph. He was sitting on the bed beside her, Indian-style, his eyes still gleaming. "Best for last," she murmured, leaning forward to drop a kiss onto his rough, whisker-stubbled cheek.

As the bathroom door was slammed, he wrapped his arms around her, pulling her onto his lap. One hand snaked out, tangling in the hair at the back of her head. Holding her still, he covered her mouth with his and kissed her, loving her with his lips, his teeth, his tongue until she melted against him with a soft sigh of pleasure. Then as swiftly as he'd taken her, he released her. The hand in her hair moved to cup her cheek, and his thumb traced the full, wet line of her lower lip.

"*Querida*, the best is yet to be," he muttered. In one fluid movement, he dumped her out of his lap and rolled off the bed to chase Danny out of the bathroom.

Chapter Eight

It was nearly eight o'clock and still raining steadily by the time everyone had finished in the bathroom and they'd re-packed the waterproof bags. Experienced traveler that he was, Joseph had produced a disposable razor, a miniature can of shaving cream, three individually wrapped toothbrushes and a tiny tube of toothpaste from the bottom of his pack. Emily had teased him about being ready for anything as she'd watched him tuck away the hunting knife. He had glanced at Danny, rolled his eyes and assured her that he hadn't been ready for some things at all.

Bundled into their jackets, packs in tow, they jogged along the path and into the lodge, their shouts and laughter and Greta's barking a joyous counterpoint to the rustle of the wind in the trees and the patter of raindrops on the ground. They settled Greta and their packs in the lobby, and enjoyed a huge, hot breakfast in the lodge dining room, their high spirits lingering as they talked and teased and shared one smile after another.

Soon after they finished eating, the rain stopped long

enough for Joseph and Emily to secure the canoe atop the Jeep. Joseph settled their account with Mr. Carson, thanking the man for his consideration and promising to bring his family back again soon. A short time later they climbed into the Jeep, and Joseph headed for the highway back to Duluth.

Their exuberance lasted a while longer despite the renewed vigor of the rain that slanted across the windshield and the wind that tugged and pulled at the Jeep, slowing their progress. Eventually, however, Danny fell asleep in the back seat, leaving Emily and Joseph with a confusion of thoughts and feelings they weren't yet ready to share.

Emily, her head supported by the headrest, stared at the passing scenery. Joseph opened his window a crack and lighted one of his thin, black cigars. Once she thought she felt his hand on her hair, but when she glanced at him, his eyes were on the road, and his hands gripped the steering wheel.

She wanted to say something... but what?

He wanted to tell her... so many things.

Yet the farther they traveled from the cabin on Gunflint Lake, the more their silence deepened. The early-morning hours, the kisses, the caresses, became more fantasy than reality, and very, very carefully they retreated from each other.

He's a stranger, Emily warned herself for the umpteenth time, as Joseph guided the Jeep off Highway 61 and into the maze of streets that led to her house. He wouldn't talk about his past, nor did he talk about the future. He had made a point of letting her know at the very beginning that he couldn't guarantee how long he'd be around. It might be a few weeks or a few months, but it wouldn't be forever. He had offered her friendship, but had at the same time avoided being alone with her. In so many ways he had told her that he didn't want a permanent relationship with her.

As they waited for a light to change, Emily felt her face flush. Suddenly she was ashamed of the way she had provoked him earlier, teasing him with her hands and her eyes. He had offered to be her friend and nothing more, yet at the first opportunity she had thrown herself at him. He had tried to control himself, and he had tried to warn her, but she had refused to listen. She had all but begged him to kiss her, and she had done so with her son sleeping in the bed across the room. Her fingers clenched into fists, her nails biting into her palms, and a wave of remorse washed over her.

Tempting Joseph Cortez had been a stupid, thoughtless thing to do. He would be a part of their lives for only a short time, and then he would be gone. A sexual relationship with him could be nothing more than a casual affair, and she was wise enough to know that making love with Joseph would be anything but casual, at least for herself. In the end it would leave her heart aching and her soul shattered.

As it was, the thought of life without him already pressed on her like a painful, bruising weight. How much worse would it be if they made love? Yet each time she thought of their moments together in the cabin, her pulse pounded, her body throbbed with desire, and her spirit was filled with a longing so intense that it made her shake.

No, she should never have provoked him, but given the same circumstances, she knew in her heart of hearts that she would do it again. She wanted his love, needed his love, and if she didn't let him know it, risked losing him forever.

I had no right to touch her, Joseph chided himself, crushing the butt of yet another cigar in the ashtray as he pulled away from the stoplight. Out of the corner of his eye he saw her staring out the window, her face turned away from him. He'd had some nerve kissing her the way he had, as if he had a right to love her, to care for her, to claim her as his own.

Where Emily Anderson was concerned, he had no rights at all until he told her about his past. She had offered him her love, a true and honest love. What would happen when he added honesty and truth to what he offered her? Was there any possibility she'd belong to him then?

But she *had* belonged to him in the cabin on Gunflint Lake, he argued silently. Far from the memory of Eric Anderson and the house on Third Street, she had been his. She had wanted him, needed him, as much as he'd wanted and needed her. She had given and taken in equal measure, her hands and mouth as eager and demanding as his own.

Joseph's grip on the steering wheel tightened; he forced himself to turn onto Third Street. What he really wanted was to retrace their journey, to drag Emily, kicking and screaming if necessary, back to the cabin to finish what they'd started. *Then try to come between us,* he challenged the dead man.

But he pulled into the driveway and slowed to a stop. The house loomed before him, dark and silent against the gray sky. An aching emptiness clawed at his gut—an emptiness born of the feeling that Eric Anderson would always come between them.

They sat together for a long moment, staring at the house, knowing neither what to say nor what to do, the stillness of late afternoon stretching between them like a gossamer web.

Talk to him, touch him, tell…

…her how much you love her.

Slowly, quietly, Emily opened her door, waiting for him to stop her. When he didn't, she slipped out and away, running across the lawn and up the front porch steps, fumbling in her jacket pocket for her door key. A moment later the door clicked open. She stepped into the cool, dim hallway, turned into the living room, and stopped at the small table full of pictures.

With trembling fingers, she picked up the largest photograph, the one of herself in Eric's arms. She would never stop loving him, but the time was coming when she would have to say goodbye. She was ready to love again, and rightly or wrongly, for however long he would have her, the man she loved was Joseph Cortez.

He watched her run across the lawn and disappear inside the house, and felt the hard, cold hand of reality wrap itself around his heart. Only hours ago she had come to him with love and desire, yet suddenly she seemed desperate to get away from him. The dead man and the dead man's house had a hold on her so tight that he could never hope to break it. He ran a hand over his eyes, then turned to the sleeping duo in the back seat.

"Come on, you two. We're home." He knew that his voice

was as dull and flat as his spirit as he opened his door and climbed out of the jeep.

Muttering and grumbling, Danny and Greta hopped out and raced each other into the house. Moving more slowly, Joseph gathered up the packs and turned to follow them. The canoe could stay put until morning.

As he walked through the front door, he heard boy and dog upstairs, but the downstairs was dark and quiet. Where had she gone? Limping slowly down the hallway toward the kitchen, he glanced into the living room and froze.

He saw her sitting in the wing chair, saw the photograph in her lap, saw her staring at it, saw her twisting, twisting the wide gold band on her ring finger. And he saw again the blond, blue-eyed prince claiming her. The hand around his heart squeezed with shattering intensity.

"Joseph?"

Emily felt his presence, but when she looked up, her eyes met the cold, hard eyes of a stranger. She set the photograph on the table and stood. She wanted to go to him, to touch him, reassure him, but the look on his face kept her still. The man in the hallway wasn't the same man who had held her in his arms and promised that the best was yet to be. The man in the hallway frightened her, because he was so far away and would never know how much she loved him.

"Joseph, I—"

He turned without a word and walked away. A few moments later Emily heard the studio door close with a quiet, forbidding finality. The bright bloom of hope that she had nourished through one perfect day withered and died.

"How do you know the words to that song, Mom?" Danny asked, as he wandered into Emily's bedroom and jumped onto her bed.

It was Friday afternoon, the sky was clear and the air was frosty cold with the first hint of winter. The previous weekend at Gunflint Lake was nothing more than a memory. Joseph Cortez had become a cool, quiet stranger, intent on avoiding her at all costs.

When she spoke to him, his responses were monosyllabic. When she entered his line of vision, his gaze slid up and over her like a chunk of ice. When her hand brushed his at the dinner table, he drew away as if he'd been burned. And when she'd accidentally run into him in the hallway outside her bedroom door on Wednesay night, her body hitting his so hard that his arms went around her for a moment to steady her, he had shuddered with revulsion. Then yesterday morning he'd muttered something about going to Minneapolis, and Emily hadn't seen him since.

"Mom, I asked you a question."

"I'm sorry, Danny. I was daydreaming. What do you want to know?" Emily turned from her perusal of the inside of her closet to offer her son an apologetic smile.

"How come you know the words to that song that was on the radio?"

"Song?" Emily frowned for a moment, trying to remember. "Oh, 'Be my Baby'? That's an old, old song. I've been listening to it for years, and eventually I learned all the words."

"Is it as old as *Mr. Ed* and *Leave It to Beaver*? If they play it on MTV, will it be in black and white?"

"Danny, that's good, real good." Emily laughed out loud for the first time in days as she reached for a pair of slacks and a sweater. Crossing over to stand beside the bed, she looked down at her son. "I think 'Be My Baby' is too old for MTV, kiddo. Do you have your pajamas in your backpack and your sleeping bag rolled up and ready to take to Jimmy's house?"

"Yes. Are you gonna leave a note for Joseph to tell him where we are?"

"No." Emily slipped out of her robe, reached for her tailored, gray wool slacks, and pulled them on over her pink silk tap pants. At the same time, she tried to convince herself that she was looking forward to her night out with Cathy.

Hank had offered to baby-sit, so the two women could have dinner, see a movie, and maybe even stop at Grandma's, a popular hangout near the aerial lift bridge, for a nightcap. It had been Cathy's idea, and Emily appreciated her thoughtfulness. A night out certainly would be different.

"Mommy, you *should* leave a note for him. What if he comes home?" Danny, sprawled in the center of her bed, sounded to Emily like a little old man as he chastised her. "And what about Greta?"

"I'm not leaving a note for Mr. Cortez, Danny. I don't have to report to him." As if he cared, Emily thought. And if he did, it would do him good to come home to an empty house. A *dark*, empty house, she amended with a gleam in her eye. Let him be the one to wait and wonder. "And Greta will be all right. She has food and water in the kitchen, and you can take her out one more time before we leave. In fact, you can get off the bed and do that right now. We're due at Cathy's at five."

"He's going to worry about us, Mom."

"I don't care, Danny."

"Are you mad at him, Mom?"

"No." Emily zipped up her pants with unusual force, then crossed to her dresser. "And you shut up." She spoke to the radio, switching it off with a flick of her wrist. The last thing she needed tonight was a song about losing that loving feeling.

"Mom, you're not supposed to say shut up."

"*Danny!*"

Amazing what tone of voice and facial expression could accomplish, she thought, watching her son roll off the bed and scamper out of the room without another word. He was a good kid, but his dedication to Joseph Cortez was beginning to get on her nerves.

Breathing a sigh, Emily leaned against the dresser and closed her eyes. She wasn't in the mood for a night out with Cathy, no matter how hard she tried to tell herself she was. However, the alternative was another night at home alone, replaying every moment of the previous weekend in her head until she wanted to scream. So she straightened and walked to the bed to retrieve her sweater.

It was pale, pink cashmere, with full, elbow-length sleeves and a deep V front and back. Wearing it always made her feel sexy and sophisticated. She slipped it on over her pink silk camisole, then returned to the dresser to add a pearl choker and gold and pearl button earrings. She admired her reflection in the mirror for a few moments, then began to wonder if she'd used too much makeup. Perhaps she ought to tame her wild curls a little. No, she decided, tossing her head defiantly as she returned to the bed, sat down and slipped into her shoes. She'd worked on her hair and makeup for over an hour. If the results made her look as though she was on the prowl, well, maybe she was, and about time, too.

The smile she pasted on her face got her into her coat, out of the house, and on her way to Cathy's place with Danny in tow. Her son chattered like a magpie as they walked the short distance down the street, and Emily tried to pay attention. But somewhere along the way her smile must have slipped. When Cathy opened the door, her first words weren't the cheerful greeting Emily expected, but a quiet question.

"Want to talk about it?"

"Yeah, I want to talk about it, Mendoza. Why else would I be here at five o'clock on a Friday afternoon?"

"Well come in, then. Sit down. What did the doctor say about your leg?" Joseph could almost feel Richard Mendoza's eyes on his back as he limped across the office to slump into the ancient wing chair in front of the professor's desk.

"Leg's fine. Mind if I smoke?" Not waiting for an answer, Joseph pulled a thin cigar from his jacket pocket and lighted it. He inhaled, exhaled, stretched his legs in front of him, slid lower in the chair, tipped back his head and closed his eyes.

"I thought you wanted to talk."

"Talk about what?"

"To start with, how about this?" With a quick motion, as if he was angry, Richard flipped over the canvas that had been lying facedown on his desk. Harsh, black brush strokes slashed across the white background to form a grotesque vision of horror and destruction. Joseph had handed it to him after class on Wednesday.

"You used to like that kind of stuff, Mendoza." Joseph

glanced at the painting through slitted eyelids. He drew on his cigar, then closed his eyes again. "Getting soft in your old age? Or would you prefer I take out my *aggression* on some poor slob on the street?" When Richard failed to respond to the taunting tone, he sat up and rubbed a hand over his eyes. "Sorry, friend. It's been one hell of a week."

"I gathered that, especially when I found these." Richard picked up a manila folder and opened it to reveal two torn sketches of Emily.

Joseph's hand moved as if he wanted to touch the shredded drawings. He looked at Mendoza, then looked away. "Since when did you start digging around in trash cans, old man?" Now his tone was bitter and filled with contempt.

Again Richard remained silent, apparently content to wait until Joseph turned to meet his gaze. "What happened at Gunflint Lake last weekend?"

"How do you know about Gunflint Lake?"

"Emily mentioned your canoe trip when she stopped by the office on Tuesday."

"You've seen her, talked to her?" Joseph's eyes bored into Richard's.

"She comes to visit for a few minutes whenever she's on campus, and she's on campus two or three times a week, picking up or delivering typing projects."

"Well, since you're all of a sudden such good friends, Mendoza, why don't you play twenty questions with her? As far as I'm concerned, not a damned thing happened." Joseph's words sent Richard a clear warning.

"I don't believe you. This time last Friday you were almost a human being again. A week later and you're well on your way back to where you were after Vietnam." The old professor tapped his finger against the dark canvas for emphasis. "Something happened last weekend, and you damn well better talk about it before it destroys you."

"You want to know what happened?" The quiet roar of Richard's voice had succeeded in destroying Joseph's carefully maintained composure. "I'll tell you what happened. I think I'm falling in love with her."

"And you don't think she feels the same way about you?"

"It doesn't matter how she feels about me now. It's how she's going to feel when she finds out who I am, *what* I am. She loved her husband, really loved him, and they had a good life together. No matter how you look at it, I'm... responsible...for the end of their life together." Joseph focused his attention on the cigar in his hand, only vaguely aware that it was trembling. "I think I'm going to move out of her house tomorrow."

"Perhaps that's the best thing you can do for her. As it is, you've got her so tied up in knots, she doesn't know what to think or do. You've been playing cat and mouse with her for weeks, haven't you? And you've got her convinced there's something wrong with her. The longer you stay in her house, the longer you keep her from finding a man able and willing to return the love she's trying to give to you."

"What are you talking about? She still loves her husband."

"Yes, she will always love Eric. He was a wonderful man, worthy of her love. But you are worthy, too, Joseph, whether you want to believe it or not. You did not kill her husband, nor did you wish him dead. In fact, if you had it in your power, you'd bring him back, wouldn't you?"

Joseph turned away, staring out the window. Yes, if he had it in his power, he would do anything to bring her happiness—even that.

"You're a smart man, Joseph. You know everything there is to know about winning wars. But you're a fool, too. Rather than take a chance, rather than fight for what you want, you're going to walk away from the one woman who loves you. And she does love you, Joseph. I can hear it in her voice and see it in her eyes when she comes to see me."

"You're not making this easy, Richard."

"It's not my intention to make it easy. I warned you to move out of her house weeks ago. You refused to do it. Now you're going to have to accept what's happened between you. One way or another you're going to hurt her. If you walk away without any explanation, the pain you'll cause her as well as yourself will be permanent, and the damage you do will be irreparable."

"So what should I do, wise one?" With an impatient gesture, Joseph leaned forward and stubbed out his cigar in the ashtray on Richard's desk. Pushing himself out of the chair, he limped to the row of tall, narrow windows along one wall and stood looking out, his hands in his pockets.

"Talk to her. Tell her…everything. Tell her who you are and why you're living in her house. Let her know how much you care for her. She'll be hurt and confused, but if she cares for you as much as I suspect she does, you'll be able to work through it. At this point you have nothing to lose, do you?"

"No, I have nothing to lose."

"You'll do it soon, won't you?"

"I'm not going to have a choice. I talked to Washington again. It's been fairly stable down south, but they want me to be ready to move on short notice. The leg is healing. I can't put them off, even if I wanted to. When they're ready for me, I'll have to leave."

"So what are you going to do?" Joseph heard his old friend get to his feet.

"I'm going to go back to the house. I've got a few fences to mend. Then I'll talk to her." Joseph turned to watch his friend slip into his overcoat.

"Don't let it go too long, Joseph," Richard warned again, picking up his briefcase. "It's not going to get any easier, and she's going to need some time to sort out her feelings. Do you understand what I'm saying?"

"Yeah, I understand. She's going to hate me when I tell her, but with luck, it'll only be temporary, right?" Joseph muttered. Head down, he followed Mendoza out of the office, and walked with him to the parking lot where he'd left his Jeep.

It was almost dark by the time he turned onto Third Street and pulled into the driveway of Emily's house. Against the twilight sky, the house looked cold and stark and empty. Not a single light shone through the windows; even the front porch light was off. Frowning, Joseph reached for the garage door opener that was hooked to the visor.

As the garage door opened, revealing Emily's car parked inside, his frown deepened. He drove the Jeep into the empty space beside it and climbed out. A trickle of fear raced along his spine as he headed for the house. What the hell was going on? Even when he'd wandered in at two in the morning, the porch light had been on, along with the one in the hall and the light above the stove in the kitchen. He had been gone since early Thursday morning, hadn't called, hadn't bothered to tell her where he was going—*couldn't* tell her where he was going. What if something had happened to them?

Fumbling with his keys, he finally managed to let himself in through the back door. The kitchen, normally so warm and cheerful, so full of Emily and Danny and the aroma of good food, was dark and empty. Only Greta, nails tapping against the tile floor, was there to greet him. Switching on lights along the way, Greta trailing along behind him, Joseph roamed from one room to another, searching for Emily and Danny. When his search proved futile, he went through the rooms again, looking for some sort of note or message.

He ended his journey where he'd begun, in the kitchen. He shrugged out of his down jacket, tossed it onto a chair and opened the refrigerator. Ignoring the labeled containers of leftovers, he grabbed a beer and slammed the door. Damn it. Of all the nights for Emily to decide to disappear, it would have to be tonight. She never went out...*never*. And where could she have gone without her car?

As he popped the top of his beer, Joseph thought of her friend, Cathy. More than likely, Emily had taken Danny to Cathy's house and stayed to visit. Taking a long swallow of beer, he eyed the clock above the refrigerator. It was just past seven. Pivoting on his heel, he walked out of the kitchen, down the hallway, and picked up the telephone. He would call there and let her know he was home.

He found Cathy's number in Emily's address book, dialed, and counted twenty rings before he finally hung up. So much for that theory. Maybe he ought to try Glen Roberts. His number was in her book. With a savage curse, he crushed the empty can in one hand and headed back to the kitchen for another beer. Moments later he was at the telephone again, dialing Richard's number, but again he got no answer. Slamming down the receiver, Joseph muttered another savage curse and began to pace.

He tried Cathy's telephone number five times, giving up only at ten o'clock. At eleven he gave up on Richard Mendoza. At two in the morning he was on the verge of calling the police, when he heard a car pull into the driveway, heard Emily's voice calling good-night, heard her footsteps on the front porch.

Flinging himself out of the wing chair by the living-room window, ignoring the pain in his left leg, he strode to the front door and wrenched it open before she could fit her key into the lock. In those few, short steps anger at the worry she had caused him overshadowed his relief at having her home safe.

"Where the hell have you been?"

"Hey, magic," Emily murmured. She swayed ever so slightly, and stared at the door key in her hand as if mesmerized. If she wasn't mistaken, it hadn't made contact, yet the front door was open. "Neat, huh?" She gazed up into the angry eyes of Joseph Cortez and offered him a wide, innocent smile.

"I'll show you magic," he growled, wrapping his fingers around her wrist and hauling her into the brightly lighted hallway.

God, she was pretty, with her hair all wild and windblown, her cheeks the same pale pink as the sweater peeping from under her coat, and her eyes suddenly shooting daggers. But damn it, he wanted to shake her until her teeth rattled. Instead he slammed the door with a violence that made her shudder, dropped her wrist, stepped back, and looked her up and down.

"Where have you been?" he asked again, his anger growing as she stood there staring at him silently, as if *she* was the injured party. "And where's Danny?"

"Although it's none of your business where I've been, I went out with Cathy. Danny's spending the night with

Jimmy." The margaritas she'd sampled and the three-inch heels she wore conspired to add a note of flippancy to her voice. He wasn't so overwhelming, after all. But he was angry, *really* angry, and Emily was perversely pleased by that fact. She eased herself around him and headed for the staircase, slipping out of her coat as she went.

"I called there five times. There wasn't any answer." Joseph followed Emily down the hallway, stopping right behind her.

"Five times? You must have been worried." Emily allowed herself a smug, little smile as she slung her coat over the banister. "Hank took the boys out for pizza and a movie. I guess they were late getting home, too." Ignoring Joseph, she sat down on the steps, eager to slip out of the shoes she'd been tottering around in all night. Much as she appreciated the added height, her feet were killing her.

"That explains Danny's whereabouts. What about you?" he propped an arm on the stair rail and watched Emily fight with the buckle on her shoe.

She had done it intentionally. She had deliberately gone out without leaving a note, without turning on the lights. The urge to shake her was overwhelming, but only for an instant. The sight of her sitting on the steps, so small and soft and fragile stirred other urges. He wanted to kiss the nape of her neck, where her hair curled in wild disarray. He wanted to hold her in his arms and run his hands under the soft, sexy sweater she was wearing.

"What's it to you, Cortez?" Emily managed to unfasten both shoes and ease them off before she slanted a glance up at him. "You've made it clear that you're not interested in me, that you don't care about me. And I'm not going to beg you to…"

Somewhere in the back of her mind, Emily regretted the two-too-many margaritas she'd downed since ten-thirty. They were taking control of her mouth, a mouth suddenly intent on uttering her thoughts of the past week to the very last person on earth who should be hearing them.

"Emily I care about you."

"No, you don't!" The sudden gentling of Joseph's voice caught her off guard, triggering her rage as his anger hadn't. She hurled her words at him as she hurled her shoes to the floor, then stood up. "If you did, you wouldn't have…you would have…" Glaring at him through the sudden glitter of tears and a crazy wave of dizziness, Emily settled her hands on her hips and stomped one small, stockinged foot on the floor. "Just stop playing with me, will you? Just…stop."

Whirling, she stalked down the hallway, trying to ignore the spinning motion in her head. Why couldn't he leave her alone? He hadn't come near her all week, but now, when everything she'd held inside so long threatened to spill out, *now* he was overflowing with care and concern.

In the kitchen, she headed for the refrigerator. "I'm going to have a beer," she muttered to herself, opening the door. But before she could reach in and grab one, the door was slammed.

"I think you've had enough to drink, don't you?"

"What you think is of no concern to me." Once again his gentle voice was rattling her self-control. Concentrating on the white enamel surface in front of her, Emily spoke slowly, enunciating each word as if she were speaking to a very small, very stubborn child. "What I do, where I go, when and *if* I come home, are none of your business." Taking a deep breath, she turned around, and made the mistake of looking up into Joseph's eyes.

They were so dark, so soft, so warm. They were the eyes of the man who had held her in his arms in the cabin on Gunflint Lake. They were the eyes of the man she loved. But tomorrow, the next day or the next, they would turn cold and distant again. Flattening herself against the refrigerator door, she closed her eyes, trying to shut him out, trying to avoid his heat, his scent, the very sight and sound of him. "Go away. Please…go…away."

"No way, *querida*," he murmured, his head close to hers, his breath warm against her cheek. He pressed his palms against the refrigerator door, his arms on either side of her, trapping her. "No way in hell."

"Don't do this to me, Cortez. I can't..." With her last ounce of willpower, Emily took a deep, shuddering breath and tried to hang on to her self-control.

"Shh, Emily, it's going to be all right." He brushed his lips against her cheek. "We're going to be all right."

"No! No, it's not going to be all right," Emily cried, flinching from him as if he'd slapped her. "I don't want you, Cortez. I don't need you." Now her words were spilling out, a sudden, violent flow to match the tears running down her cheeks. "I don't need you or any man. Let me go." She brought her fists down hard on his chest once, twice. "Let me go!"

"I need *you*, Emily. I need you so much," Joseph whispered. He wrapped his arms around her. "No matter what you say or do, I'm never going to let you go, Emily...never."

She shuddered with the force of her sobs, struggling wildly, trying to get away, but he held on to her, firmly yet gently. As her body moved against his, weeks of loneliness and longing welled up inside her, begging for release, and finally she gave in. Sagging against his chest she wrapped her arms around his neck and clung to him, her tears soaking his shirt.

Without a word, he lifted her into his arms. He carried her across the kitchen, sat down in a chair and settled her on his lap. He stroked her hair and murmured soft, Spanish words, rocking her like a child. She curled into him. He cursed himself for the pain he'd caused her, and he cursed himself for being a fool. It was his duty to care for her, and somehow, some way, he would work out the rest. He had meant what he said. He would never let her go.

After what seemed an eternity, Emily shuddered one last time and was still. A few moments later she eased away from him. "I think I'd better...better...go...." Her voice was small and shakey, muffled by his shirt.

"Not yet," he said softly. His hand smoothed her tangled curls, his fingers touched her cheek, gathering tears. Then he pushed back her head against his chest.

"I'm sorry for the way I treated you the past week. I didn't want to hurt you, but it seemed like the only choice I had. It's been hell for me not being able to touch you, talk to you, but things are going to change, I promise you. Will you trust me?''

She didn't speak, but nodded slightly, wrapping her arms around him, pressing her hot, damp cheek against his neck. She wanted to trust him more than she'd ever wanted anything.

"We're going to have to talk, *querida*. There are some things I have to tell you, about myself and the past, but not right now. In a few days, all right?'' He stroked her back, savoring the softness of her sweater and the warmth of her skin beneath it.

Emily sat in his lap, sharing the silence with him, trying to understand what he was saying. But her head felt heavy, and her mind refused to function. Too much alcohol and too many tears were a deadly combination. She wanted nothing more than to close her eyes and sleep.

"I think I'd better go to bed.'' Her voice sounded thick and hoarse to her as she sat up. Suddenly self-conscious, she wiped the last of the tears from her face.

"Sounds like a good idea,'' Joseph agreed. He set her on her feet, then stood up himself. "I'd offer to carry you, but...''

"It's all right. I can walk.'' When Joseph settled an arm around her shoulders, she gave him a watery smile and wrapped an arm around his waist.

They switched off lights along the way, ending up in the dimly lighted hallway outside Emily's bedroom. For an instant Joseph pulled her into his arms, holding her tight. Then he stepped away from her, resting his hands on her shoulders. His lips brushed hers in a gentle kiss.

"Good night, Emily.'' He traced her lips with a fingertip, then turned her around and pushed her into her bedroom. It was one of the hardest things he'd ever done.

She wanted to call him back, and knew if she did, he would come to her and love her. But she let him go. She didn't want to make love with him when she felt so fragile. She wanted her loving to be as strong and sure and steady as she knew his own would be.

As if fighting her way through a fog, Emily undressed and pulled a nightgown over her head. She slipped into bed, curling deep under the wool blanket and heavy quilt. She was going to feel like hell in the morning, but at the moment she was too exhausted to care. Breathing a heavy sigh, she closed her gritty eyes and drifted into a deep sleep.

Chapter Nine

"Hi, Mommy. Are you awake yet?"

The sound of her son's voice, soft and tentative, brought Emily the last few yards into a consciousness she had been trying hard to avoid. She opened hot, gritty eyes, and saw Danny standing beside the bed, peering at her, his bright, blue eyes shadowed with fear. She forced her lips into a reassuring smile despite the pounding in her head, the sour taste in her mouth, and the rolling in her stomach. Raising one hand, she brushed a lock of curly, blond hair off his forehead.

"Hi, sweetie." Damn it, she must be coming down with the flu. Added to her gritty eyes, headache and upset stomach, her voice sounded funny, as if she'd been screaming. Screaming...? *Let me go...let me go...let me go.* Frowning, Emily tried to remember, but Danny's small hand, twirling one of her curls round and round his fingers, brought her attention back to him.

"Are you sick, Mommy? Joseph said you didn't feel good and we should let you sleep. But it's almost lunchtime."

Joseph? His name triggered memories she'd rather forget.

The anger in his voice that didn't quite mask the worry in his eyes as he hauled her into the house. Her fists striking him again and again. His arms around her, holding her, as sobs shook her to her very soul. Words she didn't understand, whispered in a language she'd never learned, easing away her rage and pain.

Joseph. What had she said and done last night? Closing her eyes, Emily wished herself into a hole in the ground, but only for an instant. She could luxuriate in self-contempt later. Right now she had a very worried little boy standing beside her bed, a little boy frightened by the idea of losing his mother as he had lost his father.

"I'm all right, Danny." Forcing herself into a sitting position, propping her pillows behind her, she managed another smile for her son. Danny scrambled up beside her, throwing his arms around her, his relief evident in his brightening eyes. Resting her cheek atop his head, she hugged him close. "I've got a bit of a headache and my tummy's upset, but once I take a shower and get into some clothes, I think I'll feel a lot better."

That and about half a bottle of aspirin ought to do it, she thought as she glanced around the room. Her clothes were piled on the rocking chair, and she was wearing a long, pale blue, flannel nightgown. Fingering the lace edging the gown's high neck, she tried to remember if she'd entered the bedroom alone. He had held her in his arms, he had asked her to trust him, and he had promised that they would talk, but she was sure he hadn't followed her into her bedroom.

"Where's Joseph?" she asked, giving in to her growing curiosity.

"Right here."

His deep, quiet voice answered her question from the bedroom doorway. Emily's head snapped up as Danny broke away from her and leaped off the bed.

"He picked me up at Jimmy's house. We've been watching cartoons and playing games... Candy Land, Uno, Dominos, Monotony."

Head and stomach rebelling against the sudden motion of

the bed, Emily fell back on the pile of pillows. Groaning, she closed her eyes again, effectively blotting out the sympathy and amusement that were warring in Joseph's dark eyes, but not before the warmth in their depths touched her heart.

"Mommy...?" Danny's voice was full of anxiety again as he touched her cheek.

"Sweetheart, I'm all right. Honest. Just give me a few minutes, and I'll be up and around like always." Opening her eyes once more, Emily summoned a fresh smile for her son. "Okay, buddy?"

"Okay, Mom," he agreed, then darted out of the room and down the stairs.

Closing her eyes yet again, Emily willed Joseph to follow her son out of the bedroom, but she knew that hoping for his cooperation was hoping for too much. She felt the mattress shift as he sat down beside her. The scent of spice and cigars teased her nose. His fingers, warm and hard, brushed gently against her cheek, smoothing her tumbled curls away from her face. Her eyes fluttered open. There was so much she wanted to say, but she could only stare at him, feeling suddenly shy, embarrassed, and just the other side of miserable.

"Sure you're all right?" His words touched her as gently as his hands. Her face was so pale, her eyes shadowed. Tucked into the big bed, she looked as small and fragile as a porcelain doll. He wanted to pull her into his arms, but if he moved any closer to her, his slim hold on his self-control would snap.

"Yes," she replied, looking down at her fingers. Somehow they'd gotten all twisted together in her lap. When he didn't move or speak, she mustered her courage and continued. "I'm really sorry about last night. All of it. It was childish of me not to leave a note for you. And if I live to be a hundred, I'll never drink another margarita." Her heartbeat measured the silence between them.

"How many did you have?"

"Two, maybe three." She blessed him for the teasing tone of his voice, blessed him for the firm hand covering hers, stilling her nervous fingers. "I honestly can't remember." She slanted an embarrassed glance at him. "I'm sorry."

"Don't apologize to me. I had it coming." His hand squeezed hers as his lips brushed her forehead. Releasing her, he stood up and set a small bottle on the nightstand. "Take one of those and a hot shower, and you should start to feel better. I'll be downstairs if you need me. And don't worry about Danny. I'll look after him."

He was gone before Emily could reply, before she could form the words to thank him, before she could tell him how much he meant to her—but not before she admitted to herself, once and for all, that she loved him. And she trusted him, trusted what she saw in his eyes and what she felt when he touched her.

She loved and trusted the man he was today. That he was still a stranger, with an unknown past and an unsettled future, no longer mattered. The future could be shaped to suit them. She could imagine nothing that might change how she felt about him.

With sudden determination, Emily vowed she would never let Joseph shut her out again. If he wanted to talk about his past, she would listen. But if it caused him pain, if it threatened to keep them apart, she would force him to forget about it in any way she could. She would force him to forget about the yesterdays. Then they could look forward to tomorrow, a tomorrow they would share.

"Hi." He strolled into the kitchen late Tuesday afternoon, his voice soft, warm, and barely audible above the music playing on the radio.

"Hi, yourself." Emily glanced over her shoulder, offering Joseph a tentative smile before returning her attention to the potato she was peeling.

The sudden tension that seared through her at the sound of his voice eased the instant she reassured herself that his eyes hadn't grown cold and hard again. She had been waiting for it to happen, waiting as a condemned man awaits his executioner, but it had been three days, and his eyes continued to meet hers with gentle warmth and deep desire.

He was in and out of the house the same as always, and he

still spent his evenings in the studio, but since Saturday their basic relationship had changed. A bond had begun to form between them, strengthening as one day led into another. He had begun to seek her company, finding reasons to talk to her, to touch her, brushing his fingers against her cheek, moving curls away from her face, placing a warm hand on her shoulder. Slowly, steadily, he was drawing her closer and closer. Despite her hope for the future, Emily tried to hold back a part of herself, preparing for the day when he would try to shut her out again, but it was getting harder and harder to do.

"Roast beef for dinner tonight," she said, plopping the last, peeled potato into the pot of water in the kitchen sink, as Joseph settled himself against the counter beside her.

"Sounds good." He felt her hesitation at his presence, and cursed himself for the uncertainty he'd bred into her over the past weeks. He was the one who had put the look of a frightened fawn in her eyes. He would be the one to banish it forever. He edged a little closer to her, his cotton shirt sleeve barely brushing hers. "Doing anything Friday night?"

"No, I don't think so." She shrugged her shoulders, glancing at him with wide, curious eyes. He was up to something, but what? No good, if the smile touching the lips beneath the full, black mustache was any indication. It was a wicked smile, one that shot through her like lightning in a stormy sky.

With shaking hands she picked up the pot of potatoes and set it on the stove, then crossed the kitchen to the refrigerator. Digging into the freezer, she found a package of frozen spinach. "This okay?" she asked, dangling the bag in one hand. At his nod, she closed the refrigerator and returned to the kitchen sink. "Why?"

"I like spinach," he teased.

"No, why…Friday night?" she demanded, her exasperated glance catching his for an instant before she turned her attention to the bag in her hands.

"I'd like to take you out to dinner, just the two of us, someplace nice and quiet where we can talk."

Emily gazed at Joseph, her mouth open. He was asking her out on a date. She blinked. She blushed.

He waited, watching her with calm, quiet eyes, willing her to say yes. He had considered his options for days and had decided it would be easier for both of them if he talked to her on neutral ground. He could detach himself from Eric Anderson away from the house they had both shared with Emily. And in a public place she would be forced to control her initial anger and outrage. It would give him that much more time to convince her how much he cared for her.

"Really?" She stared at the bag of spinach in her hands, holding onto it as if it had grown arms and legs and was about to walk away.

"Yes, really." The teasing note in his voice reassured Joseph as much as it did Emily.

"Yes…yes, I'd like that…a lot." Emily offered him a wide, sweet smile, her eyes glistening with sudden pleasure. "I'll call around and find a sitter for Danny."

"Maybe he could spend the night at Jimmy's house."

He was asking for more than a dinner date, so much more. Emily heard the unspoken question and saw it in his eyes. The silence stretched between them, measured only by the rhythms on the radio. Phil Collins sang about being in too deep, about playing for keeps, the yearning in his voice matching that in Emily's heart. Her smile shifted into something soft and dreamy.

"Yes, of course. What a wonderful idea. Cathy owes me a few."

Desire flared in his eyes, so hotly, so brightly that Emily had to look away or risk being burned to ash. Her hands trembled as she tried to tear open the bag of spinach. Without a word, Joseph moved to stand behind her. His arms reached around her on either side, and he eased the bag out of her fingers. Quickly, efficiently, he ripped the bag open, dumped the contents into the pan on the counter, and dropped the empty bag next to it. His hands rested on her shoulders, his head was bent close to hers. She stared at their reflection in the window above the sink and shivered.

"Friday night, then. About seven."

He wrapped an arm around her waist, pressing her body

close to his. As Emily stood rooted to the spot, watching him in the dark glass, he brushed his lips against her cheek in gentle promise. He traced the line of her jaw with his lips, outlined her ear with his tongue, grazed the nape of her neck with his teeth. She closed her eyes, leaning into him, her hands gripping the counter, hanging on like a cat caught on a limb.

He held her a moment longer, savoring her sweetness. Then, barely containing a groan of frustration, Joseph released her and walked out of the kitchen. He could wait until Friday night. He could keep his hands off her. He could endure three more days of pure, unadulterated hell. He could and he would. As if to emphasize his masterful self-control, he closed the studio door with an unusually violent shove.

The slamming door brought Emily out of her trance. Her heart eased its wild pounding, she opened her eyes and relaxed her grip on the countertop. Once again she was alone in the kitchen. In fact, had it not been for the warmth tingling along her spine and the scent of spice and cigars mingling with the aroma of roast beef, she could have persuaded herself that she'd conjured up the entire scene. But it had been real, so very, very real. Her soft, dreamy smile back in place, Emily opened a cabinet and reached for a stack of plates.

Inserting his key into the front-door lock, Joseph let himself into the house. Though it was quiet except for the faint sound of a radio playing upstairs, the warm glow of lamplight from the living room and hallway welcomed him. Checking his watch, he found that it wasn't quite seven o'clock. He shrugged out of the black, wool overcoat he'd worn to walk Danny to his friend's house, and settled it across the back of the sofa. Crossing the living room, he sank into the wing chair near the window. The reservation at Fitger's Inn was for seven-thirty, so they had plenty of time.

As he sat down in the chair, the framed photographs on the small, round table beside him caught his eye. There was something different about the arrangement tonight. Studying the array of pictures, he realized that some had been removed. The three that had included Eric were no longer on the table.

Aside from the photos in Danny's room and Emily's bedroom, they had been the only pictures of Eric in the house. She had chosen to put them away. Had she chosen to put away the one in her bedroom, too?

Hope and desire surged through him hard and fast. If she was ready to put away the photographs, surely she was also ready to accept Eric's death. Surely she was ready to discard the anger and bitterness she'd clung to for so long. If she could do that, and if she cared for him as he thought she did, then she would understand and accept him for what he was. He could tell her the truth about Eric's death, and she would believe him.

And if she believed him, she would also realize that he hadn't intentionally harmed her husband. She would recognize that Eric's death was the result of his being in the wrong place at the wrong time. Joseph knew how much he cared for her. She had to believe he would never hurt her on purpose.

Sitting forward in the chair, Joseph clasped his hands between his legs and stared at the floor. At forty-two, he'd had his fair share of women, yet tonight he felt like a teenager about to embark on his first date. His heart beat a rapid tattoo, his palms were hot and damp, and his hands trembled ever so slightly. He wanted to smoke so badly that it hurt. His future depended on Emily's trust, understanding and love. Not for the first time Joseph wondered if he was expecting too much of a woman who had lived with bitterness and anger for so long.

"I'm ready." Emily spoke the words softly, tentatively. She was almost afraid to disturb him. He seemed so far away, lost in painful thoughts that deepened the lines on his face. For once, she had taken *him* by surprise.

Joseph stood up, his eyes finding her where she waited in the lamplight's pale glow. He stared at her as if he'd never seen her before, and couldn't seem to catch his breath.

"I'm ready," she repeated, offering a smile as she presented herself for his approval.

She had wished for the money to splurge on something new, something special to wear just for him. In the end she had

only been able to afford new lingerie. The slim, black wool
skirt that flared at midcalf and the simple, white, high-necked
blouse were mainstays of her wardrobe, but it gave her great
pleasure to know that underneath, the soft, shimmering silk
brushing against her body was just for him.

And he looked wonderful, she thought, as he continued to
stand and stare at her, his eyes devouring her inch by inch.
He wore dark gray, wool pants, a gray- and black-striped shirt,
and a black, pullover sweater. A blush crept up her neck and
spread across her cheeks as she caught herself wondering what
he was wearing underneath. Black or white? She'd lay odds
on the black. Her blush deepened. There was only one way to
find out, and Emily had every intention of following that path.

She looked almost old-fashioned in the classic black skirt,
white blouse, dark stockings and very high heels, a ladylike
blush tinting her cheeks, but the feelings she evoked in Joseph
were anything but old-fashioned. Already he was anticipating
unbuttoning the row of tiny, pearl buttons that graced the front
of her blouse. It was going to take forever, and he was going
to savor every moment. Already he was anticipating sliding
her slender skirt over her slim hips, his lips following wherever his hands chose to lead. Already he was anticipating the
feel of her naked body in his arms. As if responding to his
thoughts, he saw her nipples harden beneath the sheer fabric
of the blouse.

Pulling his eyes away, Joseph glanced at his watch, cleared
his throat, and walked across the living room to pick up his
overcoat. "We'd better get going, or they'll give our table
away."

Emily nodded her agreement, then crossed the hallway to
retrieve her red, wool jacket from the coat closet. As Joseph
helped her into it, she thought she detected a slight trembling
in his hands, but when she glanced at him, he seemed totally
in control. His eyes were warm, and all trace of the pain that
had shadowed his features was gone. With a light touch, he
guided her out of the house and into the Jeep, and they were
on their way.

They started the journey to the restaurant in silence. Emily's heart beat in her chest slowly, steadily, expectantly. She shifted slightly in her seat so that she could gaze at Joseph's profile. He looked hard and rather cold in the clear, dark night. But when he halted at a stoplight and his eyes met hers, they showered her with the same hot blaze as the summer sun. Her body tightened with desire.

When the light changed and Joseph directed his attention back to the road, Emily glanced out the window at the passing cars, a smile touching her lips. Her hand moved instinctively to meet his, her fingers twining with his as he brought their clasped hands to rest against his thigh.

"You put away the pictures." His voice broke the stillness surrounding them, but he kept his eyes on the road.

"Yes."

"And you took off your ring." His thumb stroked the length of her bare finger as he spoke out the realization that had come to him a moment earlier.

"Yes."

"And the box. Did you open the box?"

She hesitated—too long. "No, not yet, but I will."

"Perhaps if we did it together..."

"Yes."

His hand tightened around hers, holding on to her until he was forced to release her to maneuver the Jeep into a parking space.

"You look very pretty tonight." Joseph offered the compliment as he helped her down.

The simple words sent a thrill of pleasure through Emily, banishing the spark of uncertainty his mention of the box had ignited. Standing very close to him, she lifted her face, intent on thanking him. But before she could utter a word, his mouth claimed hers in a slow, gentle kiss. His tongue soothed and promised; his mustache tickled. Her hands rested lightly on his chest. His hands, equally undemanding, roamed along her back from shoulders to waist.

When he drew away, much too soon, Emily had to grit her teeth against the protest that was rising in her. She didn't want dinner in a fancy restaurant. She wanted Joseph, naked in her

bed. She wanted to love him with her heart and soul and body
before it was too late.

Too late? Her forehead against his chest, she took a deep
breath, trying to steady the wild beating of her heart, trying to
still the sudden whisper of fear that was riding across the night
sky.

"Later, *niña,* after we talk. I promise you." His words were
a vow of love.

Stepping out of his arms, Emily nodded her agreement.
"Later."

Hand in hand, they crossed the small parking lot and entered
the restaurant.

Fitger's Inn was the perfect setting for a romantic dinner.
During the nineteenth century, the brick building, located on
the shore of Lake Superior north of downtown Duluth, had
housed a brewery. Restored, the complex now included the
inn, an indoor shopping mall full of tiny shops and stores, and
a restaurant.

The restaurant had a distinct aura of elegance. Four wide
windows along a beige brick wall overlooked the lake. Dark
green wallpaper, splashed with beige and rust cabbage roses
covered the remaining walls, matching the heavy draperies that
framed the windows. Square, oak tables, dark green, uphol-
stered chairs, globe lights with brass fixtures, and a roaring
fire in the huge fireplace added a comfortable warmth and a
touch of intimacy to the room.

Seated at a small table near one of the windows, with a
view of the city lights sparkling off the lake, Emily felt as if
she'd traveled into another time and space. Joseph sat beside
her, so with their backs to the rest of the room, their privacy
was almost complete. A quick, quiet waiter attended to their
needs with easy efficiency, then discreetly disappeared.

They demolished plates of Caesar salad, prime rib, and
baked potatoes oozing with butter and sour cream. They drank
red wine, warm and heavy and entirely satisfying. They
splurged on maple pecan pie topped with thick, rich cream,

and drank cups of hot, black coffee. And they talked, sharing pieces of their past, laying the groundwork for the future.

With an ease she had never felt before, Emily talked about her childhood, a time she had spent moving from one city to another. From St. Louis to Houston to Denver to San Francisco to Chicago, her mother, her older sister, and she had followed her father as he climbed the corporate ladder of a major insurance company. Two years here, three years there.

Sitting beside Joseph, she could laugh at the tears and fears she'd suffered through, leaving old friends behind, wondering about new friends yet to be found. Chicago had been the final move, corporate headquarters the final rung on the ladder. Emily had completed two years of high school there. Then, tired of big cities, she had chosen the University of Minnesota in Duluth for her college education. There she'd met and married Eric Anderson.

"And I've been here ever since." Emily's voice trailed away as she stared out the window.

Joseph saw the far-off look in her eyes, and knew that she was remembering all the years of happiness in the only real home she'd ever had, surrounded by good friends and neighbors and the university community. But the house was her past; he had every intention of being her future.

"Have you ever considered moving away from Duluth?"

"My family wanted me to move back to Chicago after Eric…" She shrugged her shoulders and continued to stare out the window. "But it would have been silly. I've never been close to my parents, and my sister is busy with her law practice and her husband, a doctor. Eric's parents are settled in a retirement community in Florida. We had to get special permission from the owners' association to bring Danny with us when we visited them." Emily smiled and shook her head. "No, I've never thought about leaving Duluth."

"*Would* you consider it?" He settled one hard, warm hand over hers, where it rested on the table.

I'd go anywhere in the world with you if you asked me, Emily thought. Turning her hand palm up, she twined her fingers with Joseph's and nodded her head. "Yes, I would."

The waiter chose that moment to clear away their dessert plates, refill their coffee cups and serve large snifters of brandy. They waited in silence, gazing out the window, holding onto each other until he drifted away to check on another table. Then Emily turned to Joseph again.

"I've done all the talking. Will you tell me about yourself, too?"

That was why he'd brought her to the restaurant, he thought, reaching for the brandy with his free hand. Yet each time she'd tried to turn the conversation in his direction, he'd backed away, asking Emily another question or making a comment sure to deflect her interest.

He swallowed a mouthful of the liquor, savoring its bite. He set the glass down, ran a finger around the rim, picked it up again and considered the true meaning of the word coward. As he tasted the amber liquid once more, he felt Emily's fingers tighten around his.

"I want to know everything," she said in a soft, teasing voice, refusing to accept the withdrawal she sensed in him. She gazed at him with wide, clear eyes, unwilling to let him go. "We can start at the very beginning. Were you born with those beautiful, brown eyes and that bandit's mustache, or did you acquire them later in life?"

"I was born with the eyes," he said. He set the brandy glass on the table and turned to face her. She was making it easy, as easy as it would ever be. He shrugged and smiled. "I think I decided to grow the mustache when I was about five or six."

Emily's soft, sweet laughter was all the encouragement Joseph needed. He had wanted to tell her about the ranch for weeks, to offer her all that he had to give. So, as she sipped her brandy and listened in quiet fascination, he talked about his boyhood, growing up on a working ranch in the Texas hill country.

Although he had done well in school, he had preferred the long, hot summers spent learning the skills of a rancher from his father and grandfather. But he had always made time for drawing, and later for the paintings that had so pleased his mother and her friend, Professor Mendoza.

The ranch had been his only home until he'd gone to the University of Texas in Austin to study business and agriculture, and to perfect his artistic talent. He had been close to his parents, who had died within months of each other two years ago, and he was still close to his younger sister, Elaina. She had married her childhood sweetheart, the boy next door, and together they worked his family's ranch and took turns spoiling their two young daughters.

"What did you do after college?" Emily asked, as Joseph paused for a moment to drain the last of the brandy from his glass. "Did you go back to the ranch?"

He had expected the questions. In fact he had been preparing for them for weeks. He hadn't, however, anticipated the jolt of apprehension that shot through him when he heard Emily asking them aloud. Suddenly there was no going back, no avoiding the truth and the need to tell it.

"About the time I finished at the university, the war in Vietnam was heating up...." He paused again, once more staring out the window, his eyes cold and distant.

"What happened, Joseph? Please tell me," Emily asked, her voice full of quiet concern.

When the silence lengthened, she tightened her hold on his hand. Once again she could feel him drawing away, closing in on himself, shutting her out. She could see the pain in his eyes, could sense the sadness shadowing his soul. She wanted to banish both forever. And she chose to ignore the tiny warning bell that went off in her head at the mention of Vietnam. Surely he didn't think she'd be upset about any association he'd had with the military so long ago?

He owed her the answers to her questions, he thought. She had a right to know how he'd spent the past twenty years. But he had been wrong to think that it would be easier to tell her in a restaurant. If she turned away from him, ran from him, he didn't want her doing it in front of strangers.

"It's a long story, and in parts not a very pretty one. I

thought it would be easier…here. But I think I'd rather tell you about it back at the house. All right?''

Emily sensed his hesitation, saw the bitter twisting of his lips, felt his fingers crushing hers as if he feared she'd run away. He turned to her, his eyes bleak and weary, and she reached out, wanting to comfort him, touching his face with gentle fingers. But he flinched as if she'd slapped him.

"All right," she agreed, dropping her eyes, freeing her hand and reaching for her purse.

Once again he was using some imaginary problem in his past to distance himself from her, attempting to break the bond that had been forming between them. But he wasn't going to succeed the way he had after the canoe trip, not this time. Her love for him was too strong to be threatened by anything he had done, and she was going to prove it to him once and for all.

"I'm going to the ladies' room. I'll be back in a few minutes."

Joseph stood and watched her cross the restaurant, her back straight, her walk smooth and graceful, her chin up, her eyes and mouth set with determination. With a silent groan of despair, he signaled the waiter. Then, giving in to the urge to smoke that had been riding him since early evening, he sat down and pulled a cigar out of his coat pocket.

His heart was pounding, his palms were sweating, and the food he'd eaten rolled and tumbled in his belly. He had faced death a half dozen times in his military career, but he had never felt fear as intensely as he did now, facing the probable death of Emily's love for him.

He drew deeply on the cigar, allowing the smoke to drift slowly out of his lips as he checked the total for their meal and counted out bills accordingly. He nodded his thanks to the waiter, drew again on his cigar, and watched the thin trail of smoke curling off its bright, red tip.

He felt her hands on his shoulders, small and warm through the fabric of his shirt and sweater, before he sensed her presence. He glanced up and saw their images reflected in the window, much as they'd been at the house Tuesday evening.

But this time it was Emily who bent to kiss his cheek, trace the outline of his ear with her tongue and nip at the nape of his neck with sharp teeth, leaving him shivery, hot and hard and aching.

"I'm ready," she murmured, her breath tickling his cheek for an instant before she moved away.

With a muttered curse, Joseph crushed his cigar in the heavy, crystal ashtray on the table, pushed out of his chair, wrapped his fingers around her forearm and all but dragged her out of the restaurant. From the corner of his eye he could see her smile. It was the kind of smile that spoke of cats and canaries, the kind of smile that went straight to a man's soul and stayed there forever.

Chapter Ten

He stopped in the lobby just long enough to collect their coats. He helped Emily into hers without a word, consciously avoiding her eyes, trying to ignore the dreamy smile that was tipping up the corners of her mouth. Then, his coat in one hand, he caught Emily by her upper arm and headed for the door.

"You're going to end up with pneumonia," Emily murmured, fumbling with the buttons on her coat as she attempted to keep up with his rapid pace across the parking lot. The night air was crisp and very cold.

"I'm going to end up in a rubber room." He stopped beside the Jeep, released Emily's arm and unlocked the door. He tossed his overcoat onto the back seat, caught Emily around the waist and lifted her onto the front seat, then slammed the door. A few seconds later, he was sitting beside her, turning the key in the ignition.

They traveled the short distance to Emily's house in silence, a silence full of apprehension and uncertainty. Emily's smile faded. He was retreating again, drawing away from her bit by bit as he guided the Jeep along the city streets, but she refused to let him go. She had to tell him, had to let him know....

"Joseph?" she whispered, turning to look at him, reaching out to touch his face.

"No," he muttered, pulling away from her as he had in the restaurant, tightening the fragile hold he had on himself.

A moment later he turned into the driveway and switched off the engine. He helped her out of the Jeep, but he didn't touch her as they walked across the lawn and up the front steps. The night air clutched at him as he pulled the door key from his pocket and inserted it into the lock. He felt the cold, inside and out, and suddenly he was anxious to get in, anxious to get it over and done with, once and for all. But as the lock clicked, Emily's small, warm hand covered his, preventing him from pushing the door open. He glanced down at her, his dark eyes full of impatience.

In the soft glow of the porch light, her gaze met his, strong and steady and full of reassurance. She stepped closer to him, moving her hand along his arm and across his shoulders, her fingers threading themselves into the long, dark hair at the nape of his neck. He tensed against her, wanting to pull away, but she moved closer still, refusing to let him go.

"It won't make any difference." Her voice was soft but firm in the cold, clear night. "No matter where you've been, no matter what you've done, it won't change how I feel about you. I love you, Joseph."

"You don't know what you're saying," he groaned, trying to deny her words, though every part of him wanted to believe her.

"Oh, yes, I do," she murmured softly, smiling.

With a low moan of pleasure that was tempered by pain, he wrapped his arms around her, holding her as if he'd never let her go. "You...don't know...what you're saying," he repeated, tilting up her face with one hand.

"I know," Emily assured him. She rested her hands on his chest, her eyes meeting his, feeling strong and safe and sure in his embrace. "Trust me."

Though one small part of his mind shouted a warning, Joseph ignored it. She loved him, and he wanted her, needed her so much. And whether it was right or wrong, he was going to have her, for now and for always. He lowered his head, claiming her, his kiss hot and deep and slow as he held her in the circle of his arms. His body tightened with desire, a desire he no longer tried to control. Tonight, this night with her, was his. He would take all that she offered him, and give her everything he had to offer.

He lifted his head, cupping her face in his hands. "Will you make love with me, Emily?" he asked, his eyes searching hers. "I need you so much, *querida*. Will you let me love you?"

"Yes," she whispered. "Yes, please."

The sudden warmth of the hallway after the cold night air was almost unbearable. As Joseph pulled his sweater over his head, Emily tried to unfasten the buttons on her coat. Leaning against the front door, she willed her trembling fingers to obey, but they refused.

"Here, let me help," Joseph offered. He tossed his sweater over the stair rail and moved to stand in front of her.

The light from the porch lamp glowed through the glass door panel, softening the harsh lines of his face as he eased open the buttons. Spreading the coat wide, he trailed one finger down the line of tiny, pearl buttons on her blouse. Then he cupped her breasts in his hands, gently brushing his thumbs over her nipples. He felt her instant response through the fine, sheer fabric, heard her breath catch in her throat.

"Joseph," she whispered, covering his hands with hers, holding them against her. Her heart danced against her ribs. She was afraid to breathe, afraid to say more than his name, afraid he would turn and walk away.

As if to reassure her, he bent his head, slanting his lips over hers first one way and then another, his mouth searching, surrendering, while his hands continued to stroke her.

He tasted of fine brandy and rich tobacco. He tasted like Joseph. Emily parted her lips, welcoming the slow sweep of his tongue, arching her body against the intensifying pleasure of his hands on her breasts.

She moved against him, clinging to him, her hands moving restlessly along his shoulders and down his back. She wanted to touch him, wanted to stroke his naked body. She plucked at his shirt, tugging it free, then slid her palms along the firm plane of his chest, tangling her fingers in the crisp, dark hair.

As suddenly as he had pulled her into his arms, Joseph released her, easing her hands from under his shirt. He slipped the heavy coat off her shivering body and turned to hang it in the closet. Sagging against the front door, Emily watched in fascination as he closed the closet door and turned back to her. With a quick, unexpected movement, he scooped her into his arms and headed for the staircase, seemingly unaware of his injured left leg.

She wrapped her arms around his neck, holding onto him as he limped slowly up the stairs. She traced the outline of his jaw with swift, sweet kisses, then teased his earlobe with her teeth and tongue until he groaned and turned to capture her mouth with his.

He carried her into his bedroom and laid her on the bed. Sitting beside her, he reached out and switched on the bedside lamp. He smoothed her tumbled curls away from her face.

"All right?" he asked, brushing a thumb over her swollen lips.

"Oh, yes," she murmured, her eyes wide and shining with love and desire.

With infinite care he released the tiny, pearl buttons one by one. Emily could neither speak nor move as he parted her blouse, but when he touched her, his hands hard and warm on her breasts through the thin, silk camisole, she reached for him, pulling him into her arms. With a rough sound, he bent his head, covering her breast with his mouth, rubbing his tongue over her silk-clad nipple again and again until she cried out.

Though she tried to hold him, he sat back, once again smoothing her hair away from her face. He had waited so long for her. It seemed he had waited all of his life. He wanted to go slowly, wanted to love her thoroughly and completely. But he was losing the battle with his self-control. Tonight and forever after she would be his.

With swift, steady hands he removed her shoes and unfastened her skirt, slipping it and everything under it off as she struggled out of her blouse and camisole. When she was naked, he gazed at her for a long moment, his hand following the line of her torso from shoulder to hip and back again.

"You are beautiful, Emily, so beautiful," he murmured. Then, mindful of the cool air in the bedroom, he reached under her, pulling the blanket and quilt back and over her.

As he stood up and stripped off his clothes with quick efficiency, a secret smile lifted Emily's lips. But when he pulled the black T-shirt over his head, and she saw the evidence of his desire pressing against his black briefs, her smile shifted into something else altogether.

Shivering slightly, she slid across the bed, the sheets crisp and cool against her fevered skin as she gazed at him. His body was dark and lean and hard in the lamplight, and there were other scars besides the one on his leg. Her smile faded. He had been hurt more than once.

"Emily?"

The quiet concern in his voice tugged at her heart. Her eyes met his, and she smiled once again, opening her arms to him as he slid beneath the quilt. Whoever he was, whatever he'd done, she loved him. She would always love him.

He stretched out beside her, gathering her into his arms, holding her close, her body smooth and soft and warm against him. As his hand traveled from her breast to her belly and back again, he kissed her forehead, her cheek, her lips. Easing her onto her back, he bent his head, teasing one nipple with his tongue, then drawing it into his mouth, suckling. She arched against him, threading her fingers through his hair, her body trembling. Turning his mouth to her other breast, he moved his hand between her thighs, his fingers stroking her with a slow, steady rhythm that left her aching with desire.

"Love me, Joseph. Love me now," she begged, twisting beneath his hands and mouth. Desperate for him to fill her emptiness, she urged him closer with her hands and hips.

"Wait, *querida*. Let me protect you," he muttered, rolling away from her.

"No," she murmured, cradling his face with her hands, tracing his thick, dark mustache with her thumb. "It's all right. I—I took care of it...before we left...." She smiled shyly, running her fingers through his hair. "I didn't want you to...I didn't want anything... I love you, Joseph. I love you so much."

"And I love you, Emily. For always, no matter what happens. For always," he vowed, his voice low and rough as he slid an arm under her, lifting her. His eyes held hers, and slowly, very slowly, he entered her.

She shuddered with pleasure as he filled her, her legs wrapping around him, her hands caressing his back, his buttocks, urging him closer and deeper. She wanted to move beneath him, but he held her still, teasing her with his lips, his teeth, his tongue until she was shaking with need.

"You belong to me now, Emily. I will always care for you. No matter what...always...."

Then he began to move inside her, his body claiming hers slowly, steadily. Her fingers dug into his shoulders as she arched under him, into him, her hunger plainly as fierce as his own. Suddenly the last thread of his careful control snapped. He was powerless to hold back. He drove into her, hard and fast, driven by desire and desperation, taking her. *His*. She belonged to him, now and forever. She was calling his name, coming apart in his arms, and he couldn't...couldn't...stop.

They held each other long after their breathing steadied and their heartbeats settled into quieter rhythms, Joseph levering his weight onto his elbows, Emily sliding her legs along his thighs. They didn't speak, each afraid to break the magic spell surrounding them. When Joseph finally eased onto his side, Emily moved with him, unwilling to relinquish her body's hold on him. He tightened his arms around her, resting his cheek against her hair, and she knew once again that she was well and truly loved.

"Emily—"

"No, don't talk," she pleaded, brushing her lips against the hard plane of his chest. "Just hold me. Let me sleep with you tonight. We can talk in the morning."

His hand smoothed over her hair and moved down the length of her back to rest at her waist. Pressing her close, he whispered her name again. She was so soft, so warm, and now she was his. His to protect and to care for for the rest of his life. And he wanted the night with her so much. He had already waited to talk to her too long. What could a few more hours hurt? He moved his hand from her waist to her breast.

"Are you sure you want to sleep, *querida*?"

"It was just a thought," she murmured, as her tongue, then her teeth teased his nipple.

"Better not to think," he groaned, rolling onto his back, taking Emily with him, filling her once again with his love and desire.

She awakened to the tangy scent of cigar smoke and to early-morning sunlight slanting across the polished oak floor, brightening the blues and greens of the quilt on Joseph's bed. *Joseph's bed?* Emily blinked once, then again, focusing on the man staring out the window as he drew on the small, thin cigar he held in one hand. He was dressed in jeans, a dark blue sweatshirt and low-heeled, black boots. His hair was still damp from the shower, and he had shaved.

Emily curled into the warmth of her cocoon, her body tightening with desire as she traced the inside of her thigh with the fingers of one hand. They had made love a second time, exploring each other slowly and completely. And then, in the deep darkness before dawn, Emily had awakened to the exquisite pleasure of Joseph's mouth on her, hot and fierce and so unbelievably tender, loving her until she cried out in ecstasy again and again.

"So, you're not going to sleep all day, after all?" His voice, low and faintly teasing, broke her reverie, but he didn't turn away from the window.

Smiling softly, Emily slipped out of bed and padded across the bedroom naked. She wrapped her arms around him, pressing her body close to his, rubbing her cheek against his shoulder. Rough denim brushed her legs, and soft, fleece-lined cotton cradled her breasts as she savored his warmth and tried to ignore his sudden tensing at her touch.

"Come back to bed."

With a quick movement, Joseph crushed his cigar in the ashtray he'd set on the windowsill. Turning, he gathered Emily into his arms, holding her still when she would have reached up to kiss him. In the clear light of day, despite her words of reassurance, he knew it had been wrong to make love with her. He had violated his personal code of honor. But he was only human, and she was everything he'd ever wanted in a woman. Given the same circumstances, he'd do it again. But he would not compound the error.

"Emily, *querida,* you know how much I care for you?" His voice was rough, the teasing replaced by a fine edge of desperation. He rested his cheek against her hair and stroked her back.

"Yes." She curled her fingers into the fabric of his sweatshirt, listening to the slow, steady beat of his heart. "I love you, too." His heartbeat quickened, and she felt the faint flicker of his smile.

"I want to marry you. I want to raise your son. I want to watch my child growing inside you. But Emily, we have to talk. There are some things I have to tell you. And then we're going to open the box Eric sent before he was killed."

"But it doesn't matter—!" Emily cried, her joy overshadowed by a subtle fear, a clawing uncertainty. Why was he coupling his past with Eric? Somewhere, deep inside, she didn't want to know the answer.

"Believe me, it matters," Joseph muttered, stepping away from her. It took every ounce of willpower he possessed. Hands on her shoulders, his eyes holding hers, he silenced her protests with a gentle shake. "It matters. By the time you take a shower and dress, I'll have breakfast ready. All right?"

"All right, but..." Emily hesitated, her hands resting on Joseph's chest, her eyes searching his for reassurance. "Will you kiss me?" she whispered.

Without a word, Joseph pulled her into his arms again and

did as she asked, his mouth as soothing and caressing and possessing as the hand he settled on her breast. But even as she indulged in the pleasure he gave her, Emily sensed his urgency, as if this might be the last time he held her in his arms. And when he released her, the sadness in his dark eyes settled in her soul, leaving her shivering with apprehension as he walked out of the room.

She found her clothes neatly folded at the foot of the bed. Scooping them up, her fingers carelessly crushing the fine, silk lingerie, she strode out of Joseph's bedroom and crossed the hallway. She showered, washed the last traces of makeup off her face, brushed her teeth, and ran a comb through her tangled curls. She pulled on fresh jeans, a red- and white-striped shirt, and a red, pullover sweater. She moved quickly, keeping her mind a careful blank, but as she slipped on thick, wool socks and leather loafers, her sense of foreboding was almost overwhelming in its intensity.

She was halfway down the staircase, lured as well as lulled by the aroma of freshly brewed coffee, when the telephone began to ring. She stopped and stared at the instrument, startled by its shattering sound. She willed it to stop, it was much too early in the morning to be anything but bad news.

"Answer it," Joseph advised in a low voice. He stood in the kitchen doorway, watching her, his eyes warm and reassuring.

"No." Crossing her arms in front of her, Emily shook her head, the single word more plea than refusal.

"Emily, you have to answer the phone. What if Danny's sick?"

Cursing her foolishness, she ran down the steps and crossed the hall, yanking the receiver off the hook. She hadn't considered the most likely possibility.

"Hello?" Her voice was breathless and as unsteady as her heartbeat. In the few seconds of silence that followed, she recognized the faint buzz and crackle of a long-distance line. Immediately her worry shifted away from Danny toward her parents, Eric's parents, her sister. "Hello? Who's calling, please?" she asked on a high note of anxiety.

"Hello, ma'am. This is Lieutenant Capwell. Is the colonel there, ma'am?"

Emily sagged against the wall in relief. The gruff voice on the other end of the line was that of a stranger. He had dialed the wrong number. "I'm sorry, sir. You must have the wrong number."

"Is this 555-348-9553?" He listed the numbers slowly, enunciating carefully, as if speaking to a small child.

"Yes." Emily frowned down at the telephone table, vaguely aware that Joseph was standing very close to her. It *was* her telephone number, but…

"Well, damn it. Uh, sorry, ma'am. But that's the number he gave me, and the colonel rarely makes a mistake. You're sure Colonel Cortez isn't there?"

"Colonel…Cortez?" Her frown deepening, her murmured question reflected in her eyes, Emily met Joseph's steady gaze. Her stomach rolled and lurched, and she couldn't seem to catch her breath. The room swayed and spun around her for one soul-shattering instant.

Colonel Cortez.

If he had struck her, if he had cracked his hand across her face, the blow would have been no more stunning than those two words. Colonel Cortez. Government…. Military…. Murderer…. She dropped the receiver. Its clatter as it hit the table was an explosion of sound in the silent hallway. She backed away from him, her face white, her eyes wide, her mouth a thin, narrow line.

Joseph saw the anger and confusion in her eyes. He understood her sense of betrayal. He wanted to go to her and pull her into his arms and assure her that everything would be all right. But first, because of who and what he was, he had to deal with the man on the telephone. He picked up the receiver.

"Hello, Cappy? Hold on a minute." He covered the mouthpiece with one hand, his eyes on Emily. "Go upstairs." He issued the order to her as he'd issued the order to Lieutenant Capwell, his tone brooking no argument.

Emily wanted to refuse, to rebel against his assumption that he could order her around, but she couldn't do it. Tears itched at the back of her eyes, tears she wouldn't, couldn't shed, and her legs wobbled as she moved across the hall. A sickening sense of shame overwhelmed her. She had seduced him, and she had slept with him. She had slept with the enemy, and in doing so, she had betrayed her husband. She wanted to run, to hide, and her bedroom was as good a place as any.

She didn't hear the thud of the receiver against the hall table, but as she started up the staircase she felt Joseph's hands on her shoulders, stopping her, turning her. She flinched away from him, trying to break free, but he was too strong for her. When he pulled her into his arms, crushing her against his chest, she stopped fighting, her body rigid in his embrace.

"Emily, *querida,* I'm sorry. I didn't want you to find out this way." His voice was low and rough and pleading. He stepped away from her, his hands on her shoulders, his eyes searching her face, but she refused to look at him, refused to touch him or acknowledge him in any way.

"I know you're hurt and angry, and I don't blame you." He moved his hands from her shoulders, cradling her face, his thumbs stroking her cheeks. "But Emily, we can deal with it, put it behind us. Trust me."

Trust? She had to bite back a howl of laughter, had to clench her fingers against the urge to strike him, had to swallow the tears that clogged her throat at the sudden gentling of his voice and hands. What did *Colonel Cortez* know about trust, except how to use it against her?

He was losing her. He could feel it in the rigid way she held her body. He could see it in the shimmery stillness of her eyes as she avoided his steady gaze. He wanted to shout at her, wanted to shake her. Instead, he released her.

"I have to talk to Lieutenant Capwell. Will you wait for me upstairs, please?"

Without a word, Emily nodded her head, turned and continued up the staircase, unaware that Joseph's eyes followed her until she disappeared from view.

She walked into her bedroom and settled into her big, old rocking chair. She sat there for a long time, the rhythm of the rocker soothing her soul. The only sound in the quiet house was the click of Greta's nails against the hardwood floor. When the dog rested her head in Emily's lap, she somehow felt comforted. Greta seemed to know as surely as did Emily that he was leaving. He was the enemy, and he was going away, and Emily, curled up in the rocking chair, wasn't sure which thought hurt her more.

Finally she heard his footsteps on the stairs, heard him cross the hall and enter his bedroom. Greta nudged her hand one last time, then trotted out of the room. Emily sat alone, rocking, waiting, listening to the sounds of drawers being opened and closed, of the closet door swinging back and forth on its hinges, until she couldn't stand it another moment. Slipping out of the rocking chair, she padded out of her bedroom and across the hallway.

Stopping in the doorway of his room, she saw the suitcase open on his bed, a dark green, uniform jacket, gleaming with medals and ribbons, lying beside it. The sight of it was enough to make her want to laugh...or cry.

A sudden snap and click drew her attention to Joseph, standing at the dresser. Unaware of her presence, he was methodically checking a black handgun, releasing the magazine clip from the butt, replacing it. What kind of army officer carried a handgun? The kind of officer who spent more time at war than at peace, she assured herself. The kind of officer who, as a result, had an angry red weal of scar tissue running up the side of his left leg.

As if sensing her presence, Joseph turned to look at her, his face expressionless. He had so little time and so much he had to say to her, but she was looking at him as if he were something nasty smeared on a sidewalk. His heart twisted with pain. Turning away from her, he fitted the Beretta into a sleek, black leather holster.

"I have to leave this morning, Emily. A car will be coming for me in about thirty minutes." Holster in hand, he crossed the room to stand in front of the suitcase, waiting for her reply. When she didn't respond, he glanced over his shoulder.

"How were you hurt?" Her voice was soft, strained, belying the look in her eyes.

"I was in a restaurant in Santa Maria, the capital of Norteña." He met her gaze, his voice steady, answering her with the honesty he'd owed her from the start. "I was with two of my men. We'd been there many times. It was a popular place with military personnel. Everybody knew it, including the person or persons who lobbed a couple of hand grenades near our table. Both of my men were killed instantly. I was buried under a pile of rubble, knocked out. My leg...my leg was shattered."

She took a step back, not saying another word. She raised one hand, as if she wanted to touch him. Then, her face pale, she dropped her hand to her side, turned and walked away.

The house was silent, as if anticipating his departure. With a muttered curse, Joseph tossed the holster into the suitcase. *Damned rotten timing.* For a moment he rested both hands on his hips, bent his head, and closed his eyes. Mendoza had warned him, but he hadn't had the good sense to listen.

Then he moved across the room again, pulling on his jacket. He didn't blame her for being upset. He was upset himself. But if he hurried, he might have time to explain.

Emily sat on the bottom step of the staircase. It was as far as she'd gotten before her trembling body had called a halt. Legs drawn up, her head resting on her knees, she listened again to the sounds emanating from Joseph's bedroom. Her thoughts and feelings spun out of control, pulling her first one way, then another.

Eric and Joseph, anger and exhilaration, pain and comfort, love—and something too near to hate, guilt and a fine edge of fear. One had left and never come back. Now the other was leaving, too. She heard him close and lock his suitcase, switch off the light and start down the stairs.

As he passed her on the steps, Emily sat up, staring at him, but he didn't meet her eyes. He carried his suitcase in one hand, his cap in the other. He crossed the hall to stand in front of the oval mirror. He set down his suitcase, balancing the cap on it, then knotted his tie with quick, deft movements. He buttoned his jacket, then picked up his cap and settled it firmly on his head.

When he faced Emily at last, she could do nothing but stare at him, her eyes wide, as if he were an alien from another planet. He wore the uniform well. Despite the fact that his hair was a shade too long, he was a real military man, no doubt about it.

"You knew how I felt about the government and the military," she accused him, her voice low and harsh and hurting as she stood up to face him. "Why didn't you tell me?"

"At first it didn't seem necessary. I needed a place to live, you needed the money. I didn't expect to fall in love with you. When I realized what was happening, I tried to stay away from you. When that didn't work, I knew I had to tell you. I meant to tell you at dinner last night."

"Why didn't you?" Emily asked, brushing past him, turning her back on him, desperate to put some distance between them.

"I tried to tell you, Emily."

"You didn't try very hard, *Colonel.*"

"No, maybe not. But last night you told me the past didn't matter. I wanted to believe you. I wanted to believe you when you told me you loved me. And I wanted you so much, Emily. I needed you so much. I'm only human." He came up behind her and rested his hands on her shoulders. "I love you, Emily."

"Don't talk to me about love!" She spat the words at him, wrenching away from his touch, rounding on him, her eyes glinting with a fierce, wild light. "You didn't tell me because you were afraid of what I'd do, or rather what I wouldn't do, once I knew you were part of the military machine that murdered my husband."

He came at her then, his anger far surpassing hers. He wrapped his fingers around her upper arms and shook her, hard. "First and foremost, I didn't trick you into bed, *niña.* We made *love*, together...you and I...together. Nothing changes that...*nothing.*" He gave her another shake to emphasize his words. "Second, your husband wasn't murdered by the military. He was running with a band of Arteagan soldiers when he was killed. He got caught in the cross fire, when they decided to ambush a U.S. Army unit stationed in Norteña.''

"You're lying," she cried, trying to pull away from him without success. "He wouldn't do something like that. He *wouldn't*. And the State Department—"

"Damn the State Department. I'm telling you the truth."

She searched his dark, steady eyes as silence stretched between them. "How can you be so sure?" she whispered. Then, recalling what he'd just said about how he'd been injured, another puzzle piece slid into place. "You were there...."

"I've been stationed in Norteña off and on over the past three years, working as a military adviser. The army unit that exchanged fire with the Arteagan soldiers was under my command. It's possible one of my men fired the shot that killed Eric, or he may have been killed by the Arteagans. In any case, we found his body among the dead, and I ordered my lieutenant to send it to the embassy to be shipped home."

"You're telling me that you were there when Eric was killed? You're telling me that *you* were responsible for Eric's death?"

"I'm telling you that your husband was participating in a military action against the United States Army. I don't know why, but he was. Maybe the answer is in that box he sent you. In any case, he ended up in the wrong place at the wrong time. He ended up dead, and it was his own damned fault."

"No!" Emily cried, wrenching free of Joseph's hold on her. "I don't believe you. You're lying to me. He wouldn't have risked his life. He promised.... And the State Department would have told me...." She leaned against the wall, wrapping her arms around herself, pain and anger and uncertainty warring within her.

"I may have avoided talking about my past, but I've never lied to you, Emily. I'm not lying now. Maybe he didn't know what he was getting into, but that's the way he died. As far as the State Department goes, their main concern is avoiding international incidents at any cost." He took a step toward her, intent on holding her, comforting her, but the cold, dead look in her eyes stopped him.

"Why did you come here, Cortez? Why did you move into my house?"

"I didn't kill your husband, Emily, but I *was* indirectly responsible for his death. He...he haunted me. I don't know why, but he did. I found out all I could about him, and I found out about Danny and you, too. I came to Duluth to make sure you were all right, to take care of you if you weren't—"

"Oh, Cortez, you certainly did that. You certainly did take care of me," Emily cut in, her voice soft and full of bitterness. "And now that you've done your duty, now that you've accepted your responsibility and taken care of the little widow in *every* way, you can get out of my house." Her words fell from her lips like chips of ice and were punctuated by the chiming of the doorbell. "Get out of my house, Colonel Cortez, and don't ever come back."

He had waited for a woman like Emily Anderson all of his life. He wasn't going to give her up without a fight. Ignoring the officer on the front porch, ignoring her orders to get out, he pulled her into his arms. Holding her rigid body close, he claimed her mouth with savage desperation, forcing her to respond.

"I haven't even begun to care for you," he muttered, his hands on her shoulders holding her in a viselike grip. "What I feel for you has nothing to do with duty or honor or any debt I thought I owed. Believe me, if it did, my part would be over, and you'd never see me again. But I'm coming back, Emily. I promise you, I'll be back, and we'll work it out. Somehow we'll work through the past."

She had ordered him out of her house, yet suddenly, perversely, she was clinging to him, her fingers wrapped around the lapels of his jacket. What if they sent him back to Norteña?

"Don't go. Please, don't go. Don't be a part of it anymore," she pleaded, her eyes locked with his. "If you're not a part of it—"

He bent his head and kissed her again, his lips warm and gentle on hers, stopping the flow of her words. "I have to go, *querida*. I don't have a choice. I *am* a part of it. It's not something I can change. It's not something I want to change.

I've served my country with pride for almost twenty years, and I'll continue to do so. But I'll be back.''

He eased away from her, touched her face, her hair, then bent to pick up his suitcase. He walked down the hallway and rested his hand on the doorknob. He glanced at her over his shoulder.

"While I'm gone I want you to do something for me...for us. I want you to open the box Eric sent you.''

She flinched as if he'd struck her, closing her eyes for an instant, then met his gaze with renewed determination. "If you leave, Cortez, there is no 'us.' If you walk through that door, I never want to see you again.''

He held her gaze for a long moment, then turned away from her and opened the door. He stopped for a moment, taking a deep breath, squaring his shoulders, blinking back the moisture that blurred his vision. Then, with a nod to the young lieutenant standing on the porch, he slipped through the doorway, closing the door behind him.

As the door closed, Emily took one step, then another down the narrow hallway. But by the time she reached the door, he was gone. She rested her forehead against the cool glass panel, her eyes dry, her throat aching with unshed tears, her heart cracking into a thousand tiny pieces.

"I can't love you, Joseph,'' she whispered in a sad, broken voice. "Don't you understand? I can't love you anymore.''

Chapter Eleven

Long after he had gone, Emily stood at the front door, oblivious to the cold glass beneath her cheek, waiting for him to return. If he loved her, if he really loved her as he said he did, how could he choose to be a part of the military machine that had murdered her husband? And how could he leave her without once, not even once apologizing for what he'd done? There had been regret for her pain and suffering, but no sympathy for Eric, none at all.

And what about the details of Eric's death that Joseph had revealed? Eric had been a pacifist, and he had promised to be careful. He had planned to visit a colleague at the university in the Arteagan capital, but that was a long way from the Norteñian border. It was impossible to believe he had been part of a band of Arteagan soldiers, yet Emily knew in her heart of hearts that Joseph Cortez had not lied to her.

It was Greta's wet nose nuzzling her hand that brought Emily out of her reverie. He wasn't coming back, not today. And if he heeded her bitter, angry words, he'd never come back. It was just as well, she thought, opening the door so the dog could go out. Or was it? Rubbing a hand over her forehead, she turned and walked down the hallway into the kitchen.

What she wanted, what she *needed*, was a cup of strong, black coffee and a handful of aspirin. Her head felt thick and heavy, but her mind was whirling a mile a minute. And deep inside a strange, sick sadness gripped and churned as she fought to deny that she'd made a mistake when she told Joseph to go away and stay away.

Somehow Emily got through the remainder of the day. She stayed downstairs all morning, scrubbing the kitchen from top to bottom, emptying cabinets, washing windows and mopping the floor like a madwoman. She couldn't face Joseph's empty bedroom, nor did she have any desire to enter her office. There, crouched in the closet, waiting for her was the box Eric had sent before he was killed.

Late in the afternoon she walked to her friend's house to pick up Danny. She avoided Cathy's bright eyes and teasing questions, cursing herself for being rude and ungrateful. But she simply couldn't discuss the events of early morning, even with her best friend. As Cathy's curiosity turned to concern, Emily hustled her son out the door with nothing more than an apologetic shrug of her shoulders. Back home again, she unplugged the telephone.

Avoiding Danny and his questions was even more difficult. In fact it was next to impossible. If he uttered Joseph's name once, he uttered it a hundred times before he finally tumbled into bed that night.

"Where's Joseph?" he asked, racing up the staircase moments after they walked in the door, Greta right behind him.

"He had to go away." Reluctantly Emily followed her son to the second floor, and found him in the doorway of Joseph's bedroom. She stood beside him, wrapping an arm around his shoulders as she surveyed the empty room, her heart twisting as her gaze rested on the rumpled bed, the jeans and sweatshirt and the black T-shirt he'd been wearing earlier tossed at its foot.

"Where?"

"I don't know."

"When's he coming back?"

"I don't know."

"He *is* coming back, isn't he, Mom?" Danny's bright eyes caught at Emily's, pleading.

"I...don't know, Danny." But she did know. He would never come back, not after the way she'd behaved that morning. She had destroyed his love for her with words as sharp as swords, as bitter as poison. Despite the sunlight pouring through the bedroom windows, despite the warmth of her son's body pressed close to hers, Emily shivered. Without Joseph the old house was once again a cold and lonely place to be.

"What about Greta? He'll come back for her, won't he?" Slipping away from Emily, Danny knelt beside the dog and wrapped his arms around her neck. "He won't forget about you, girl. He won't forget about us. I know he won't. He loves us. He said so lots of times."

Emily folded her empty arms across her chest, leaned against the door frame and closed her eyes, trying to steady herself against the tears she saw sparkling in her son's eyes. A twist of pain gouged her heart. *Danny, sweet Danny, what can I say? I sent him away. I sent him away.* The rhythm of the words and their reality rolled through her head again and again, until she thought she'd scream.

"Mommy, are you okay?" Danny's soft, worried voice tugged at her soul as his hand tugged at her shirt sleeve.

"Yes, I'm okay," Emily assured her son, pulling him into her arms for a fierce hug.

"What about Greta and Joseph?"

"Don't worry about Greta. We'll take care of her." She smoothed Danny's curls away from his face and offered him a reassuring smile. "Joseph...Joseph's a colonel in the army—"

"Like GI Joe?"

"Um, sort of. Anyway, he...he had to go...back to work. He had to leave right away. We didn't have time to... to...talk." Emily's eyes flicked away from her son's for an instant. She hated lying to him. The truth was, if she hadn't been so busy hurling accusations and insults Joseph's way, they would have had time to talk. "So I honestly don't know where he is or when he'll be back. All right?"

Danny nodded his head, but Emily could see the unasked questions in his eyes, questions that marked his young face with sadness and a trace of fear. Emily knew instinctively that he was thinking about Eric.

"He'll be okay, Danny. And he'll be back." Emily spoke the words with determination, as much for herself as for her son. Reaching out, she caught hold of the doorknob and closed the bedroom door with a decisive click. "Come on, buddy. Why don't we bake some brownies? Then maybe we can take Greta for a long, long walk. He wouldn't want us to sit around, worrying about him, you know."

"Okay, Mom," Danny agreed, nodding his tousled, blond head once more, his worried frown replaced by a big grin. "Can we play Candy Land, too?"

"You're pushing it, kid, really pushing it," Emily teased as she followed him down the stairs. Actually she welcomed any activity, even a game of dreaded Candy Land, if it took her mind off Joseph Cortez and the increasing certainty that she'd made a very serious, possibly irreparable error in judgment.

It was well past midnight, almost one o'clock in the morning, and Emily couldn't sleep. Her head hurt despite more aspirin than allowed by law, her eyes were gritty with unshed tears, and she ached from her heart to her soul. She was bone weary from thinking and trying not to think in a house that was too quiet and a bed that was too big and too empty. With a groan she pushed the blankets away, swung her legs around and stood up. As if drawn by a magnet, she crossed the hallway and opened the door to Joseph's bedroom.

Moonlight pierced the shadowy darkness, highlighting the unmade bed. She moved slowly, hesitantly, to stand beside it, gathering into her arms the clothes Joseph had left at its foot, burying her face in their cool, clean depths. She inhaled his scent, the scent of spice and cigars, and shuddered, her longing laced with despair.

Setting aside his black T-shirt, she hung his jeans and sweat-shirt over a hanger and tucked them into the closet. Returning to the bed, she pulled her long, flannel nightgown over her head and dropped it onto the floor. Naked, she reached for the black T-shirt.

As the soft cotton caressed her skin, her nipples hardened into tight peaks, as if accepting a lover's touch. She smoothed her hands over her body, molding the shirt to her breasts, her belly, her thighs. The ache inside her eased a bit. One hot, wet tear etched a long, slow trail down her cheek. Quickly, before she had time to analyze her foolishness, she pulled back the blankets and quilt and slid beneath them. Head resting on his pillow, she burrowed under his blankets, his scent, mingled with her own, surrounding her.

She closed her eyes and uttered a deep, heavy sigh. Her mind stopped whirling in mad confusion, the throbbing in her head faded away, the edge of pain in her heart dulled slightly. Here they had blocked out the past, here they had held each other and loved, and here they had hoped for the future. Here they had been good and right and wonderful together. With that knowledge, Emily found some small measure of peace, and finally drifted into sleep.

"Hi."

"Hi, yourself." Cathy eyed her friend through the narrow crack in Emily's front door. "Your telephone's out of order."

Reluctantly Emily opened the door so Cathy and Jimmy could enter. It was early Sunday afternoon, and the gray sky and cold wind suited her unwelcoming mood. The peace she had found in Joseph's bed had faded with the dawn light, leaving her as full of pain and confusion as she'd ever been. How could she love Joseph Cortez, knowing who and what he was, without betraying her love for Eric? The impossibility of it overwhelmed her.

If it had been anyone but her best friend, Emily would have slammed the door in their faces. As it was, it took her last ounce of effort to dredge up a smile for Jimmy. "Danny's out in the backyard with Greta. He'll be glad to see you." As the boy disappeared down the hallway, she closed the door, her smile fading fast.

"How about you? Aren't you glad to see me?" Cathy asked, frowning at the purple shadows smudging Emily's eyes and the faint, fine lines that drew down the corners of her mouth.

"The telephone isn't out of order. I unplugged it," Emily muttered, leading the way to the kitchen.

"If that's a hint, I'm not taking it. What's going on? What happened Friday night? Where's Joseph?" With a flip of her wrist, Cathy plugged in the telephone, then followed Emily down the hallway.

"October, 1987. Duluth, Minnesota. The Inquisition, Part Two. You are there." Emily flopped into a chair and ruefully eyed her friend.

Ignoring Emily, Cathy opened a cabinet and took down two long-stemmed glasses. Filling them from the jug of wine in the refrigerator, she set one in front of her friend and kept one for herself. Sitting in a chair across from Emily, she sipped her wine and waited with the patience and understanding of a true friend.

"He's gone."

"Mmm. So I gathered. I didn't think he'd scare so easy."

"It wasn't fear. Duty called." Emily's hand snaked out, her fingers wrapping around the glass. She swallowed a mouthful of the cold, clear wine. Its effect was so soothing that she drank again.

"Duty?" Cathy twirled her wineglass, hesitating. "Wife? Mother? Mistress?"

Emily laughed, but the sound was without joy. It was harsh and brittle. "Orders from the United States Army for Colonel Joseph Cortez, military adviser extraordinaire, assigned to Central America."

Cathy's glass hit the table with a tinkle of almost-breaking glass as she turned to meet Emily's cold, dry eyes. "Oh, Emily, no."

"Oh, Cathy, yes. And do you want to hear the best of it?" Emily's lips twitched into a tight, little smile. "He was there when Eric was killed. Right there. It's quite possible someone under his command killed my husband. He moved into my house, he let me fall in love with him, he took me to bed, and all the time he knew he was responsible for Eric's death." Emily drained the wine in her glass and set it on the table with a small, final click.

"You're telling me Joseph Cortez ordered Eric's assassination, then moved into your house and seduced you?" Cathy's face was pale, her eyes grim, as she gazed at Emily across the kitchen table.

"According to Cortez, Eric wasn't assassinated." Emily turned away from her friend's probing eyes. "He...he told me Eric was part of a band of Arteagan soldiers that crossed the border into Norteña to ambush the army unit Cortez was commanding. Eric was killed during an exchange of fire. Cortez claimed the State Department didn't tell me the details because of the possible political implications."

Cathy was quiet for a long time. She finished her wine, then crossed to the refrigerator to retrieve the jug and refill their glasses. "Do you think Joseph lied to you about Eric?"

Emily shrugged her shoulders and reached for her glass. Her head was spinning slightly; she hadn't eaten since dinner Friday night. "Eric promised to be careful. He *was* going into Arteaga to visit a friend at the university in the capital. But I can't believe he ended up with a band of soldiers."

"So you *do* believe Joseph lied to you."

Emily shrugged her shoulders again, a bewildered look in her eyes as she turned away from her friend.

"If Eric *was* part of a military action down there, for whatever reason, even accidentally, then he's the one responsible for his death, Emily. Not the United States government, not the army, not Joseph Cortez." At the stricken look on Emily's face, Cathy left her chair and knelt in front of her, grasping her hands. "What did you say to him, Emily? What did you say to Joseph?"

"I accused him of lying to me. Then I told him, if he left, he should never come back."

"And what did he say to you?"

"At first he said he cared for me and he'd be back. He said he never lied to me. Then he didn't say anything. He just walked out the door."

"Oh, Emily, what are you going to do?"

"I don't know."

"Do you love him?"

"How can I? If I allow myself to love him, then I'm betraying Eric."

"That's crazy. If what Joseph told you is true, and I think we both know he wouldn't lie to you, then no one is to blame for Eric's death but Eric. For whatever reason, he was in the wrong place at the wrong time. You'll probably never know why he was with a band of soldiers, but apparently he was.

"You've mourned him for over a year. Stop waiting for him to come home, Emily. Accept the fact that he's dead. Let him go, and let yourself love again. It's what he would have wanted, and knowing Eric, he would have been relieved and happy to know you found a man like Joseph Cortez." Her hands tightened on Emily's for an instant before she stood up. "Where's Joseph? Can you contact him?"

"I think he's gone back to Norteña, but I have no idea how to contact him." Emily's eyes had brightened considerably, and for the first time in almost forty-eight hours she felt the first stirrings of hope. "But he did say he'd come back. He left all his things and Greta, too. I'll wait...."

"Don't wait too long," Cathy advised, returning to her chair and her glass of wine.

"No, I won't," Emily promised. Just long enough to do as Joseph had suggested. She would go through the box Eric had sent, she would then face the fact that Eric was dead, she would lay to rest her anger and her bitterness, and she would free herself from the past, once and for all. Then she would seek out Professor Mendoza and ask him to help her find Joseph.

* * *

As it turned out, Richard Mendoza found Emily first. He telephoned late Sunday evening, shortly after she had tucked Danny into bed. He offered the usual small talk. Then he asked her if she could be at home at nine o'clock the next morning. She said that she could. However, when she tried to question him, he told her they would talk in the morning. That night, filled with a sick sense of foreboding, Emily found it impossible to sleep, even in Joseph's bed.

The next day she dressed carefully, pulling on navy, wool pants, a plaid flannel shirt, a thick, red sweater, socks and boots. To ward off the cold wind and blowing snow outside, she told herself, as she walked down the hallway to greet Richard Mendoza at the front door. But the flakes of snow that grazed her face were warm compared to the icy hand that clutched at her heart when she glanced over his shoulder. A Mayflower moving van was parked at the curb.

"What...?" she murmured, her eyes wide, her face pale, as she stepped back into the hallway.

"He asked me to come and collect his things as soon as possible, so you wouldn't be burdened with them." Not waiting for a reply, the professor turned and waved to the two men in the van's cab. They returned his wave, then settled down to wait, the running motor a dull drone in the early-morning quiet.

"But he said he was coming back," Emily protested, her voice wavering slightly. "Joseph said he'd be back."

"Do you want him to come back, Emily?"

"I—I don't...know." Emily's voice wavered even more as she met Richard Mendoza's steady gaze.

"He moved into your house without telling you why, without telling you anything about his past. He did so because he felt responsible for you and Danny. He came to Duluth to secure your future, not to hurt you nor to fall in love with you. But he did both. He fell in love with you. And he hurt you, didn't he?"

"He let me fall in love with him, knowing all the time that he was the last man on earth I should love."

"Do you really believe that, Emily? Do you really believe you shouldn't love Joseph Cortez?"

"He was responsible for Eric's death."

"Yes, you could say that," Mendoza replied, catching Emily's arm, holding her still when she would have walked away. "But what about Eric himself? Do you think Joseph lied about the circumstances surrounding his death?"

"I don't know what to think anymore," Emily murmured, her voice soft and low.

"If you don't believe what Joseph told you, if you can't trust in him and his love for you, then you're better off apart. He came to Duluth out of a sense of duty and responsibility. He stayed much longer than he'd planned, because he cares for you so much. But if you can't return his love, it's better that he make a clean break now rather than grow bitter, feeding off false hope."

"Is that what you told him?"

"Yes." Taking Emily's elbow, the old professor guided her up the staircase to Joseph's bedroom. "In the end, he agreed with me. He asked me to pack his things and arrange to have them shipped back to Texas."

"Where...where is he?" Emily leaned against the door frame, as Richard pulled a large suitcase from the closet shelf and began to fill it with Joseph's clothes.

"In Norteña."

"I thought we were trying to hammer out some sort of peace agreement down there."

"He's been asked to work with the military leaders of several Central American countries to insure that the peace will be a lasting one. If each country has a sufficiently strong peacetime force, they won't be tempted to trample on one another in the future."

"That should be a nice change of pace for Cortez. But once it's settled down in Central America, I guess he'll be ready to head for another hot spot...Beirut, the Philippines."

"When he completes his assignment in Central America, he's retiring from the army. It's a decision he made long before he met you." Emily saw Richard glance at her as if to emphasize his point, then he moved to the dresser and opened a drawer. "He didn't kill your husband, Emily. He's a good, honest man. He has served his country well. And he would never, never do anything to hurt you."

"But he lied to me—"

"He didn't lie to you. He waited to tell you about his past, because he knew you'd never accept his help if you knew he was an army officer."

"But what about Eric? Eric promised…." Emily strode into the bedroom, stopping in front of Richard, her hands clenched at her sides.

"Eric was bright and funny and very, very charming," Richard said, gently placing his hands on Emily's shoulders. "He was also adept at getting whatever he wanted and avoiding whatever he didn't. His position at the university was guaranteed by generations of Andersons, and you helped him maintain it. At least he had the good grace to acknowledge that fact."

He stared at her for a long moment. Her silence was probably all the encouragement he needed, Emily reflected. "You were a team, weren't you? You worked together. You agreed he should go to Central America, didn't you? And you knew he was going to end up in Arteaga, not the safest place to be. He had a reputation for researching both sides of any story. If you're honest, you'll admit it's not impossible that he ended up part of a military action."

Though kindly spoken, the professor's words left Emily numb with shock. Everything he'd said was true; she had no rebuttal. So she watched in silence as he pulled a small, black leather case from a dresser drawer and crossed to the suitcase on the bed. She saw him open the case, slip something out and into his coat pocket. Then he set the case atop the clothes, shut the lid, and snapped the locks with quick efficiency.

Without a word, she stood aside so he could leave the room, then followed him across the hallway to the studio. For the first time since Joseph had walked out her front door, Emily admitted the enormity of her error in calling Joseph a liar and blaming him for Eric's death. The admission left her feeling cold and empty and alone.

Richard moved around the studio, gathering art supplies into a large box, apparently ignoring Emily as she wandered the room. She stopped at the wall of windows, arms crossed in front of her, staring at nothing, the hiss of falling snow against the panes grating on her nerves, the clouds as gray and heavy as her heart. With a sigh, she turned away from the bleak, dull day, and came face to face with the light, bright warmth of love and laughter and longing.

The painting on the canvas perched on the easel was of Danny and herself. He'd used shades of pale green, rose and brown, periwinkle and sunny gold, then added splashes of denim blue, red and kelly green as he showed them walking through the woods, their arms around each other. She touched the canvas with shaking fingers, then turned to bury her face against Richard's chest. His arms wrapped around her.

"I've made a terrible mistake, Professor," she muttered, pressing her cheek against the coarse wool of his overcoat.

"You've *both* made mistakes, Emily. There's nothing you can do to change that. But you can avoid making similar mistakes in the future."

He held her for a moment longer, then released her and lifted the painting from the easel. "Joseph said he left a set of keys for the Jeep in the kitchen. Will you get them for me?"

Not trusting her voice, Emily nodded her head and left the studio.

Ten minutes later, the moving men had removed all of Joseph's things and were busy loading the Jeep into the van. Emily had no idea what Richard had done with the painting, but obviously it wasn't meant for her to keep.

"What about Greta?" she asked in a small voice, as the men closed and locked the van doors and climbed into the cab. The dog had been pacing through the house, eyeing Richard and the moving men with obvious suspicion.

"Joseph thought Danny and you would need her more than

he. He was hoping you would take care of her for him until he returns.''

"Yes, of course," she agreed, her fingers digging into Greta's soft fur, even as her heart clutched at the faint promise that Joseph would return. One day he'd come back for Greta, and maybe by then...

"Well, I guess that's everything." She followed the old professor to the front door and reached for the doorknob. "Goodbye, Professor."

"Not quite everything." He caught her hand before she could open the door. "What are you going to do?"

"What *can* I do but wait and...hope?"

"That depends on what you want."

"I think, my friend, that it's much too late for me to get what I want." Emily's lips twisted into a sad little smile.

"As long as you're alive, it's never too late to get what you want. Do you love him?"

"Yes." For the first time since Saturday morning, she could say it without a shadow of uncertainty, without a twist of guilt. She might not agree with his political beliefs and she would never be fond of the military, but she loved Joseph Cortez. And she couldn't deny the fact that his political beliefs and his military background had shaped him into the man she loved.

"Well, then, use this time apart to finish with the past. And when you're done with it, when you've answered all your questions and come to terms with all your doubts, when you've banished the last of your anger and pain, when you've finally accepted the fact that Eric is gone forever, then go to Joseph." He pulled a small, white card from his pocket. "He asked me to give you this." He handed Emily the card. It bore Joseph's address and telephone number. "Also this." Reaching into his pocket again, Richard withdrew a large, oval locket on a slim gold chain and pressed it into Emily's hand. "It was his mother's. He wanted you to have it. No matter what happens in the future, it's yours to keep."

Emily stood silent as Richard slipped out the front door and walked down the porch steps. Then, clutching the card in one hand and the locket in the other, she started up the staircase. Halfway up she stumbled, then sat down hard on one of the narrow steps. With trembling fingers, she fastened the chain around her neck and slipped the gold oval inside her blouse. As the cool metal nestled between her breasts, she rested her head against the stair rail. She sat for a long time, listening to the sighs and whispers of the old house, while outside the wind picked up, piling thick drifts of snow over everything.

With a last hug and kiss, Emily tucked Danny into bed and said good-night. Joseph's bedroom across the hall—the bed made up with fresh sheets and blankets—was now nothing more than an extra bedroom. The studio was stark and empty. The pale glow of a street light was reflected off the snow and into the room through the wall of windows, sending shadows into every corner. He was gone, and he wasn't coming back. If she wanted to see him again, if she had any hope of facing him, whole and free and ready for the future, she knew what she had to do.

Silly to be so afraid of a cardboard box, she thought, switching on her desk lamp and opening the closet door. But maybe it wasn't the box or even what it contained that frightened her so. Maybe it was finally accepting the brutal reality of Eric's death, honestly and intelligently, without anger and blame, as Joseph had urged her to do so many weeks ago. Though she had told herself over and over that Eric was never coming home, had she been waiting for him somewhere at the edge of her mind, somewhere deep in her heart and soul?

Waiting for him to walk through the door? Waiting for him to swing her into his arms...?

He was such a tall man, such a big man, a huge, cuddly teddy bear. He would lift her off her feet, hold her high in the air, his blue eyes bright with love, his laughter a deep, rich counterpoint to her own, echoing through the house. Together they would open the box; together they would pore over the notes and diary, listen to the tapes, study the photographs and maps, sorting, selecting, arguing, agreeing, sharing smiles and cup after cup of strong, black coffee.

She scooped the box off the closet floor and dumped it onto her desk. Picking up a sturdy pair of scissors, she plunged them into the heavy strapping tape that sealed the edges.

"Damn you, Eric. Why did you have to die?" She raised the scissors and stabbed at the box. "I loved you...loved you...love him." Again she raised the scissors, attacking the box as if it were an enemy she desperately needed to destroy. "Dear God, I love him, and he isn't you, Eric."

Dropping the scissors, she tore at the flaps, bruising her fingers, breaking her nails as she ripped through the thick cardboard. She pulled out the wads of cheap newsprint he had used to cushion the contents, her eyes blurring with tears.

Inside she found a smaller box, full of plastic cylinders holding rolls of undeveloped film. Setting it aside, she reached for the large, padded, brown envelope. It had almost fifty photographs Eric had developed during his six-week journey. She sifted through them slowly, searching for his face, but he wasn't in any of them.

There were photographs of soldiers and civilians, men, women, children, sleepy village side streets and bustling, big city thoroughfares, farmers' fields, dense jungle, mountains and sandy beaches. Each one was marked with a date and place name in Eric's clean, free-flowing script. She traced a finger over the words he'd written on one. She closed her eyes, and could see him sitting at the desk, writing, writing.

She set the pictures aside with a sigh, and reached into the box yet again to pull out three spiral notebooks, a diary, and four cassette tapes. She found the cassette marked with a # 1, and tucked it into her tape player. She closed the office door, switched off the desk lamp, and stumbled into her chair. Groping in the darkness, she started the tape. In the still night, his voice vibrated through the room, offering first impressions of his first day in Central America.

She tipped back her head, closed her eyes and listened, as she had so many times, to the sound of Eric's voice. If she moved her hand, she almost believed she could touch him. But when at last she moved her hand, it was to wrap her fingers around the locket that rested on her sweater.

"Goodbye, Eric...goodbye," she whispered, her words breaking the sudden silence as the tape whined to its end.

She sat in the darkness a few moments longer. Then, with a new sense of determination, she brushed the last of the tears from her eyes and reached for the desk lamp. She would listen to the rest of the tapes another time. Tonight she would read through the notebooks and the diary. It would take her most of the night, but she didn't mind. The sooner she got an idea of what she had ahead of her, the earlier she could give Steve Muehler an estimate of the time she'd need to complete the writing. And the faster she finished the book, the sooner she could face Joseph Cortez and start her new life, free of the past, prepared for whatever the future might have to offer.

Gathering up the notebooks and diary, Emily headed for the stairs. If she planned to read all night, she might as well do it in comfort. She showered and changed into a nightgown, then turned off all the lights except the bedside lamp. She crawled beneath the blankets and comforter on her bed, propped her pillows behind her back, and settled the first notebook on her knees. Opening it, she began to read, one hand holding it in place, the other cradling the locket that dangled from the chain she wore around her neck.

"Wake up, Mom, wake up. I'm going to miss the bus. It's almost seven-thirty."

Pushing herself up against her tumbled pillows, Emily opened her eyes and smiled at her son. "Don't worry about the bus. I'll take you in the car. Hurry and get dressed, and I'll have your cereal ready in a flash."

As Danny raced from the room, she rubbed a hand over her eyes, then reached for the diary lying beside her. Turning to the last page, she read again the final entry.

"Tomorrow I'm going into Arteaga to meet with Martin Estrada as planned. He has set up meetings with several high-level officials there and he has promised me a firsthand look at the war from their point of view. Must listen to both sides if I want to be fair. Then in a few days I will be heading home again. I miss you so much."

"I miss you, too," Emily murmured, closing the diary and setting it aside. But sometime during the night, as she read his notes and followed his journey through Central America, she had said her final farewell to Eric Anderson.

His spirit had shown through page after page of his research. He had been a good and honest man, a man worthy of her love and respect. He had been cheerful, lighthearted, relatively carefree, but deep inside he had been as steady, as dependable as a rock. He had been firm in his beliefs, yet willing, always willing to listen to both sides of any argument. That willingness to listen, that ability to care had led him into Arteaga.

What had she told Danny so many weeks ago? That his father would have liked Joseph Cortez. It was true. Joseph, too, was a good and honest man, equally worthy of her love and respect. His humor was more subdued, and his life had been shadowed with physical and emotional pain that Eric had never known in his more sheltered life. But Joseph had a core of stability and dependability as strong and solid as Eric's, and he, too, knew how to listen, and most of all how to care. Eric and Joseph might have argued politics, disagreeing into the night, but at the end they would have shaken hands and wished each other well, even as they anticipated their next meeting.

In many, many ways they were so different, shaped as they were by the different lives they had led. Yet she loved them both, would always love them, each in a special way. Eric was gone forever; her love for him was tucked into a safe place all its own. But Joseph was alive, and so was she, alive and finally free to truly love again.

Sitting in a pool of early-morning sunshine, Emily Anderson realized that the anger, the bitterness, the pain she'd lived with for so long had faded away, replaced by a sense of determination and a small, bright ray of hope.

She would get dressed, feed Danny and take him to school. Then she would call Eric's editor. She had a book to write... for Eric, for Danny, for herself, and also for Joseph Cortez. By completing Eric's work, she would guarantee that he hadn't died in vain. Then maybe one day she would be able to face Joseph again, heart-whole and soul-free. For just a moment her fingers grazed the locket, then she threw back her blankets and slipped out of bed.

Chapter Twelve

He shifted on the seat of another rented car, this time trying unsuccessfully to beat down the uneasiness that was building inside him. It had been nine months since he'd first seen Emily's house, and although he had expected changes, he hadn't been prepared to find it looking quite so...abandoned. No car in the driveway, no bicycle on the sidewalk, no pots of brightly colored flowers on the stone porch railing. And every window that should have been open to the warm summer breeze was closed.

Should have called first, he thought, as he drew deeply on the thin, black cigar. Should have written to her, called her, weeks ago...months ago. Initially his pride had prevented him from making the first move. Mendoza had told him she needed time. Well, damn it, she could have all the time in the world, he'd thought.

But then as the days passed, as he completed his assignment in Norteña and moved to Washington to serve his last months at the Pentagon, a letter or a telephone call seemed so inadequate. So he had waited, hoping, praying that Emily had finally accepted Eric's death and would be willing to see him, to talk to him once he had fulfilled his commitment to the army.

Through Richard he knew that she was all right, but the old professor had refused to provide any other information about her. Mendoza knew that Joseph was planning to come to Duluth. Surely he would have said something if he thought Emily had made plans to leave town in June.

Crushing his cigar in the car's ashtray, Joseph forced himself to stop thinking and start acting. Just because the house wouldn't have looked any more deserted if the windows had been boarded up didn't mean she was gone forever.

But she *was* gone. Joseph tried the doorbell several times without success. He peered into her office window, only to see her desk cleared and her computer covered. He walked around to the back door and rattled the knob. Where were they? And where was Greta? he wondered as he walked down the driveway. If she had been in the house, she'd be barking her head off.

"Damn it," he cursed, running a hand through his hair and stopping to stare at the rental car parked at the curb.

What *had* he been thinking, flying to Duluth on the spur of the moment without contacting her first? That she'd be waiting for him, as he had waited for her until he couldn't stand the waiting any longer?

"Damn it," he swore again. "Where are you? And how the hell am I going to find you?"

When he had talked to Mendoza over a week ago, the professor had been planning to head out on his annual driving tour of Mexico within a day or two. Perhaps someone at the university would know if Emily was gone for the day, the week or the month. He'd go so far as to find Glen Roberts.... Then he remembered Cathy Stewart. Turning away from the car, he started down the sidewalk.

He covered the block to her house in less than two minutes, his stride long and steady as he ignored the faint twinge of protest from his left leg. He only felt the pain occasionally now. His finger stabbed the doorbell once, twice, a third time; a new wave of desperation washed over him.

"Oh, no," Cathy murmured, as she opened her front door—

to find Joseph Cortez standing on her porch, feeling like a stick of dynamite about to explode.

"Oh, yes," he replied, his voice harsh. "Where is she?"

"On her way to Texas." Joseph saw Cathy run her fingers through her hair, heard her hesitate for a moment before she went on. "It's my fault. I badgered her into it. Through Richard she knew you had retired from the army and returned to the ranch at the end of May. She thought...well...she thought you might come to Duluth, and she had Eric's book to finish, so she waited. When you didn't come, I told her she owed it to herself and to you to go to you and apologize."

"Apologize? For what?"

"For blaming you for Eric's death. She realized how wrong she was even before she read through Eric's notebook and listened to his tapes. Anyway, she finished the book, and she was beginning to give up on ever seeing you again. So, I convinced her to drive to Texas so she could apologize to you and one way or another put an end to that chapter of her life once and for all."

"When did she leave?" Joseph demanded, his hands on Cathy's shoulders, his dark eyes bright as he realized what she was saying.

But before Cathy could reply, Joseph heard a vehicle pull into the driveway. His attention diverted by the sudden noise, Joseph turned just in time to catch the little demon with sparkling blue eyes and shaggy blond curls who launched himself into his arms.

"You came back...you came back!" Danny cried, holding on to Joseph with all the strength of a sturdy seven-year-old boy. "I told her you'd come back. I told her not to be sad. I told her, Joseph, I told her."

"Oh, Danny, I've missed you. I've missed you so much," Joseph muttered, his arms around the boy, his eyes closed. "My God, you've grown at least six inches," he continued, loosening his hold at last and stepping back. "And you've taken good care of Greta, haven't you?" He acknowledged the dog who was wagging and whining around his legs.

"Of course I'm bigger. I'm seven now. And I took real good care of Greta. She's my buddy. And Jimmy's buddy," he added, grinning at his friend. "You aren't going to take her away, are you?"

"No, of course not. She's your dog now. I came to see you and your mother."

"She's not here. She went to Texas to see you. She didn't believe me when I told her you'd come back. First she was going to my grandma's in Chicago, then she was going to Texas. I don't know when she's coming home. Are you gonna wait for her?"

"When did she leave?" Joseph asked, meeting Cathy's eyes over Danny's head and resting a hand on the boy's shoulder.

"Last Saturday. She planned to stop in Chicago for a few days to see her parents and her sister. Then she was going on to Texas. If I'm not mistaken, she planned to be in the San Antonio area by today, tomorrow at the latest."

"Are you gonna wait?" Danny asked again, gazing up at Joseph.

"No, I've waited too long already," Joseph replied. "If I leave now, I may be able to make it back to the ranch before she gets there."

"Then what are you gonna do?" Danny's eyes reflected his sudden uncertainty.

"Then I'm going to do everything in my power to guarantee that the three of us spend the rest of our lives together. Is that all right with you, Danny?"

"Oh, yes," the boy replied, throwing his arms around Joseph, hugging him fiercely. "Oh, yes."

"Okay, then. I've got to go." Joseph freed himself from the boy's hold and turned to face Cathy and Hank. "I'll call you as soon as I get to the ranch. And if by some chance I miss her, and she calls here, tell her, tell her…"

"I don't think my wife will have any trouble finding the right words," Hank advised, offering Joseph his hand.

"Thanks." Joseph shook Hank's hand, then turned to squeeze Cathy's shoulder, matching the smile on her face. "I owe you one, lady."

"Send us a wedding invitation," Cathy said, as he started down the porch steps. "That should definitely cancel all debts."

Though he was already halfway down the sidewalk, and

intent on nothing more than getting back to the airport as fast as possible, he stopped and turned. "You got it," he promised, saluting smartly. "You got it."

Of all the idiotic things she'd done in her life, surely this took first prize, Emily thought, swiping at the trickle of perspiration that was easing down the side of her face. Though it was almost sundown, she'd bet her last nickel it was ninety degrees outside. Damp curls clung to her face and the back of her neck, her khaki skirt and white camp shirt had wilted into wrinkles, and her feet felt as if they'd swollen to twice their normal size inside her soft, leather moccasins. Until she'd started the drive across Texas, Emily had never understood the need for air conditioning in automobiles. Two days later, she was a believer.

She was hot and tired and dusty. If she'd had any sense at all, she wouldn't have attempted to find the ranch so late in the afternoon. She would have stopped at a motel in Bandera, gone for a swim, had an early dinner, and gotten a good night's sleep.

But the thought of seeing Joseph Cortez after so many months of waiting had been too much for her. Though her head told her another day wouldn't make any difference, her heart urged her on. What she had to say to him had waited too long already. And good, old-fashioned common sense had eluded her for so long that she saw no reason to change now.

So here she was, out in the middle of nowhere with nothing but a service station attendant's crudely drawn map to guide her. If she was heading in the right direction, that dirt road up ahead to the right should lead to the ranch. It was hard to judge distances here, and she hadn't thought to check her odometer when she'd left the main highway and started down the two-lane, asphalt road, but surely she'd covered the ten miles indicated on the little map.

Slowing the car, she turned onto the dirt road. Bracing herself against the sudden bumping and thumping, she squinted into the setting sun. In the distance, she thought she saw a house, barns and a cluster of outbuildings.

A mile farther, the dirt road divided into several smaller

tracks. Emily followed the one that curved toward the front of the house and pulled to a stop near the stone path leading to the front door. Switching off the engine, she allowed the hush of early evening to settle around her as she studied the long, low lines of the white, stucco house with the red-tiled roof. For just a moment she admired its simple beauty and elegance. Then she opened her car door and started up the path.

She rang the doorbell once and then again, wondering suddenly at the early-evening quiet. She glanced at the barns off to the left, but didn't see anyone there. Cattle and horses grazed in the pastures, but the men must have finished work for the day.

Suddenly unsure, she crossed her arms in front of her. What if she had made a mistake? What if this wasn't Joseph's ranch? Or worse, what if it was, and no one was at home?

"Yes? May I help you?" The dark, heavy wooden door swung wide, and a short, gray-haired woman in a housedress and apron greeted Emily with a friendly smile. She glanced over Emily's shoulder, as if searching for someone. Then, clearly not recognizing the car in the drive, she settled her gaze on Emily, her dark eyes bright with curiosity. "Are you lost?"

"I don't know," Emily replied, returning the woman's smile. "Does Joseph Cortez live here?"

"Yes. Yes, of course. Are you looking for Mr. Cortez?"

Emily nodded her head, her smile widening. "Is he here?" Through the open doorway the house seemed unusually dark and quiet, but mouth-watering aromas were wafting out, reminding her that it was dinnertime. She was probably interrupting his evening meal.

"No, I'm sorry, he's away." The housekeeper's smile faded and was replaced by a puzzled frown. "Was he expecting you? It's not like him to forget to tell me he's invited guests. I'm Maria Gomez, his housekeeper."

"He wasn't expecting me. I just thought…I…actually, I didn't think at all," Emily admitted, her own smile slipping as she spoke her thoughts aloud. The warm, evening breeze ruffled her curls, sending a shiver along her spine after the oppressive heat of the day. "When will he be back?"

"I'm not sure." The woman hesitated a moment. Then,

perhaps seeing in Emily's eyes the uncertainty she was feeling, Maria continued. "He left early this morning. He was in a big hurry, but he didn't say where he was going. He did mention he might be bringing someone back with him, but he didn't say *when*."

"I see," Emily murmured, taking a step back. Bringing someone back with him? Oh, God, she'd waited too long, and now it was too late. She took another step back. "Well, thank you. I'm sorry I bothered you." She offered a faint smile, took yet another step back and turned away.

"Wait, miss. Please wait." The housekeeper touched Emily's arm. Her voice was full of concern, and as Emily glanced over her shoulder, she saw that the other woman's eyes were kind. "It's getting late, and it's a long drive to anywhere from here. You shouldn't be on these back roads alone. Why don't you stay for dinner and spend the night? Mr. Cortez would want that."

"Oh, no, I couldn't...." *Couldn't bear to be here if Joseph returned with another woman. Couldn't bear to face the fact that she'd lost him forever because of her pride and stupidity.* "But thank you, anyway." With a wave that was intended to be cheery, Emily ran down the stone path and climbed into her car.

Without a backward glance, she started the car, eased it into gear and headed away from the house. She gripped the steering wheel with one hand, reaching out to switch on the headlights with the other. The sun was setting behind her, and the road ahead wound away into blurry darkness. She blinked, trying to clear her vision.

"What am I going to do?" she whispered. "What am I going to do?"

She touched the locket that she wore tucked under her blouse. Despite the angry, hateful words she'd flung at him, she had clung to the belief that he had loved her enough to wait. But maybe what he'd felt hadn't been love. Maybe he'd cared for her only out of a sense of duty and responsibility, after all.

If only she had listened all those months ago. She would have heard the truth in his words, the love and longing in his voice, would have understood his pride in his military background. She would never have accused him of killing her husband. And she would never have asked him to choose between his duty to his country and his love for her.

She stopped the car at the end of the dirt road. The sun had disappeared, and the car's headlights barely made a dent in the ink-black night. Glancing first one way, then the other, Emily hesitated. Had she turned onto the dirt road from the right or the left?

Shifting the car into Park, she switched on the interior light. She searched the front seat, the floor, felt in her skirt pockets, even opened the glove compartment, but the scrap of paper with the map on it had disappeared. Blinking rapidly, she switched off the light. *Think, Emily, think. Right or left?*

Her head propped on the steering wheel, she squeezed her eyes shut, trying not to cry. It was too late for tears, much, much too late, but that fact didn't stop them from trickling down her cheeks.

She didn't hear the Jeep roaring up the asphalt road, nor did she hear the screech of brakes or the slam of the door. But the deep, demanding voice that greeted her through the open car window wouldn't be denied.

"Well, if this isn't a pretty picture!"

Emily grew very still. Then, opening her eyes, she turned her head to see Joseph opening her car door. His eyes held hers for what seemed like an eternity. Then, without another word, he reached for her, pulling her out of the car and into his arms, whispering her name over and over again.

She would have held on to him forever, but as suddenly as his arms had gone around her, she found herself released. His hands resting on her shoulders, she saw his eyes search her face in the dim light from the car's interior. "What are you doing out here? Are you lost? Why didn't you call me? I was so afraid—"

"I'm not lost," Emily cut in, tilting her chin at a defiant angle. "Not exactly... You weren't home, so I...left."

"You left?" Joseph's hands tightened on her shoulders and he shook her once, gently. "Maria let you leave? She didn't ask you to stay?"

"She did invite me to stay," Emily admitted, stepping away from Joseph, freeing herself from his hold. Crossing her arms in front of her, she stared at the hard, dusty ground. "But she said you were bringing someone home with you, and I... couldn't..."

"*Madre de Dios*... I ought to shake you until your teeth rattle." The grip of the hands on her arms was no less threatening than the tone of his voice, and she stared at him in surprise. "But after flying to Duluth and back in one day, I'm too damned tired."

"You flew to Duluth?" Her eyes widened even more, and her soft mouth trembled slightly.

"Yes, and you and Danny are the ones I intended to bring back with me," he growled, an instant before his mouth closed over hers in swift, silencing possession.

At Joseph's request, Maria led Emily through a large living room, down a wide hallway and into a cool, spacious bedroom with a connecting bathroom. As she followed the housekeeper, Emily saw white walls, dark, wooden beams, arched windows and splashes of bright color. The house would be light and airy through the long, hot Texas summers, but warm and cozy during the short winter months.

After pointing out stacks of towels in one bathroom cabinet and every conceivable toilet article in another, Maria led Emily into the bedroom. There the older woman turned and smiled softly, apologetically.

"I didn't realize until you'd left that you were the one he's been waiting for. I'm so glad you found each other." As Emily expressed surprise, she saw the dark eyes twinkle with warmth and humor. "He's a good man, Mr. Cortez, but he's been like a caged animal the past few weeks. Now that you're here, maybe he'll settle down."

"But first he's going to fire the meddling busybody who calls herself his housekeeper," Joseph growled as he walked into the bedroom and dropped Emily's suitcase onto the bed.

"Hah, that'll be the day. Dinner in thirty minutes?" Maria asked, her eyes on Emily. At Emily's nod, she bustled out, ignoring Joseph's scowl.

"Joseph, I—"

"Later, *querida*. We'll talk later." For a moment he studied her face, feature by feature. Then, a smile lighting his dark eyes and lifting the corners of his mustache, he turned and left the room.

It was almost midnight by the time they finished eating, then Emily insisted on helping Maria with the dishes. She had used the time before dinner to shower and change into a pale pink, cotton sundress; her only jewelry was the simple, gold locket. So after bidding Maria good-night, there was nothing left to do but find Joseph.

Her heart thumping in her chest, she wandered through the quiet house, stopping in the living room, where she saw that the French doors were slightly ajar. The faint aroma of cigar smoke, drifting in with the warm night air, beckoned her. Taking a deep breath to steady herself, she stepped into the moon-lit darkness.

He was sitting on a wide chaise lounge on the wooden deck, the red glow at the tip of his cigar a tiny beacon. Walking past him, Emily stopped at the railing. Pressing her palms against the rough wood, still warm from the day's heat, she leaned forward, lifting her face to the diamond-studded sky. Now that the moment had arrived, she couldn't seem to find the words she wanted to say.

"Maria's gone to bed?" Joseph's deep, soft voice caressed her as surely as the warm breeze that lifted her curls.

"Yes." Emily dropped her head, her hands gripping the railing. "Joseph, I…" She hesitated, closing her eyes, shaking her head. "What I said that day…I was wrong not to believe you, wrong to blame you for Eric's death. I realized it almost at once, even before I went through his notebooks and tapes.

"And then, when I finally opened the box he'd sent, I realized why I'd been so bitter, so angry, so intent on laying blame. I'd been waiting for him to come home. I had never really accepted his death. Blaming the government and the military for his death was my way of avoiding finishing the work we had started together. Fueling my anger and bitterness kept him alive for me."

She waited for Joseph to say something, but only the rustle of the breeze in the trees and the small sounds of night animals broke the silence surrounding them. "I know saying I'm sorry now is too little, too late. But Joseph, I *am* sorry."

Releasing her hold on the railing, she turned to face him, and found him standing less than a foot away.

"I'm sorry, too, Emily." He brushed a hand over her curls, traced the line of her jaw with one fingertip. "I should have told you about myself and why I'd come to your house as soon as I realized how much I cared for you. I knew how you felt about the government and the military, and I knew you trusted me. But I told myself you didn't have to know, as long as we were nothing more than friends." His hand tangled in her hair, tipping her face up, forcing her to meet his eyes.

"Nothing more than friends…God, I was only fooling myself. I think I fell in love with you the moment I laid eyes on you. And I was afraid that if you had to choose between Eric and me, I would be the loser."

Without a word, Emily stepped into Joseph's arms, resting her head on his shoulder, her palms flat against his chest. She listened to the gentle rhythm of his heart as his hands traveled up and down her back in long, soothing strokes. He *had* loved her, then. But what if her anger and bitterness had destroyed that love? What if she had destroyed all hope for them to be together?

"Have you made any plans for the future?" he asked, his voice soft.

She stiffened in his arms, forcing herself to accept the unacceptable. He *had* loved her once, but no more. "I haven't decided yet. With the money from the book, I can afford to go back to school, finish my Ph.D." Her hands clenched into fists as she tried to push away from him. "I don't expect anything from you, Joseph. I came here to apologize to you, nothing more, nothing less." With a violent twist she freed herself, refusing to meet his eyes. "I realize your feelings for me have changed, and I don't blame you—"

"Damn right my feelings for you have changed," Joseph growled, pacing after her as she took a step back, then another and another. "And it's time I showed you just how much."

Catching her in his arms, Joseph swung her off her feet and tossed her over his shoulder. Ignoring her whispered protest, he carried her into the house, through the living room and down a long, narrow hallway. Once in his bedroom, he kicked the door shut, locked it, then dumped Emily onto his bed.

Standing over her, he switched on a lamp, then turned to face her.

In the dim light her eyes were wide and full of uncertainty. Joseph hesitated, suddenly unsure of himself. Perhaps she *had* come to Texas to do nothing more than apologize. Perhaps he had destroyed her love for him when he betrayed her trust. The thought was almost more than he could bear.

"I'm sorry I acted like a caveman, Emily," he muttered, running a hand through his hair. He sat on the edge of the bed, his back to her, resting his elbows on his knees, rubbing his forehead against his clasped hands. "If you don't want to stay here with me, you're free to go back to your bedroom. You can stay at the house as long as you like. I won't bother you again."

It seemed like an eternity before the bed shifted with her weight. But when he expected to hear her feet hit the floor, instead he felt her cheek pressed against his shoulder and the fullness of her breasts nudging his back.

"Joseph?" She brushed the back of her hand against his face, her touch as light and gentle as her voice. "You hung the painting in here."

"Yes." He hesitated a moment, then reached up to catch her hand in his. "You're wearing the locket."

"Always." She pressed her lips against the back of his neck, and waited.

"Joseph?" When he didn't respond, she pressed her cheek against his shoulder once again. "There's nowhere else on earth I'd rather be than here with you...if you want me...us."

He faced her then, wrapping his hands around her upper arms in a firm, possessive hold, his dark eyes hot and bright. "Emily, *querida,* I love you. I want you here with me. I want you and your son here with me for the rest of our lives. Will you stay with me? Will you marry me?"

"Oh, Joseph, I love you, too." She cradled his face in her hands, her eyes gleaming, her lips trembling. "Of course I'll stay. And yes, I'll marry you."

Threading her fingers through his thick, dark hair, she pulled his head down until his lips met hers, and together, in the pale glow of the lamplight, they left the past behind.

Epilogue

Outside it was cold and wet, but inside the long, low ranch house it was warm and cozy. As Emily opened the oven door to retrieve a pan of cookies, the aroma of sugar and spice and other things nice wafted into the kitchen. Just two weeks until Christmas, she thought, smiling slightly as she popped another pan into the oven. As she turned back to the kitchen table, she saw Maria return her smile, though the other woman's eyes were visibly shadowed with concern.

"Maybe you should sit down for a while, Emily. He'll be angry if I let you wear yourself out."

"I'm not wearing myself out, Maria," Emily laughed, but she did settle herself in a chair beside the table. Her pregnancy had been an easy one so far, and the baby wasn't due until the end of March, but she wasn't taking any chances.

"When will they be back?"

"I'm expecting them anytime." Joseph and Danny had gone to San Antonio early that morning to do their Christmas shopping, and Joseph had promised they'd be home before dark. As Emily glanced at the clock, Greta trotted into the kitchen and sat at the back door, her ears pricked expectantly. "In fact, I think they're home now," Emily added, her smile widening as she pushed herself out of the chair.

Man and boy burst through the door, arms full of packages, as well as handfuls of cards and letters they'd picked up at the mailbox. Dropping his load onto the kitchen table, Danny ran to Emily and hugged her.

"I can hardly get my arms around you, Mom," he teased, then yelped when she landed a swat on his bottom.

"All in a good cause, son," Joseph said, adding his things to the pile.

"As long as it's a boy," Danny muttered. "I already have girls for cousins. A sister would be a real pain."

"Oh, you might be surprised, Danny. Sometimes girls aren't so bad," Joseph replied, as he wrapped his arms around his wife and kissed her. "Feeling all right?"

"Aw, mushy stuff. Come on, Greta. Let's go hide Mom's presents."

"I'll help," Maria offered, and the trio slipped away.

"I'm fine," Emily insisted. "What came in the mail?"

"Notes from Richard and Cathy." He handed her the envelopes, and she tore into them, reading first one, then the other.

"Cathy says the couple renting the house is taking good care of it. Hank, Jimmy and she will be arriving in San Antonio on the twenty-second, and Richard will be here on the twenty-third." Her voice was high with excitement as her gaze met Joseph's. "With your sister and her family, we'll have a full house for Christmas. I can't wait."

"It's not going to be too much for you, is it?" Joseph asked, his eyes shadowed.

"No, it's going to be wonderful." When her enthusiasm failed to dispel the shadows, Emily touched his arm. "Don't worry. I'm healthy as a horse, the baby's fine, and I'm taking it easy." But despite her reassurance, the shadows seemed to linger.

"Something else came in the mail for you." Turning away from her, Joseph retrieved a large, padded envelope from the pile on the table, and handed it to Emily.

As she glanced at the return address, she realized why Joseph was concerned. It wasn't just her health or the houseful of guests. He was still afraid that the past might return to haunt them. Without a word, she tore into the envelope and pulled out the book.

On a glossy, dark blue background, white, block letters spelled out the title: *Give Peace a Chance; Another Time, Another Place.* Beneath it, her name joined Eric's. Turning the book over, she stared at the picture of Eric on the back cover. She traced his handsome features with a finger, her smile soft and sad.

Then, her smile widening with all the joy of her new life, her new love, Emily opened the book to the dedication page. Turning to face her husband, she offered it to him without a word.

He accepted it, his eyes questioning, but she simply smiled. Standing very still she watched as he read the words printed there, watched as the shadows fled once and for all, replaced by a warm, soft glow that would never fade.

For Joseph, with all my love,

                                    for always Emily Cortez

* * * * *

SPECIAL EDITION

Stories of love and life, these powerful novels are tales that you can identify with—romances with "something special" added in!

Fall in love with the stories of authors such as **Nora Roberts, Diana Palmer, Ginna Gray** and many more of your special favorites—as well as wonderful new voices!

Special Edition brings you entertainment for the heart!

SSE-GEN

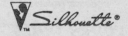

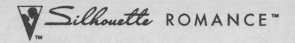

What's a single dad to do when he needs a wife by next Thursday?

Who's a confirmed bachelor to call when he finds a baby on his doorstep?

How does a plain Jane in love with her gorgeous boss get him to notice her?

From classic love stories to romantic comedies to emotional heart tuggers, **Silhouette Romance** offers six irresistible novels every month by some of your favorite authors! Such as…beloved bestsellers **Diana Palmer, Annette Broadrick, Suzanne Carey, Elizabeth August** and **Marie Ferrarella,** to name just a few—and some sure to become favorites!

Fabulous Fathers…Bundles of Joy…Miniseries… Months of blushing brides and convenient weddings… Holiday celebrations… You'll find all this and much more in **Silhouette Romance**—always emotional, always enjoyable, always about love!

Listen to whispers of sweet romance with

Best of the Best™ Audio

Order now for your listening pleasure!

Best of the Best™ AUDIO

#15295 FIRE AND ICE
$11.99 U.S. ☐ $14.99 CAN. ☐
Written by Janet Dailey.
Read by Erin Gray.

#15292 THE ARISTOCRAT
$11.99 U.S. ☐ $14.99 CAN. ☐
Written by Catherine Coulter.
Read by Marcia Strassman.

#15293 RAGGED RAINBOWS
$11.99 U.S. ☐ $14.99 CAN. ☐
Written by Linda Lael Miller.
Read by Erin Gray.

#15294 THE MAIN ATTRACTION
$11.99 U.S. ☐ $14.99 CAN. ☐
Written by Jayne Ann Krentz.
Read by Marcia Strassman.

(limited quantities available on certain titles)

TOTAL AMOUNT $
POSTAGE & HANDLING $
($1.00 for one audio, 50¢ for each additional)
APPLICABLE TAXES* $
TOTAL PAYABLE $______
(check or money order—please do not send cash)

To order, complete this form and send it, along with a check or money order for the total above, payable to Best of the Best Audio, to: **In the U.S.:** 3010 Walden Avenue, P.O. Box 9077, Buffalo, NY 14269-9077; **In Canada:** P.O. Box 636, Fort Erie, Ontario, L2A 5X3.

Name:______

Address:______ City:______

State/Prov.:______ Zip/Postal Code:______

*New York residents remit applicable sales taxes. Canadian residents remit applicable GST and provincial taxes.

Available wherever audio books are sold. AUDB

NORMANDALE COMMUNITY COLLEGE
LIBRARY
9700 FRANCE AVENUE SOUTH
BLOOMINGTON, MN 55431-4399